# The Elenauts

By
Tarek Masud
Copyright Registration Number: CRL-26554
Date of Issue: June 08, 2022
https://tarekmasud.com/
+8801706401667
Cover Design by Simul Chowdhury (Drik Gallery)

## Table of Contents

# Chapter One

The hollow feeling in the chest struck Cindy like an electric shock as she stepped out of the aircraft. From ten thousand feet in the air, she could hardly make out the details of the homes and the surrounding area. Her heartbeat was on fast track due to the adrenaline secretion. On her face, the rushing wind slammed like a hammer while she plummeted at four hundred kilometers an hour towards the ground below. Her goggles allowed her to have a clear view despite the force of the wind hitting her countenance.

Cindy had her digital altimeter on her left wrist. She folded her arm to have a look at the gadget. In ten seconds, she plummeted five hundred meters. After thirty seconds of free fall the activation device was going to open the primary chute. The noise of the chute opening behind her was like getting a new contract on life. Every time she did it, on the back of her mind a question was always there, "Is the chute going to open?" The jolt of the chords was followed by the expected deceleration. Upon deployment of the chute, it was time for her to enjoy the scene below her feet. Close to the horizon, the eastern bank of Lake Tahoe was visible. She was at a safe distance from the lake. Cindy began manipulating the chords to guide her descent to the desired location. The open field, roughly a kilometer from the lake bank, was the designated spot for touchdown for her and her team.

Cindy looked up over her right shoulder. Approximately two hundred meters above her, she spotted Tim's red and blue chute descending. Another two to three hundred meters above Tim, was Stacy, and then Ed, Kimberly and

Greg followed. They had jumped from the aircraft at an interval of ten seconds. Cindy pointed her finger at the designated spot where they had planned to land. The outer compound of the South Lake Tahoe High was also within their sight. In another two or three minutes, they were going to come down on the grassy field.

At three meters per sec, Cindy's feet crashed down onto the ground. She was used to it. Like always, she took a few quick steps before her to divert the force of the momentum. Managing the puffed-up chute was the next task. She pulled one of the chords to let the trapped air out of the chute. While folding her chute, a few yards from her, one by one, her students touched down.

"Yahoo!" Tim yelled at Cindy, expressing his sheer joy. Cindy yelled back, "Well done guys! It was a wonderful drop."

About fifty meters from Tim, Stacy cried out, "My ankle!"

Accidentally, Stacy landed on a bump on the ground, making her losing balance. By then Cindy was almost done folding her chute. She unbuckled and ran to assist Stacy. Unable to keep herself on her feet, Stacy had been dragged to the ground by her chute. Very swiftly, Cindy held the chords of Stacy's chute and told her to unbuckle. Once the chute had been taken care of, Cindy began to take off Stacy's sneaker for a closer look at her injury. Cindy was a licensed first aid administrator with first aid and CPR certification. Very gently, she held Stacy's right ankle. As she touched it, she asked if it hurt. An affirmative reply made Cindy communicate with her drone.

"Robert, do you hear me?" As the tiny wireless microphone relayed her voice to the drone attached to the roof of her vehicle, the hidden speaker in her suit crackled, "I'm on my way. I'll be there in a minute."

Cindy's vehicle had been parked in the concrete parkway of South Tahoe High. From there it took less than a minute for the robot to fly to its owner. The robot was licensed to inspect and diagnose physical injuries. In no time, it hovered over Stacy and Cindy when Cindy made way for the robot to scan its patient. For a couple of seconds, it scanned Stacy's ankle, and then its mechanical voice was activated. "No fractures found. It's a case of a mild sprained ankle. The patient requires ice on the injured spot, and bed rest for the next forty-eight hours," the robot reported.

"Go fetch the icebox from my vehicle," Cindy commanded her robot. In five minutes, Robert returned with the first aid box and ice. Cindy took out a pain-relieving ointment and a roll of bandage from the box. Very gently, she administered the ointment, and then wrapped the injured spot with the bandage.

By the time Cindy had finished treating Stacy's injury with ice, the team members surrounded them with helping hands. They had no stretcher or clutches with them. Tim and Ed helped Stacy up on their shoulders. Though Stacy's vehicle was also in the parking lot, they figured she was in no condition to drive. Tim had to drive her to her home while Cindy discussed with the rest of her team the schedule of their next drop.

"Have you ever heard of anyone breaking their neck during the landing?" Kimberley asked Cindy.

"No, I haven't. It's unlikely because the feet touchdown first," replied Cindy with a smile.

"Once I heard of a case like that. The lady was from Ohio. It happened on her first jump. I even saw the images of her landing. Later she went through surgery to replace the part of the broken spine," Kimberly narrated.

"Most probably it happened when she had lost balance and subsequently got dragged by the chute on the ground," remarked Cindy.

"Yes, that's exactly how it happened," Kimberly confirmed.

Cindy could sense the unease in Kimberly. She knew it had the potential to infect others. So, she decided to address her fears.

"Listen guys, in this kind of sport, there's always the possibility of mishaps. As a matter of fact, we have this risk in every sport. If you go for a horse ride, the chances are there that you might fall. If you swim, you might have muscle spasm and drown. In a race, you might have a heart attack and collapse. In a seemingly harmless game like ping pong, your partner's bat can hit your head. Now are you going to stop living because of these possibilities of mishaps? The possibility of mishaps is an integral part of life. You cannot imagine one without the other. Even a hermit, fleeing from this kind of risk, and living a secluded life in a jungle, cannot tell if he's not going to be devoured by a tiger. Therefore, it's not only pointless, but a waste of our precious energy and spirit, unnecessarily thinking about these risks," Cindy explained.

Greg joined Cindy in addressing Kimberly's fears, and added, "That's exactly how it is Kim. As the proverb goes, life is not a bed of roses. I think the risk only enhances the thrill. Why do you think we love to dive from an aircraft? Why do you think we love roller coaster rides? Why do you think we love to race down the lane in our vehicles instead of walking? The answer is thrill. It's an inherent human gene. Where there's no risk, there's no gain." At this point

Greg paused before adding with a smirk on his lips, "I think before you go for a jump from the aircraft, you should practice jumping from a six feet high wall. It's good practice, and remember, practice makes perfect. It'll also help manage your anxieties." ***

On her way back home, Cindy thought about what Greg had said. Indeed, it was true. Life would not be worth living, had it been totally risk free. While flying back home at more than four hundred kilometers an hour, something could go horribly wrong, and the vehicle could simply drop from the sky like a piece of rock. It happened to so many aircraft in the past. It can happen at any moment.

Cindy looked through the window. At fifteen hundred feet, low white clouds beckoned to her to come out of her shell. Cindy wished she had a pair of wings. All day she would play with the clouds. She heard that inside the clouds, it was very humid and uncomfortably warm. A friend who flew a hand glider from the Sierra Mountains told her this. Often, he described to her how it felt to be flying with the clouds and the kites, drifting high up in the troposphere.

Cindy's flying vehicle, XJ-9200, was equipped with the latest version of the facial recognition software. Hence, the vehicle's operating system was able to read the facial expressions of its driver or the passengers. Cameras embedded in the cabin were connected to the onboard computer with the help of the radio signals. This way, the system could sense if the driver or the passengers were in any kind of physical or mental stress. Once it had gained the necessary inputs from the sensors, the vehicle's onboard computer would suggest to the driver or the passengers' various options to reduce their stress. The chips enabled the computer to have intelligent conversations with the riders, at the same time, providing information if they needed it.

Cindy had been in a trancelike state when she heard Stellar's soothing voice. It said, "Cindy, you look depressed. May I ask why?"

"No Stellar, you have read my expression incorrectly. I was a bit philosophical," Cindy snapped.

"The term philosophical is the adjective of the noun philosophy, a subject dealing with almost everything in life, am I right?"

"Yes, you are. Now, what do I have to do?"

"Will you please tell me, what you have been thinking?"

"I haven't been thinking, I was just enjoying the view outside."

"You love the sky, don't you?"

"Yes, I do, but not without the ground I stand on. Without the solid ground underneath my feet, it's kind of frightening," with a smile on her lips, Cindy replied.

"Man has always been afraid of heights."

"Yet man has managed to conquer the heights, hasn't he? Why do you say, 'man has been afraid'? I'm a woman."

"If I said women, you would say, there were men in this world too."

"You should have used the term people."

"But that's not how the proverbs go."

"When these proverbs found their usage, men ruled the world. The world has changed a lot since then."

"That's true. However, in language, there's also a thing called tradition. Besides, anything that doesn't sound good, is usually avoided."

"Now tell me what you have on your mind, Stellar."

"I just want you to enjoy the ride. Shall I remove the roof over your head?" Stellar suggested.

Cindy thought about it. She glanced at the temperature readings on the display. Outside the vehicle it was sixty degrees Fahrenheit.

"Alright, clear the roof," Cindy replied in a casual tone.

As the roof slid open, the first thing which rattled her senses was the humming noise of the two turbofan jets, providing thrust to the vehicle. The cool fresh air instantly filled the cabin. Cindy felt much better.

"Thanks, Stellar. It really feels good."

"I know it does. It makes me happy, knowing my owner is comfortable."

The vehicle shuddered, as it fell into air pockets.

"This is what I love the most when flying. It feels like a ride at the amusement park. This aspect of the journey sets it apart from the normal drive on the road. A drive on the road is monotonous, it's boring."

"Would you like me to dive or climb steeply?"

"No, no, I don't need it. I've had enough of it today when I jumped from the aircraft."

"How did you feel when you stood at the door of the aircraft, Cindy?"

"I cannot convey it to you. It's like describing an elephant to a blind man or talking about music to a deaf. In the end, you're just a machine, Stellar. I'm sorry for being so arrogantly blunt."

"It's alright Cindy, I'm used to this kind of remarks."

"Who made this kind of remark to you? Aren't I the only owner you have had so far?"

"Before you made the purchase, the dealer at the showroom invited many prospective buyers to have a conversation with me. Whenever my intelligence had somehow offended them, they made this kind of remark. I take it as human vice. When something threatens their status or ego, they resort to this kind of verbal abuse. This way they want to establish how indispensable they are."

It was too much for Cindy. She burst out in laughter. This time she had to appreciate Stellar's wit. She asked, "Do you think I'm also like them, Stellar?"

"That I do not know, Cindy. My chips have not yet developed the skills to read your mind."

"Don't you worry about it. You're one smart computer. So far, what I have heard from you, that's more than enough. By the way, can you infer?"

"Do you mean drawing a conclusion from a hint?"

"Yes."

"Yes, I can. It required the most extensive research on the part of my system's developers."

"Then tell me what you have deduced from our conversation. I mean tell me what you think of me."

"You are exceptionally brave, frank and open minded. At times, your ego feels threatened, but you know how to tackle it, so there's no harm to it."

"Stellar, you also excel in the art of flattery!" Cindy exclaimed.

"My data tells me, the term flattery refers to sugar coated lies. No Cindy, I'm not lying. I have given you my honest opinion."

By this time, the vehicle had climbed to two thousand meters to avoid the rain clouds ahead of it. Subsequently, the temperature had dropped considerably before Stellar suggested having the roof back in its place. As soon as the roof had been restored, the vehicle began its gradual descent.

Cindy remembered Trevor once telling her he wanted to be a fighter pilot. It was before they got married. She said it was no longer an attractive profession. Nowadays, anyone could fly if he or she had a flying vehicle. She didn't want Trevor to feel disappointed. It was the reason she downplayed the impact of that incident on his life.

It was time for her to focus on her plans for the present, so she stopped reminiscing, and turned her attention back to flying her machine.

"How far are we from home?" she asked Stellar.

"In ten minutes, we'll be landing," Stellar replied coldly.

"Stellar, I would like you to change our heading, set a course for Trevor's latest project. I intend to have a look at it from the air. Do you have the coordinates of the site?"

"Yes, I do. It's Shamrock Tower, in downtown South Tahoe."

"How did you get the location? I don't remember feeding you the data."

"Mr. McLaughlin had once mentioned it during a conversation with you. I have the conversation stored in my memory."

"Have you been spying on us, Stellar?"

"I have been programmed to record what I hear, what I see, and learn from them. The data helps us to modify our programming. This is the greatest advantage of having this technology built into my system. In other words, chips with the latest version of the technology can program themselves to adjust to the changes in the exterior conditions."

"Alright, enough of your magical tech, now get me to the Shamrock Tower."

In five minutes, Cindy's flying machine was over the tallest building in Downtown South Tahoe. The vehicle made a few circles over the tower before heading for home.

The road in front of Cindy's home was wide and long enough for the flying vehicles to land like conventional aircraft. However, Cindy opted for the VTOL mode for landing. Not too many flying vehicles had the option. Her one did. This was one of the reasons why this model was larger than its predecessors. At the showroom, when she had the first look at the vehicle, she didn't like it for its size. She thought the machine had the shape of a pregnant lady. She still remembered everyone laughing at her for her peculiar, but candid remark. Indeed, the middle of the vehicle was larger for the duct which directed the thrust of the engines downward. Apart from it, she thought it was too large for many of the narrow roads of her neighborhood. The dealer was a twenty-five-year-old young man from the northeast. From his accent she could tell he was from the New England region. A brief conversation with the fairly tall dealer with dark brown hair, farther revealed that he was a graduate of Boston University from where she had graduated almost ten years back. The revelation created a natural fraternity between the two, instantly changing what she thought of the vehicle the dealer wanted to sell. Trevor, who had been with her at the time, also contributed to convincing her to buy the vehicle. Trevor was mostly interested in the vehicle's VTOL capability. He said this would allow her to land on short and narrow landing spots as well. Cindy pointed out the necessary skills required to land or take off vertically. She knew the risk associated with it. The dealer said that the onboard computer was programmed to land or lift the vehicle vertically. Hence, there was no need for anyone to be trained to do so at the beginning. However, for legal ground the driver needed to be trained to do so, and he gave assurance of assistance if she needed training before getting the special permit required by law to operate the vehicle.

Subsequently, Cindy decided to get the training before buying the vehicle. It took two weeks of training by Trevor in his flying vehicle for Cindy to acquire the necessary skills. Later, she found the VTOL option more interesting than landing or taking off like a conventional aircraft. The interior of the XJ-2900 was more luxurious, and more attractive than most of the vehicles of its class. For two people, it was sufficiently spacious. The seats of her vehicle changed color to match the climatic condition outside. In winter they changed to black, while in summer they changed to white or beige according to the owner's choice. If the day was very sunny, a mechanism was there to prevent the greenhouse effect when the vehicle was parked in open space. In winter the seats were kept warm, and in summer they were kept comfortably cool even when they had been occupied. In the end, these were not the features that finally tilted her opinion in favor of making the purchase. The day she saw it for the first time, the clever dealer had allowed Cindy to have a conversation with its onboard computer. The dealer didn't mind even though the long conversation had continued for more than an hour. At the time, the onboard computer didn't have any name, for it was up to the owner to choose a name for it. In the past, Cindy had conversations with many computers, robots and androids. This time she could not compare her experience. It was totally different. There was no way to tell that she had been talking to a machine. It sounded like it had feelings. After the conversation, she fell in love with it. She told herself, there was no way she was going to walk out on it. She even decided on a name for it. She was going to call him Stellar. For the first time in her life, she found a friend in a machine.

The yard in front of their huge garage was paved like a tarmac to allow their vehicles to land or take off vertically. The blow out from the two turbofan jet engines created a tiny storm over the landing spot as the vehicle made a controlled descent. Cindy held the joystick, though she had left the landing to Stellar. She could feel the power of the machine while gently holding the joystick very mildly vibrating in her hand. She was aware of the steps to be taken if anything went wrong. The wheels had been deployed before Stellar switched to VTOL mode. As soon as the wheels had touched the ground, the directions of the jet engine's nozzle returned to normal, before completely shutting down.

"You are always so awesome," Cindy said to Stellar.

"Thank you, Cindy. It was my pleasure. I'm one lucky machine to have an owner like you," responded Stellar.

While removing the seat belt, Cindy asked, "Why do you say, you're lucky?"

"Many people talked to me. None appreciated the way you do, what I had to offer. They saw as a threat to their intelligence. From your speech, your tone, I can tell that you see me as a dear friend. Thank you for being such a sweet friend."

"I wish you had a physical existence," said Cindy.

"I do."

"You do!"

"The half centimeter by half centimeter chip in the motherboard is my physical existence."

For a moment, Cindy just closed her eyes, and tried to visualize the chip, before saying goodbye, and getting off the vehicle. ***

The loud alarm from the bedside clock brought Trevor out of his sleep. He stared at the cube-like clock on the bedside table. Trevor focused on the time and date which glowed in the display. It was 7:00 am, August 05, 2065. Trevor was still under the spell of slumber. The previous night, Trevor planned everything for the next working day at his office. He was the owner and CEO of Zenith Elevators. It was a big day for his company. They had been working tirelessly for the last one month in order to install ten elevators of the Shamrock Tower, situated at the heart of the new commercial block in Lake Tahoe City. It's a hundred storied building, incorporating all the latest technologies of the twenty second century. The underground multi-level parking space could accommodate over two hundred vehicles. The complex over the parking space consisted of two swimming pools, a gym, and then a commercial complex and residential complex constituted the rest of the building.

For being the president, there's no need for Trevor to be physically present at the construction site. Nonetheless, he made it his habit to personally supervise the final stage of the installations. Installing elevators in a thousand feet tall structure was a challenging task, requiring precision, hard work, and flawless planning. The rails and brackets were the foundation of an elevator. If the brackets were not installed properly, the rails would be off, and every other item that was set to the rail distance would be off. Hence, precision was of prime importance. Technicians had to ensure that the rail brackets were off no more than plus minus one sixty fourth of an inch. Once the brackets had been installed, the guide rails were carefully attached with tons of ultra-high strength steel chains and cables. Constant communication between the technicians and the robots was key for a safe installation.

In fifteen minutes, Trevor was ready to leave for his office. He found a pot of hot coffee in the dispenser, along with toast and cream cheese on the kitchen table. Cindy had breakfast ready for Trevor before she left home. In front of his garage, Trevor's vehicle had been waiting for him. The vehicle's onboard computer greeted Trevor the moment its sensors picked up his presence even before he was meters from his vehicle. The vehicle's onboard computer had been given a seductive female voice. After the exchange of greetings, the onboard computer of the vehicle asked, "Should I set the course to the Shamrock Tower, Trevor?"

"Yes, back to Shamrock Tower, Debbie. Aren't you glad I'm so predictable?"

"So, I would assume you want me to drive."

"Of course, sweetheart."

"How many sweethearts do you have, Trevor?"

"How many would you like me to have?"

"It depends."

"Depends on what?" exclaimed Trevor.

"Depends on your belief, attitude, and the capacity to take the pressure."

Trevor exploded as he asked, "Where did you get all this information about men?"

"Perhaps my software designers were mostly men."

"Yeah, that explains it. Don't worry, I'll think about your suggestion, but for the time being, I think two sweethearts will do just fine. Now, let me do some calculations for the elevator installations."

A head-up display appeared out of the dashboard when Trevor was done talking. Debbie said, "Let me do the pre-flight checklist while you do your calculations."

The onboard computer switched to the auto-pilot mode before releasing the brakes. Almost noiselessly the vehicle moved forward, gradually picking up speed for takeoff. Trevor's vehicle did not have the VTOL option. Like a traditional aircraft, it had to gain sufficient speed before it could take off. Its wings spread out from the roof of the vehicle as the vehicle gained speed. From the rear luggage compartment, two attached wings appeared. They transformed into rudders. The takeoff was very gentle. A slight turn and the flying vehicle was on its way to the holoway, four kilometers from Trevor's home. There, the flying machines used holographic projections as the highway. They were developed to avoid collision. Over highway eighty-nine, five such holographic lanes had been built, one over another, with relay stations, every five miles. Each lane was two hundred meters high and hundred meters wide. A remote tower at the city center directed the traffic. The vehicles using the holoways had to ask for permissions from the remote tower for access to the holoways. The tower would then decide the lane and altitude of the vehicles. Trevor's vehicle received permission to enter HHW-5 at eight hundred meters.

Gradually, Debbie ascended to the designated altitude. Trevor told Debbie to connect him to Offisec-1, the robot at Trevor's office which performed as his private secretary. In a matter of seconds, Offisec's smooth female voice greeted Trevor, "Hello Trevor, how are you today?" it said.

"I'm okay, thanks Offisec. Now tell me if Jane has posted yesterday's transactions from petty cash book to the general ledger."

"Yes, she has. Would you like me to separately post them to the respective ledgers?"

"Yes, that'll be great. I also want you to prepare a balance sheet for the first quarter. After my visit to the Shamrock Tower, I'll collect it from Jane. Tell her to keep all the books up to date. We might have visitors from the bank."

"No problem. One more thing, how long do you think it will take for you to complete your tour of the site?"

"I don't know Offisec. It all depends on several factors. If everything goes as planned, I'll be done in a couple of hours."

"Okay then, I'll have the balance sheet ready for you."

"Thanks, Offisec."

Trevor shifted his focus back to Debbie. He said, "Connect me to Davis, Debbie. I need to talk to him before I reach the site."

For a few seconds, Trevor listened to Dave's phone ringing, and then his voice crackled, "Yes Trevor, go ahead."

"So, how is everything over there?"

"Jetpack-3 has a problem with its mechanical arm. It's getting stuck."

"What! How long has it been since we purchased it?"

"Not even a month."

"Is it a software or hardware issue?"

"Its diagnostic tools say it's a hardware related problem, and I have the same opinion because I've checked the apps, there's no problem there."

"Call Fire Tech. I spent quite a heavy amount on this latest installation robot. They better fix it fast. How about the other jetpacks, how are they functioning?"

"Jetpack-1, 2, 4 and 5 have been functioning alright. As we speak, they are installing the cables. Once the cables have been installed, we'll turn on the power and the computer."

"It's 8:15 now. Don't worry, I'll be there by 9:00, see you then."

Trevor stared at the valley down below. The winter retreat looked like a paradise. In 1960, it was the venue for the winter Olympics. The venue selection committee never thought of it. However, the spectacular natural beauty of the Tahoe Valley won over the hearts of the committee members.

Suddenly, a formation of white clouds enveloped Trevor's vehicle. The vehicle was equipped with the most sophisticated navigational devices. Hence, coordinating movement with the designated satellite, the vehicle's radar could easily steer through large cloud formations and inclement weather. Still, having his views obstructed by the clouds, it didn't take time for unease to settle in his heart. The uncomfortable blindfold was removed when the vehicle popped out of the cloud. Another half an hour passed before Debbie brought the vehicle out of the HHW-5 for gradual descent. According to the traffic code, no vehicle was supposed to change the altitude or the direction while being inside the virtual highway. The onboard computers must notify the remote tower prior to its exit from the highway.

Within a minute after leaving the holoway, Trevor sensed the gradual descent from the designated altitude, Debbie inquired if she was going to fly all the way to downtown South Tahoe City. The vehicle made a soft touch down over Lake Tahoe Boulevard upon receiving instructions from Trevor. Trevor never liked the idea of flying vehicles inside the congested city roads. In the past, numerous crashes caused plenty of casualties. He told Debbie to turn off the autopilot and switch to manual control. The steering wheel popped out of the dashboard before Trevor. He felt the wheels moving over the paved road as he held the steering wheel.

Davis and Steve had been waiting in front of the Shamrock Tower when Trevor's vehicle appeared exactly at 9:00 am. Debbie took over control as her boss stepped out. She had already been told where to park. Davis and Steve stared with signs of admiration in their eyes at the expensive flying vehicle. Almost like a UFO, the navy-blue machine drove itself to the parking lot, while Trevor's men escorted their boss into the skyscraper for an inspection.

One by one, very carefully, Trevor examined the elevators which were being prepared for a trial run. Upon a thorough inspection, he returned to elevator number one, and told Davis to hook up a jetpack to his back. Trevor planned to check if the brackets and rails had been installed properly. He would use a laser to measure the level of precision. Trevor and Davis, each put on a jet pack like backpacks. They were designed to be operated mostly by voice command.

"The top floor," was all Trevor had to say, and the two jet packs zoomed up to the mentioned floor in a minute. At the top floor, the jet packs hovered while Trevor gave a close inspection to the brackets and rails on each side of the shaft. He attached the laser pod onto one of the brackets for a reading. The readings were what he wanted to see. The alignment of the brackets and rails, throughout the shaft did not deviate more than a thousandth of an inch. The requirement was one sixty fourth of an inch. In other words, his men and robots had exceeded the standard which was expected of them. He noted down the readings in his tab before descending to the lower floors. From his smile Davis could read his boss' satisfaction. Now it was time to install the cables and connect them to the elevators. Just when he was about to descend further down, the humming noise of his jet back ceased. The mechanical voice of the power pack was heard saying, "Power failure! Back-up power malfunction!"

Davis reached out to grab the handle of Trevor's jet pack, missing it by an inch. Trevor was on a free fall from the sixtieth floor. The sinking feeling in his chest made breathing difficult. He had five seconds before impacting upon the base of the shaft. ***

Cindy walked around the garden of their luxurious mansion next to South Tahoe Lake. From their bedroom upstairs, and also their living-room downstairs, the spectacular view of the largest freshwater lake in the US, was the crown jewel of their lodge. The design of the mansion blended the latest trends with the ancient Roman architecture. The front part had the high porch supported by two Roman Doric columns with a triangular pediment and gable roof similar to ancient structures. Under the roof of the porch, from the second floor, a small balcony extended out over the garden. It was guarded by four feet high, perfectly conspicuous glass railing, giving the front part of the mansion the most charming look possible.

It was Cindy's habit. The moment she stepped out of her flying vehicle, she would begin inspecting their garden. She arrived from her work at eleven in the morning. Today, it was their second marriage anniversary. They were going to have lunch together at home, and then after scuba diving for an hour in the lake, they had a plan to have dinner at the best steak house in the town. Trevor loved steak and pasta with chicken and cheese. So, the menu for dinner would most certainly include steak and red wine. At the dinner table, Cindy intended to talk about her plans for the next few years. Since their marriage two years back, they had little thoughts about children. But lately, Cindy had been thinking about conception. To her, the home feels empty without the noises of children chirping or running around.

Cindy had a rather pale complexion. Her long black hair, big dark eyes, long nose, gave her a Semitic look. She hardly ever had sickness, perhaps because of her exceptionally strong immune system. Under her frail look, she possessed a robust and well-toned physique, fit for almost all kinds of outdoor activities one could think of. For five years, she served as an instructor at a local gym before starting her sky-diving company. Sky diving was still a very popular sport among the young generation. A friend owned an old C-130, and he came up with the idea to start a joint venture with Cindy. Within a year, they made a healthy profit by catering to the mostly twenty second century youth, craving for the ultimate thrill of life.

Cindy stared at the hedges. They needed trimming. Then she turned her attention to the lake beyond. She tried to smell the fresh air, closing her eyes and raising her hands like a yoga instructor. For about a minute, she remained motionless. Her trance was interrupted by the vibrations in her waist. One gentle touch, and her device produced the holographic representation of the message before her. It was a message she had been eagerly waiting for the last few months. Space Race sent congratulations to her and her husband Trevor for being selected for the Mission Elenaut. Six months earlier, Cindy and Trevor responded to an advertisement from Space Race, seeking applications from bold and physically fit applicants for its latest project. The description of the mission was not adequately explained in the ad. Nonetheless, it did not fail to arouse Cindy's interest. Later, when she had shown the ad to Trevor, they decided to apply. Subsequently, both went through a series of interviews and rigorous physical tests. None of them believed they had any chance, for there were hundreds of prospective candidates, queuing up before the selection committee. A month after the interviews and tests, when they had received no response, they gave up.

On their wedding anniversary, it was the most wonderful surprise Cindy could think of. With a throbbing heartbeat, she read the rest of the message. They were to report to the company's training facility on September first, at eight in the morning. She murmured to herself, "I have the sweetest surprise for you, Trevor," before turning off the device and heading for their kitchen. She was going to prepare the best pasta with chicken and cheese for their lunch. ***

Trevor had been only a few feet from the base of the shaft when the airbag set at the bottom was activated. By then, Davis hovered over his boss. He dropped to his feet once the noise of his jet pack had receded. Trevor looked at him and remarked, "You know what, I think I know what goes on inside a man when he's about to die, falling from a tall building. It's a disgusting feeling!"

Steve took off the jetpack on Trevor's back and began inspecting it when Trevor felt his communication device vibrating in his trousers' pocket. The device was in voice command mode. A holographic projection of Cindy appeared, as soon as Trevor's voice had received the call. From their kitchen, she called Trevor. She looked unusually upbeat as she said, "I have a nice surprise for you dear."

Trevor was fond of the Dobermans. He said, "Let me guess, you have got a Doberman for me."

"I could not find a Doberman puppy for you. Come home and I'll show you what it is."

She threw a flying kiss before hanging up. ***

Friday's was Trevor's favorite steak house. From the eighteenth floor where the restaurant had been, Lake Tahoe and the entire city were visible. Trevor wanted to go to the grill house next to the beach. However, Cindy insisted on going to the Friday's. She was keenly aware of her husband's taste.

Cindy never really liked red meat. Hence, she ordered grilled salmon. It was seasoned and cooked to perfection. She had asked for it to be cooked medium rare, and the chef nailed it. Trevor went for aged New York Steak. He always had his steak well done. Trevor loved the brown rice that came with it.

Cindy was a great cook herself. Trevor wasn't aware of an item she could not prepare at home. Her world-class kitchen had everything she needed. Apart from that, her Italian ancestry helped her to be a great cook. Her mother taught her to cook everything from Italian cuisine to the great American steak. Still Cindy insisted, eating at home and the experience of it at fine restaurants were two different things. She argued that people went to restaurants not only for the food. It had a lot to do with the environment and presentation. She believed serving food was an art. The restaurant owners of the twenty-second century brought this art to an unprecedented level.

Upon ordering their food, Cindy exclaimed, "Honey, we've done it!" Out of sheer excitement, she closed her eyes for a few seconds. By then, Trevor's curiosity was unstoppable.

He grinned at Cindy as he remarked, "Honey I've been wondering ever since you called me at my work. Will you reveal it to me now?"

"I got a message from the Space Race. We have been selected for the Project Elenaut, though I still don't know what that stands for," signs of extreme delight and amazement adorned her countenance as she said these words.

"What! Trevor took Cindy's hands in his own as he exclaimed. A broad grin touched his cheeks. He asked, "When do we have to report?"

"Next Monday."

"Well, we have the weekend in our hands."

"Shouldn't we celebrate the occasion?" Cindy 's eagerness was palpable.

"That's why we're here, aren't we?"

"We're here to celebrate our anniversary," protested Cindy.

"Oh yeah, I almost forgot," Trevor muttered apologetically. Then he added, "The accident must have made me forget."

"What accident!" the alarm in her voice echoed against the transparent glass window.

"My jetpack malfunctioned while we had been inspecting the brackets and guide rails in the shafts. Of course, safety measures were in place. I fell on the airbag from the sixtieth floor." Trevor paused while he reflected upon the moment, and then with a somber expression, he added, "Those who die this way, honey I know how they feel before the final moment. It's awful. Our lives are so full of uncertainty. You never know what's going to happen the next moment."

"I'm sorry honey, I had no idea you went through this," very tenderly Cindy expressed her compassion. ***

# Chapter Two

"Trevor McLaughlin, Cindy McLaughlin, Greg Austin, Mark Polanski, Andrew Ferguson, Anna Heinrich, Ted Anderson, Mehmet Ozul, Suzy Brennan, Gale Landsdale," the names of the selected candidates were read out while Professor Stan Clifford, the head of the Project Elenaut, stood by. With some files in her hand, Margie Haywood, Professor Stan's secretary stood like a statue next to him. Over their heads hovered a robot which looked more like a small-scale hovercraft.

Each candidate raised his or her hand as their names were read out. Altogether ten of them were chosen out of nine hundred and fifty who had volunteered for the mission. Inside the huge auditorium, the candidates occupied not even a quarter of the front row seats. The temperature of the auditorium was kept at 70* F, comfortable in late summer.

After the greetings, Margie stared at Trevor as she took his resume in her hand. Politely, she asked him to introduce himself. One by one, all the candidates got to know each other, and then the Professor took over the show. He said, "I'll assume, all of you have done a little bit of research on our company before attending the orientation program. I'll start with you, Mr. Polanski. Your resume says that you're a physician, and that you used to work for Mass General in Boston. Glad to have you here with us. Now please tell us what you know about us."

For the sake of courtesy, Dr. Polanski stood up before the audience, and said, "Space Race is one of the companies operating resorts in the earth orbit and the moon. It's a pioneer in the field of space tourism with annual revenue of little more than hundred billion US dollars."

"You're right Dr. Polanski, the previous year we earned over a hundred billion dollars in revenue, and indeed we're one of the pioneers in the field of space tourism. Thank you for your input. Now I would like to ask," the Professor paused, and then continued, "Anyone, please any one of you, add something more."

Trevor stood up and said, "Space Race has a settlement on Mars, plus a mining operation. The company has plans for an interstellar voyage."

"Matter of fact, as we speak, work is going on to build a vessel for the journey to Alpha Centauri with a dedicated crew. It's going to be a joint venture. The number of crew or the exact size of the vessel has not yet been finalized. I believe the number of crew will be somewhere between two hundred to five hundred. As for the size of the vessel, it will not be measured in square feet or yards, but in square kilometers. Obviously, the vessel must be self-sustainable." At this point, Professor Stan paused, expecting questions from his audience.

"Would you please explain what you mean by self-sustainable, dear Professor?" asked Cindy.

With a smile the professor said, "I was expecting a question like this. The journey would take a lifetime, or perhaps longer. Whichever way you see it, it's going to be a one-way trip for the crew. Perhaps one day their offsprings will make the return trip. Therefore, whatever the case, the vessel has to be able to sustain its crews for an indefinite period. It means the vessel must have a mini ecosystem, agriculture, water cycle, and of course, artificial gravity. For communication with earth, ultra-high energy gamma rays will be used. I hope that answers your question, Mrs. McLaughlin."

"Very interesting," remarked fighter pilot Ted Anderson.

Trevor was interested in the vessel's propulsion. He asked, "What kind of propulsion system is going to be used?"

"I knew it was bound to come," the professor remarked with a grin. Then he went on to explain, "In this case chemical propellant does not make sense. For the last couple of decades, there have been numerous debates about it. There were many who proposed particle accelerators. The problem with this system is that it will take years for the vessel to gain the kind of speed required for this mission. And gaining speed is not the only challenge. Ladies and gentlemen, we're not talking about thousands of kilometers per hour, we're talking about thousands of kilometers per sec. If the vessel needs to stop or reduce speed, theoretically it will require an equal amount of force from the opposite direction. The deceleration rate must be tolerable for the crew and the vessel. If the particle accelerators are used, it will take years for it to reach the desired speed, and in the same manner, it'll take years for it to come to stand still. This problem has been solved after the perfection of the anti-matter drive. It was tricky, getting the anti-matter where we wanted it. And then came the discovery of isolium on Mars, the only element in the periodic table the anti-matter does not annihilate, at least during the first few seconds after contact. Those few seconds provided the window we needed to harness the energy from it. The anti-matter drive can propel a vessel at speed close to speed of light. Even at that kind of speed, it would take forty-five years for the vessel to reach Alpha Centauri. Anyway, that's not our immediate concern. First, we must build the vessel, and it cannot be built down here and lifted up there. It must be built up there in space, and this would pose a logistical challenge of Herculean scale. Conventional rockets cannot carry all that load in a reasonable time frame. Hence, we have come with this plan to erect a pair of elevators to the lower orbit."

"Elevators to orbit!" Trevor could not believe his ears.

"Yes, elevators to the lower orbit, that's about eighty miles from where we are," replied Professor Stan.

Trevor laughed as he remarked, "We have not been able to build an elevator reaching a mile high, and here you are talking about an elevator going up eighty miles."

Professor Stan said, "Mr. McLaughlin, a lot has happened in the last couple of decades, and robotic drones are just one of them."

I have employed these drones in my firm," Trevor interrupted.

"Then you must know, these flying robots have no problem working at altitude you or I cannot possibly climb, let alone work."

"That's true, but even robots cannot build a structure for the shaft eighty miles up into the lower orbit. Who'll carry the building materials?" asked Trevor.

The professor looked amused. He said, "Oh Mr. McLaughlin, please do not underestimate our flying robots. They can lift tons of steel and precisely place them at an altitude of more than eighty miles. For just an elevator, we do not need to build any brick structure around the shaft. All we have to do is build the metal structure for the brackets and the guide rails. Already five steel platforms, sixteen miles apart, have been built, each one on top of another, except the one at the base. So, we're already there. Now we have to install the brackets, rails and the ultra-light, and ultra-high strength, state-of-the-art cables. These cables are further fortified with chains made of titanium and alphiron alloy. The alphiron is the unusually high strength derivative of iron extracted from the mines of Mars. Actually, no single elevator will reach the top from the base of the shaft. Five elevators on top of each other, except the one at the bottom, will rise from their respective platforms.

"Simply amazing!" remarked Greg Austin. Then he added, "I have something to show you, if you don't mind."

"Of course, go ahead," the professor responded.

"Please pass the link to your drone, I'll share the image with everyone over here," said Greg.

The drone reproduced a fifty-six-inch holographic image of an impact upon a thick steel plate. The impact spot looked like a crater. Greg explained, "This was caused by the collision with a grain size asteroid. The steel plate is two inches thick. The interplanetary or inter galactic space is full of these devils. If a grain size asteroid can do this to a two-inch-thick steel plate, what will happen to a vessel if an asteroid the size of a tennis ball, or let's say the size of a building hits a spaceship? What kind of plan do you have to prevent such catastrophe?"

"Quite confidently, the professor replied, "Large asteroids are not a problem for you can easily detect them and navigate your vessel around them. Problems arise when these objects are smaller than a golf ball and roam space at an astounding speed of more than a hundred thousand kilometers an hour. However, we have developed sensors that can detect these high velocity objects moving towards us even when they are millions of miles away. The vessel we plan to assemble in space will incorporate state-of-the-art sensors and an electromagnetic force field. The moment these objects encounter the force field, they will either disintegrate or vaporize. I hope that addresses your concern, Mr. Austin."

"If you don't mind, now let's get to the point. What's the objective of Project Elenaut?" Trevor insisted.

For a brief moment the professor glanced at his audience, and then said, "The objective of this mission is to establish the facility of this program and demonstrate to the world whether it is safe to use elevators to reach the lower orbit. Once you reach there, materials will be sent to you to commence building the plant where the space vehicle could be assembled and launched. Your stay there will last for a month. If you can prove the program safe, a steady stream of man and material will find their way to the plant, expanding in line with our plans. From now on, you might be addressed as an elephant. It stands for elevated astronauts. That's all for today, you can return to your quarters. Tomorrow, we'll visit the location where the work on this project has been going on. I think we have a nice surprise waiting for you guys over there." ***

From the control room, the progress of the work was being monitored. The brackets and rails of the topmost section were being installed at an altitude of eighty miles. The three-dimensional holographic projection reproduced all activities of the robots right before the monitors. Every time a part was installed, the respective robot focused its cameras on the installed component or section. The monitors observed the position and the measurements with their own eyes before approving the installation. The last part of the elevator was on the fifth and final platform. The platform was made of five-inch-thick titanium plate. The plate of the final platform was comparatively thinner. For zero gravity there was no need for a thick floor. Those who worked at the control room had four-hour shifts. The work had been going on round the clock. When the professor arrived at the control room for an unscheduled inspection, it was ten o'clock at night. The final stage of installing the brackets and rails had been going on. The cables were ready to be connected to the elevators at the base of the shaft. In a single shaft, two elevators were being fitted with the necessary tools. After connecting the cables, electrical and electronics devices had to be checked. Once the devices had been certified, the elevators were to be operational for a test run.

For about five minutes, Professor Stan watched the activities of the two robots. When it was time to connect the cables, he told the remote operators to stop the robots. He wanted to check the alignments of the guide rails. It took roughly two minutes to scan the sixteen-mile-long shaft. Nothing seemed out of place. The robots produced readings, confirming the professor's observation. For some reason, Professor Stan looked apprehensive. Very carefully, he read the printout of the readings sent by the two robots. He had to approve the work. Subsequently, the robots began connecting the cables. It would take several hours to install the cables. Early in the morning, Professor was going to accompany the selected elenauts to the project site. Hence, he retired from the unscheduled inspection and returned to his quarter. ***

A thirty feet high concrete wall with barbed wire at the top surrounded the entire compound. A small contingent of private contractors was in charge of the security of the compound. In the middle of the Mojave Desert, the sight of the project was like a lost and found case. The sky above the project was a no-fly zone. Hence, the three flying four-wheel drives landed on the driveway in front of the huge gate. A drone came down from the watch tower and scanned the occupants of the vehicles. Facial recognition software was used to identify. When the data matched with the data which had been earlier sent to the watch tower, it transmitted the signal to open the gate.

The three vehicles drove past the gate for about fifteen minutes. Finally, when the vehicles stopped, the elenauts were greeted by a jaw dropping sight. They had never seen anything like it. Columns made of steel went up as far as eyes could see. The platform on the ground was at the center of the columns. The view was obstructed from the spot where the vehicles stopped.

Professor Stan was at the forefront when a loud humming noise distracted the team. Fifty meters behind them, the behemoth landed on its four extended landing gears. All of them had read comics about transformers during their childhood, but for the first time, the elenauts saw what a real-life transformer looked like. It was like the wildest dream. The fifteen-meter-tall monster had just finished installing the cables alongside its associates. The professor paged the monster in order to present a stunning surprise to the visitors.

"These monsters are powered by miniature fusion reactors in them. The danger of nuclear contamination is zero. The energy is one hundred percent clean," said the professor while the spectators stared at the monster with awe. "I hope now you understand how we built the eighty-mile-tall shaft, Mr. McLaughlin," the professor boasted.

Cindy had an eerie sensation when they walked past the thick steel columns, towards the elevators. There were two of them, side by side, ten feet apart. The entrance of one of the elevators was open. It was as large as a spacious room. The ceiling was at least thirty feet high. Later, the professor explained the reason behind such a high ceiling. The space was to be used for long construction materials like fabricated beams. The insulators along the door panels ensured an air-tight environment once the door was shut. It had a clinic like arrangement with a bed and surgery lights, in case of an emergency. The closet had extra space suits neatly hung from the hangers. Two fire extinguishers were attached to the wall next to the door. Two indoor units of air conditioners were installed on the walls.

"It has the capacity to lift twenty thousand kilograms. Hence, fifty healthy elenauts with everything they need, can easily be elevated at any given time," remarked the professor. ***

In the morning, the elenauts congregated for another meeting with the staffs of the Space Race. They were given a list of the things they were expected to bring with them for their month-long training period. Forty-eight hours prior to reporting time, the candidates were told to abstain from all types of alcoholic drinks or narcotics, and this prohibition would continue during the whole program. ***

On their flight back to South Tahoe, Trevor and Cindy discussed the ways to wrap up their businesses for the next three months. They had two weeks to organize everything and report back to the Space Race training facility at Henderson, Nevada. From the aircraft, Trevor directed his flying vehicle to the parking lot of the airport. It would take roughly fifteen minutes to fly to their villa located at Lakeside Beach, on Lakeshore Boulevard. The day was unusually windy. Strong wind had been blowing from northeast. Right before getting into Trevor's vehicle, Cindy pointed at the lightning under the dark clouds, a couple of kilometers from the parking lot. Debbie received a storm warning while the vehicle had been gaining speed at the cruising altitude. Prior to getting into the hollow way at seven hundred meters, the vehicle encountered sporadic hails, hitting it from all directions. Trevor told Debbie to turn off the autopilot and hand over control of the vehicle to him. It was then that they noticed the vehicles, hundred meters behind them being tossed out of the hollow way by something.

"Trevor, it's a twister!" Cindy cried out.

By then the greenish swirling clouds of the uninvited monster became visible. It had been moving along the holoway towards Lake Tahoe.

"Control tower, we have an emergency! Need to get out of the hollow way!" Trevor's voice rattled.

In the head up display before him, Trevor saw the direction from the control tower, and began his descent out of the lane. The vehicle shook violently as it struggled to steer a course safely out of the raging storm. Air pockets made a steady descent almost impossible when the monster caught up with the vehicle. Trevor realized that even twelve hundred horsepower of the engine was not enough to outrun the chasing monster. He exerted full throttle in order to maintain control over his vehicle. For nearly a minute, the vehicle somehow made progress while its passengers held their breath. Cindy turned off the air-conditioner to conserve power. Condensation accumulated on the windshield and windows, indicating a rapid drop in temperature outside the vehicle. The two wipers moved frantically to provide a clear view of the ferocious world ahead of the vehicle. Trevor watched helplessly the debris and dust flying in the direction of the vortex along with the car. Debbie was heard saying in cold and indifferent voice, "I'm losing power."

It was the worst nightmare one could imagine. Mentally, Cindy was a very strong woman. However, as death looked in their eyes, her feminine instincts kicked in. With petrified expression in her eyes, she grabbed Trevor's arm.

The swirling dark clouds turned so dark that they could hardly see anything through it. The thermometer on the dashboard displayed temperature outside. It was close to zero. The altimeter indicated the vehicle was at two thousand meters. It was not designed to fly at that kind of altitude. How high the force of the savage twister was going to hurl the vehicle, Trevor had no idea. Cindy had never been religious. She felt like it was a good time to surrender to the will of the Providence. She closed her eyes and tried to focus her thoughts while everything around them shook violently, turning the vehicle on its left side at forty-five degrees.

Is the GPS working honey?" whimpered Cindy.

Trevor glanced through the window, there was nothing but utter darkness. Then he looked at the onboard navigation system. It was being powered by the vehicle's auxiliary power unit. The GPS indicated their location somewhere over the lake.

Trevor said, "We're already over the lake. Soon, the force of the twister is going to drop."

"Are we going to fall?" exclaimed Cindy.

"It looks that way. At least we're over the lake."

"Is it safer, landing on water without power?"

"Look at it this way, we won't be instantly crushed to death by the impact."

They could sense the vehicle dropping as Trevor finished his statement. And then, quite abruptly, the cloud outside thinned out, eventually leaving the vehicle in a free fall. Habitually, Trevor stared at the altimeter. The free fall had begun from the height of little over a thousand meters. He kept pressing the ignition for manual restart. He wasn't sure, the vehicle would survive the impact upon the lake surface. ***

# Chapter Three

At the head office of Space Race, Michael Stewart, the owner and CEO of Space Race, has been browsing through the company's financial statements since morning. He has called his secretary Stephanie to get a printout of the draft prospectus. At four in the afternoon, he has a meeting with prospective investors. For the last three months, he has been haunted by the dire prospect of a cash crunch. The debt of the company far exceeds the assets. Hence, at the moment his company's net worth is a negative figure. Within the next one month, if there's no significant infusion of funds, some of his projects will shut down, and Project Elenaut is among them. Michael is among the leading entrepreneurs from the southwest coast who has placed his bet on space exploration. He has invested all his fortunes in Project Elenaut. Either it's going to give him unprecedented level of fame and fortune or crush him to nothing. Michael is one of those few visionaries who possess the means and the determination to realize the long-cherished dream of inter-planetary or perhaps inter-stellar journeys.

The internet giant Fox Tail, global container transport LLD, and trans-continental shipping Ocean View, have expressed their interest in investing. Today, the CEOs of those companies are supposed to attend a meeting with Michael. If Michael can convince them, his financial predicament will be over for the time being. Or else he will have no choice but to go public. Michael has no desire to collect funds through IPO. He knows he'll have little control over his company once he goes public for funds. Even if he holds more than fifty percent shares, still he will have to accept the decision of the governing board. Exclusive ownership has its appeal, and Michael will do everything in his power to retain family control over his company.

When Stephanie handed over the draft copy of the prospectus, his office computer alerted him of an incoming call from Professor Stan.

"Go ahead, have him before me," Michael instructed.

In the hologram projection the professor looked anxious. Without his usual sunny grin, he looked odd. Very coldly Michael greeted him and said, "Professor Stan, don't wait. Please get to the point."

"I think you should watch the news channel seven," the professor suggested.

Michael stared at the projection before him, and a live video of the thick greenish column of swirling wind and debris plodding through South Tahoe captured his attention.

"What are those?" whispered Michael.

"Those are the vehicles picked up from route 89," replied Professor Stan from the other end. Then he added, "I've been following it for the last half an hour. The report says it has wind speeds of up to a hundred and eighty miles an hour. Very powerful storm. Haven't seen a twister of such magnitude in this region for quite some time."

"Well, it's tornado season, so I wouldn't call it a surprise. Stan, please don't tell me, you want to talk to me about the twister. I expect something a bit more substantial than this," said the boss with clear signs of impatience in his tone.

"I'm afraid it's the reason why I called you, Mike."

This time Michael did not conceal his irritation. He said, "Stan, I have been going through a nightmare of my own, collecting funds for the program that writes your paycheck. Today, I have an extremely important meeting with a number of prospective investors. If I fail to make an impression about the project, we're all in trouble. So, please spare me the extra trouble and pray for a miracle."

The old professor knew he had to be quick. He said, "Mike, what if something like this strikes the shaft, has it occurred to you? I'm kinda anxious."

"Something like what?" Michael wasn't comfortable talking about it.

"The twister."

"Come on Stan, I didn't expect it from you, not at this moment when I'm going through hell. You're a scientist. You know better than anyone the kind of force the structure can withstand. These twisters can't do a thing to those skyscrapers. And here we have a structure that hardly presents any resistance to wind."

"We could delay the launch. In winter there's no chance of twisters, it's better to be safe than sorry. There are just too many uncertainties," remarked the old professor as he gasped for air.

"My dear professor, please calm down, I think you're being unreasonably pessimistic. Uncertainty is just another term for life. At this very moment, your heart could have angina because of your anxieties. Now tell me, are you going to live the rest of your life with a pacemaker in your hand? Does it make sense? If we have the launch in winter the frosty conditions will cause more problems than the twisters. Please do not let your fears distract you from your task in hand. Keep up your good work, and in no time, we'll hit a milestone in space travel. When that happens, you'll look back at yourself and laugh."

"That's just one aspect of it, we're not too far away from the quake zone either."

"I know, we could have built it in Texas or Florida, but if something goes wrong, I don't want to see the whole thing crashing down on people's heads. There's hardly any place without settlement in those states. This is why we chose the godamn desert. No one is going to be hurt if it crashes. I hope I've managed to address your fears, professor. Now please, let me focus on my work. I'll be there personally to see the progress of your project within a very short time. See you then." ***

The two chutes popped out at three thousand feet, one from the front, another from the rear of Trevor's flying vehicle. Trevor had to press a button in his seat to deploy the chutes. For a reason there was no option to activate the device by voice command. When he pressed the button, he wasn't sure if it was going to work because it had never been tested. A sense of relief returned when a sudden jerk slowed down the violent descent. Now they had peace of mind, and above all the time to think about their next step.

By then, the dark swirling clouds were completely gone. Through the window, Trevor looked down. He could see the green waters of Lake Tahoe, and then glanced at the distant lake shores. They would have to swim for an hour if not longer to traverse that kind of distance. Trevor regretted his decision not to go for the model which offered amphibious capability. He did not feel the need to spend the extra cash on such a seemingly unnecessary option.

"Are we going to land on the lake honey?" Cindy asked anxiously.

"Yep, it looks that way," Trevor replied promptly.

"Does this vehicle have amphibious mode?"

"Nope, I never thought this could happen to us. I was wrong. I shouldn't have been so stingy. However, we do have another option." After saying this, Trevor opened the glove compartment and took out a blue kit box.

"What is it?" Cindy asked.

"It's a magic solution," with a smile Trevor replied. After a brief pause, he explained, "It's concentrated form of liquid nitrogen, oxygen, and tiny bit of water. Once we inject ourselves with this, it'll allow us to breathe underwater for more than an hour, if we remain motionless, and for an hour if we keep swimming."

"Is it safe, Trevor?"

"Of course, it's FDA approved. It has the exact ratio of the air we breathe in. Seventy eight percent nitrogen, twenty one percent oxygen, and two percent water." Taking some capsules from the file attached to the kit, he farther explained, "However, we have to take these capsules prior to injecting the solution. It is calcium oxide, designed to absorb the poisonous CO2 released from our blood cells. It will react with the CO2 and produce a substance called calcium carbonate in our kidney." Finally, Trevor showed the ultra-sonic device in the kit, and explained, "We are to use this tool to break down the by product in our kidney. Eventually, it's supposed to come out of our body with urine. But there's a catch to it. We cannot breathe in fresh air, as long as we're under the influence of the solution, or else it will burn out our lungs. Therefore, we must time our dive."

Trevor set the alarm in his watch. It would vibrate to notify the moment they could breathe air safely. The injector appeared like a handgun with an eight-inch silver barrel. Trevor inserted four capsules, two for each, into the chamber, and waited for the splash down. The splash down was rather violent, as the vehicle slammed onto the water surface at hundred and fifty feet per second.

The passengers were in their under-wears, getting ready for the long swim.

"Are there sharks in these waters?" Cindy asked with an anxious tone.

"Not that I know of. Don't worry, it's safe," Trevor reassured Cindy.

The amount of trapped air in the cabin was not sufficient to keep the heavy vehicle afloat. Gradually it began to sink. Trevor continued, "Honey, we must be very quick, because once we open the windows, the vehicle's descent will be very rapid. At places, the depth of the lake is well over two thousand feet. I hope we have not landed at one of those spots. If we cannot make a timely escape, we will be crushed to death at that kind of depth. When both had received their shots, water rushed in as Trevor opened one of the windows manually. By the time Trevor came off the vehicle, it had already sunk at least a hundred feet. Cindy was not so lucky. The force of the water rushing in trapped her inside the vehicle. The vehicle descended faster at every passing moment. Trevor tried to keep up with the sinking vehicle. He could not. It was simply too heavy. The sight of the vehicle grew dimmer and dimmer, eventually disappearing into the abyss. ***

"I think, I'm going to try hazelnut today," Professor Stan told himself as he approached the coffee dispenser. Usually, he would drop by at a local restaurant for his breakfast. Today he made an exception to that tradition. He came straight to his office on the top floor of the R&D

division. He had already placed the order for his breakfast. At any moment it would be air delivered by a drone. The moment he had stepped into his office, the melodious female voice of his robocom greeted him.

The old professor didn't pay attention to Helen's greeting. With a cup of coffee in his hand, he said, "Helen, I want you to run a simulation."

"Professor Stan, I said good morning to you. You didn't respond. Do you feel agitated? You know I have ABM-300 processors. My programming tells me how to have feelings. I'm disappointed by your indifferent attitude. Please, be kind to this very sensitive lady."

"Oh yeah, I forgot. I have a very sensitive lady here. I'm sorry Helen, I should have been more attentive to your needs. You know what, had it not been for that old, frail and intrusive lady at home, I would have married you by now. Now, let's start with the simulation, shall we?"

"You did not feed the scenario into my system."

"It's an F-5 twister, hitting the shaft."

"What would be the scale of projection?"

"Adjust to fit my office."

"If I reconstruct the entire shaft in your office, in comparison, the twister will appear quite small."

"So, what's the solution?"

"I do not see why we must reconstruct the whole shaft. We could simply reproduce the part of the shaft affected by the imaginary twister. Subsequently, I can calculate the effect of the strike upon the whole structure."

"I wanted to visualize it," the old professor insisted.

"It does not make sense to me, Professor Stan. What if I just prepare the findings? You should be able to construct an imaginary picture of it based on the report. I have data that tells me, human brain is the ultimate supercomputer."

"You got that right, beautiful lady. Here I have my Robocom trying to flatter me again," with smiling face, the old professor remarked.

"Of all the human traits I have been gifted with by the state-of-art technology, still I lack this one. Believe me, when I say you're a genius, I mean it," Helen remarked.

The old professor couldn't help but laugh when he responded, "Don't worry, it's not a virtue. It's a vice. Now, please get going. I can't wait to see the result."

"Just give me a few seconds to upload the relevant data from the global net."

In fifteen seconds, the hologram image of the bottom part of the shaft appeared before the professor. The actual size of it would have reached ten thousand feet in the stratosphere. Then a twister with wind speed of three hundred kilometers an hour could be seen approaching the shaft. The force of the twister picked up debris of destroyed structures on its way. Every detail of the shaft, such as the thickness of the titanium beams, the tensile and yield strength ductility of the metals used to erect the structure had been fed into Helen's system for evaluation of the effect.

As it had been expected, the force of the twister could not harm the structure, for the spiraling wind met little resistance, passing through the horizontal and diagonal braces the structure stood on. However, when the eye of the mile wide vortex reached the shaft, unexpectedly it picked up a heavy trailer truck like a matchbox. The trailer slammed onto the shaft with the ferocity of an approaching aircraft. The old professor's heartbeat jumped up. For his age the tension infused with some kind of devilish thrill was devastating. He gasped for air as the shaft vibrated in order to absorb the shock. The braces at the impact spot had been blown away like twigs. Nonetheless, the structure withstood the impact.

"Helen, I want you to connect me to Michael asap. Be ready to re-run the simulation before him," the professor could hardly suppress his dismay as he said this to his robocom. ***

With depth, very rapidly the water pressure had been increasing. Cindy knew she had little time. In no time the pressure inside the cabin and outside equalized, neutralizing the force which had trapped Cindy. She swam out of the sinking vehicle with relative ease. Albeit the solution had released the necessary amount of oxygen in her blood stream, the suffocating sensation caused by the water pressure presented an unpleasant prospect, and the fact that they had to endure it for quite some time, made it even more painful. Nonetheless, she thanked her luck just for being alive.

At little over a hundred and fifty feet from the surface, Cindy met Trevor descending with his hands extended towards her. He pointed at his water-proof watch on his wrist. The glowing display showed the depth, the level of oxygen in his blood stream, and the remaining time submerged. The level of oxygen was ninety percent. They could stay submerged for the next fifty-five minutes. The gadget also had GPS, indicating the distance and direction of the shore.

The slightly brackish water of the lake was more or less free from algae and other aquatic plants. Out of the depth of the lake, without any kind of warning, a couple of beavers appeared before Trevor and Cindy. One of them touched

Cindy's face with its snout, displaying a friendly gesture. In return, she stroked its head as a sign of mutual affection. The animals knew the direction their newfound friends had been heading. They turned around and began swimming in the same direction, while Cindy put her hand on the neck of one of the beavers, pulling her as it swam forward.

The experience turned out to be rather pleasant for both Cindy and Trevor. In almost an hour, they came within fifty meters from the lake shore. The vibrating diving gadget indicated to them that it was safe to hit the surface. The two beavers were still with them, they had no idea how to thank them, or say goodbye to them. ***

When Michael had finished his conversation with his wife, Mary Anne, he could see the notification before him. It was Professor Stan online. Most people in his place would simply refuse to get into a conversation with an employee who had been a constant source of annoyance to Michael lately. However, he had this uncanny ability to face even the most disturbing prospect with the sweetest of smiles. Michael saw it as his greatest strength, and he was not about to abandon it. He knew he had come this far in life because of this virtue. Michael tried to speculate what the old professor might have for him this time. The bold visionary was determined, he was not going to let anyone talk him out of his way. He organized his thoughts, in case the witty professor raised any kind of unpleasant issue.

"Alright Bob, let me hear what the nutty professor has to say," Michael said to his office computer acting more like his additional secretary. A life-size three-dimensional representation of the old professor appeared only a foot from Michael's office desk.

The speakers became alive when the professor said, "Mike, I just ran a simulation of a twister hitting our project_______,"

"And what did you find out?" inquired Michael.

"The good thing is you were right, the twister could do no harm to it________,"

"I told you so," with a smile Michael interrupted while swallowing some chow Mein from his soup bowl he had ordered from the nearby Chinese restaurant.

When Michael stopped, the professor continued, "And the bad news is, what the twister could not do, a fifty-ton trailer truck did it for the twister."

"What do you mean?" Michael sounded clearly agitated.

"On its way, the twister had picked up this trailer truck, and it crashed onto the structure like a bulldozer, severely damaging the structure."

"The twister picked up the trailer because you had programmed it to. Remember, it's a simulation," responded the boss.

Frustration and disappointment were palpable in the professor's tone. He exclaimed, "For heaven's sake Mike, be realistic! You know, these computers don't need to be programmed for such a scenario, they have AI technology built in them. They create the most logical scenario from the available data, and you know as well, in real life the highways aren't going to be devoid of vehicles."

Michael stopped and put the chopsticks in the bowl. He looked straight into the professor's eyes, and said, "Tell your simulation to step back, say eight kilometers from the shaft, and then look it."

"Why?" the professor was puzzled.

"Just do it," quite firmly Michael insisted.

"Helen, do what the man says," the professor told his robocom.

When Helen focused on the structure from eight kilometers, Michael asked, "Now tell me, how big the damage is."

"For crying out loud, you're looking at it from eight kilometers! What do you expect?" the troubled professor protested vehemently.

"But the structure doesn't look small, does it? And that's the point Stan. You have to look at the big picture. Even a dozen strikes like that can't do a thing to the structure," a bit boastfully the boss pointed out, and then added, "Apart from that, how many twisters do we have in a year in that region, and what are the chances of one of them hitting the shaft? The chances are very slim, and I'm willing to take the risk."

"You sound like it's going to be there only for a while. Wake up Mike, it's a permanent structure. Sooner or later, we're going to have something like this knocking our door."

"I told you, even a dozen of them can't do a thing to our structure. It's too big."

At this point, Michael slumped back in his seat and quietly stared at the dismayed professor. From Michael, the message was clear. It was going to be his way or the highway. Finally, the anxious professor decided to give it a rest. Something in him warned him not to drag the issue farther. It was his duty to point out the risks if anything unpleasant was to occur. His conscience was clear.

And then Michael signaled to the professor how utterly disappointed he was with the professor. His voice sank to an abyss as he said, "I never expected this from you. I knew there would be obstacles. I just couldn't imagine it would come from you. Anyway, I won't let your conscience bug you. I don't want you to be a hostage, held against your will. I can see that it was a mistake to hire you for this job. You're not the man for it ___________,"

Realizing where the conversation had been heading, the professor tried to stop it. He said, "No, no, Mike, you didn't make any mistake, I just wanted to ___________,"

Michael wouldn't let the professor finish. He resumed, "Don't bother Professor, I have already made up my mind. I always hated having to deal with unhappy employees. Since you never really approved of the project, as of today, I'm letting you go. You can pack up. I'll have Jeff take over from you before you leave the compound. From the very beginning he had been the most enthusiastic supporter of the project. I don't know why I picked you instead of him to lead the project in the first place."

Now it was the professor's turn to have the long face. He knew he had gone past the point of no return. Very gently he uttered, "I'm sorry Mike. Feel free to call me if you need any assistance."

"Just one request to you before you leave, Stan. Please don't make any kind of inconvenient remarks to the media or the public. Remember, you're still under an oath, even when you're not with us. My attorney will be watching you."

"You can trust me on that," said the old professor in a reassuring voice.

There was no response from Michael as he pressed the button to terminate the connection manually. ***

# Chapter Four

The simulator was an exact replica of the X-Elevators. However, instead of reaching the lower orbit, its rails and brackets were installed in a three-hundred-meter-tall shaft. Though the elevator could easily accommodate more than fifty people at a time, ten elenauts, along with the instructor, were chosen for each simulated lift. During the ascent, the control panel was introduced to the trainees. The movement of the elevator could be controlled from the panel inside the elevator, and also from the control room situated at the base next to the shaft. The interior looked a bit like the aircraft cockpit with two seats for the commander and his assistant, and eight for the rest of the elenauts right behind them. There was provision to eject the capsule, along with the elenauts, in case of an emergency. This mechanism could not be activated if the altitude of the X-Elevator was less than two hundred meters.

It was time for the trainees to get familiarized with the gadgets and safety procedures. Beginning with Trevor, one by one, all ten trainees were shown the devices from the joystick which controlled the rate of the ascent or descent to the CPC which maintained normal air pressure of 11-12 PSI inside the capsule. The cables connecting the elevator had oxygen supply line buried in them. There was also an emergency oxygen tank installed on the roof. The multifunction AC could automatically regulate not only the temperature of the capsule, but it had controls over the lighting and oxygen supply as well. The instructor demonstrated to the trainees how to set or change the set up. The trainees also had to familiarize themselves with the first aid tools and emergency medical procedures such as conducting CPR to check the vital signs.

The simulation went on for two hours straight. Once the selected candidates completed the simulation, the next candidates began their training session. The selected candidates were then given a break before taking the team for the next round of training for the day.

The trainees were in full space gear as they stood before the huge water tank. One standard size football field would easily fit in the gigantic water tank. Down below, submerged in thirty feet deep crystal-clear water, the elenauts could be seen working with the kind of tools they were going to use in space. Prior to getting down into the water tank, they were shown the scale model of what they were expected to assemble under water.

For the first time, the elenauts had been using the space suits. These suits had the state-of-the-art gadgets needed to ensure safety and comfort for the elenauts in the most hostile environments one could imagine. Each elenaut were attended by a humanoid robot, constantly watching the gadgets or the vital signs of the elenaut. In turn, this data was being relayed to the monitoring cell situated behind a thirty feet high glass wall, inside the complex housing the pool. Inside the monitoring cell, three humanoid technicians under one human supervisor, kept an eye on the hologram representation of the activities down in the pool.

The ten elenauts were divided into five pairs. Cindy was paired with a stunningly attractive red headed young lady from Minnesota. Gale Lansdale had completed her post graduate degree two years back before she applied to join Project Elenaut. She was a physicist, specializing in quantum mechanics. Her jolly and frank attitude helped her to easily befriend those who came in touch with this beautiful lady. She was a few inches shorter than Cindy. In her space suit, she had to struggle with her relatively small figure. Nonetheless, it couldn't stop her from doing what she had to do. Cindy observed her mate, admiring her wit and resolve. While working on the rollers of the ten by seven sliding door, they got into a conversation meant to befriend each other.

"Are you married, Gale?" Cindy asked.

"Never had the time to think about it," Gale replied with a smile under her headgear.

"Not even a boyfriend," Cindy sounded surprised by Gale's reply.

"I see it as a distraction. I don't want anything to hamper my career."

"I wish I could be dedicated to my career the way you are, Gale."

"Don't regret. At times, it gets awfully lonely."

"Really! Then why do you choose to live like a hermit?"

"Hermit's life!" Gale had to laugh at Cindy's question, then she resumed, "Naa, I won't call it a hermit's life. I do interact with my friends. It's just that I don't wanna be emotionally involved before I reach a certain stage in my career. In this field, one has to be one hundred percent focused, to achieve something substantial."

Cindy noticed the red light blinking on Gale's visor as she finished her statement. She said to Gale, "I think someone has been trying to reach you."

Gale glanced at it, and said, "I wonder what's going on. Those fellas before the monitors, they wanna see me."

"Is anything wrong?" Cindy asked anxiously.

"I don't know. I guess I'll have to find out."

The supervisor of the monitoring team sat behind his desk. His flat expression defied what he had on his mind. Quietly Gale stared at the man. He held Gale's personal file before him, browsing through it with a somber expression. Then he raised his head, throwing at Gale a calculated smile. "How are you today, Ms. Landsdale? How do you feel right now?"

"I'm alright. Is everything okay over here?"

"Oh, we're doing alright. There's something we would like you to have a look at," the hologram report of her vital signs appeared before them as the supervisor had stopped. With his laser pointer, he circled the figures indicating her pulse rate. It was unusually high.

"Something seems to have been bothering you. Are you nervous for any reason?" inquired the supervisor.

"Nope, I don't feel nervous," Gale's response was quick.

"Sometimes, we're unaware of our inner workings," the supervisor sounded suspiciously intrusive.

Gale nodded to display her attention. The next moment, the supervisor continued, "Ms. Landsdale, have you ever been to a shrink?"

"Shrink!" Gale wasn't familiar with the term.

"I mean a psychiatrist."

Gale tried to recall, and then said, "I can't remember."

The supervisor had a postgraduate degree in psychology. He was quite prepared for such a response. Right after she had failed to recollect if she ever visited a psychiatrist, the hologram image of a webpage owned by a clinic appeared before them, and then the supervisor asked, "Does this clinic look familiar to you, Ms. Landsdale?"

"Oh yeah, now I remember. Three years back I visited the clinic," Gale replied firmly.

"Would you please tell us, the reason behind your visit?"

"I had claustrophobia. I don't have it now."

"How did you develop claustrophobia, Ms. Landsdale?"

"When I was a child, my mother wouldn't have me in a daycare center. Every day, she locked me down in our tiny studio and went to work. Eventually, I developed this aversion for enclosed space."

"Didn't you have your father with you?"

"My parents were divorced."

"Well Ms. Landsdale, it may appear to you that you don't have Claustrophobia now, but we think this fear of enclosed space is causing your pulse rate to jump up while you're in that suit. Perhaps it's not a big issue. Nonetheless, there's always this possibility that the suit might put your wellbeing at risk. Therefore, we have decided to recall you from the project. We're sorry, Ms. Landsdale. It's for your own good. We would like to thank you for the cooperation we received from you. Though you will no longer be involved with the project, you'll receive your remuneration as specified by the contract for the remainder of the period." ***

At lunch time, Trevor and Cindy sat a few feet from the rest of the team. The cafeteria was on the top floor of the training facility, overlooking the countryside surrounding the compound. It occupied roughly half of the top floor, at the northern end of the building. Whenever the diners needed service, they could press a button on their arm rest, and a humanoid waitress would appear, ready to serve. These humanoid staff members managed the entire restaurant. All of them had vivaciously young look, and no matter how many times they had to respond, or how rude any particular diner was, these humanoid waiters and waitresses were as courteous as ever. They recorded every detail of their conversations with the diners, and therefore, there was absolutely no chance of misunderstanding or humanoid error.

Cindy had ordered seafood, while Trevor asked for a steak subwich with lettuce, tomato and Swiss cheese. Trevor smiled back, as the humanoid waitress served him the subwich with a smile. Trevor gazed at the humanoid waitress, courteously commenting "Arabian look! Thank you. You're very attractive. I like your hairstyle."

"Thank you, Mr. McLaughlin, I appreciate your sweet comment."

Trevor whistled as he exclaimed, "You already know my name. I suppose you know more about me than my wife does!"

"No Mr. McLaughlin, which is not wholly factual. We have been fed only the names of our clients and their food preferences."

Cindy laughed at the humanoid's response. She said, "Thank God! I was afraid my husband might fall for a humanoid if she knew everything he liked."

"Don't worry Mrs. McLaughlin, he cannot possibly convince a humanoid with his charm."

This time, Cindy broke down laughing at Trevor. Trevor had obviously been enjoying the conversation. He asked the humanoid waitress, "How should we address you? Don't you have a name?"

"My associates call me Hal, short for Halima, an Arabic name, given to me for my Arabian features."

"Well Hal, nice to meet you. Now, would you please tell us, who does the cooking here? Is the chef a humanoid or a human like us?" Trevor inquired.

"It's a collaboration. The chef tells us what is to be cooked, and watches over our shoulders as we do the actual cooking. Then he does the tasting, for the humans have not yet succeeded in developing tongues with taste buds for us."

"Humans have not yet developed tongues for you guys because you don't need one as you don't eat. You get your energy from the batteries installed inside you," Trevor pointed out while munching his meal.

"Yes Mr. McLaughlin, you're right. I can see that you're one well informed man," Hal said to Trevor.

"I have to be well informed Hal, or else I won't be in this business for long."

Cindy changed the topic abruptly. "Honey, let me introduce my new pal to you," she said to Trevor having noticed Gale approaching them. Both turned their attention to Gale. She had a handbag with her.

"Hi Gale, this is my Husband, Trevor. He' also involved with this project."

Trevor and Gale exchanged greetings when Cindy asked, "Aren't you going to have lunch with us? Where are you going at this hour with your bag?"

Gale explained to Cindy and Trevor her status. Cindy was clearly saddened by what had happened to her pal. She said, she wanted to invite Gale to their villa once they had completed their mission. Before leaving, Gale promised she was going to make time to visit Cindy and her husband, even if it meant flying from Minnesota to Lake Tahoe. She didn't forget to kiss Cindy on her cheek before the sad farewell.

Gale's unexpected departure conveyed a bitter fact to Cindy and Trevor. Their stay at the training facility also depended upon their overall fitness. Any of them could be rejected at any given time for any given reason. The standby candidates were there to replace the disqualified candidates.

"For the next three months we have to be on our heels, sweetheart," remarked Trevor.

"Let's see what happens," with a dismal face Cindy began taking her meal. ***

The following day was set to test how the candidates reacted to extreme G force. At the beginning it was just a ride. Each of the four long arms of the G force simulator had a compartment at the other end. Two trainees sat abreast in each of those compartments while the extended arms of the simulator circled around the center at high speed, producing bone crushing G-force upon the trainees sitting in the four compartments. When the arms of the simulator reached top speed, the brute force pressed on the countenance of the trainees, making their faces look like ironed clothes. For Cindy, it was a familiar experience. However, for the rest of the trainees, it was a ride through hell. For the next fifteen minutes, the candidates endured the pain caused by eight plus G-force. The uncomfortable sensation made at least one of the trainees throw up, while another lost consciousness for a few seconds. Trevor looked disoriented as he was led out of the compartment, at the end of the run. Cindy laughed at her husband, leading him to the nearby seat while tenderly stroking his back.

"It was hell of a ride, Cindy," was the first statement he made after he had calmed down.

"Yes, it was sweetheart. I guess we'll have to be prepared for any kind of eventuality."

"Don't you think it's a bit too much? After all, we'll be riding an elevator."

"If something happens up there, and we get stuck, they intend to keep the option open to bring us down the hard way."

"Yeah, I know. Let's hope our luck doesn't run out up there."

As the G-force test was over in the next half an hour, the candidates were given a short break for light refreshments. Before lunch, they went to an airfield for the parabolic flight. Two wide bodied jet aircraft had been waiting for the trainees and their instructors. During this flight, the trainees would experience zero gravity for the first time. They had been warned not to take anything heavy prior to the flight for there was a history of trainees throwing up during the parabolic flight as well.

Exactly at eleven in the morning, the aircraft were airborne. In ten minutes, the aircraft reached an altitude of thirty-nine thousand feet. From the cockpit, the pilots gave the signal that the parabolic flight was about to commence. Trevor was in the other aircraft, while Cindy got ready to record the activities inside the cabin during the parabolic flight, to share it with Trevor and her friends. Suddenly, Cindy felt like everything inside her floating in the air. She watched a packet gradually defying gravity right before her eyes. Her companions rolled, executed perfect summersaults, as Cindy told herself, *"So, this is how it feels to be out there in space! Not bad!"*

The first parabolic flight lasted forty-five seconds. The aircraft regained lost altitude, and then went for the next parabolic flight. Hence, the two aircraft executed several parabolic flights. By the time the two aircraft returned to the airfield, the trainees had been thoroughly familiarized with the zero-gravity environment. Both Trevor and Cindy loved the ride. There were no unpleasant scenarios like throwing up or losing senses. Cindy thought she had acquired enough materials to share with her friends. ***

For about an hour Jeff observed the development. Earlier, the monitors called him to the control-room. A strange phenomenon had been taking place around the shaft, at an altitude of thirty thousand feet. In an hour the formations grew thicker and larger. The de-foggers had to be turned on to have a clear view of the scene.

"What do you think?" asked the humanoid technician who oversaw the control room at the time.

"Let me see the full transcript of the report which had been sent by the scout."

"Do you want the hard copy, or the hologram image of it?" the technician asked.

"I need the hard copy," Jeff muttered after a brief pause.

It took Jeff more than five minutes to go through the whole report. He turned his attention to the technician, and said, "I think the structure has accumulated ions, and these ions are causing the unusual cloud formations."

"From the look of it, I would say cumulonimbus. At that kind of altitude, it's rare."

"Towering cumulonimbus can reach up to thirty-nine thousand feet, depending upon the location. In the desert area, the up draft is much stronger, allowing the clouds to climb higher than expected," remarked Jeff.

"If that's the case, soon the clouds are going to be ionized as well."

"Most likely. I think I should send someone with a jetpack attached to an exoskeleton. I need human input from this."

"Human input!" the humanoid technician had no idea why Jeff would want to send a human up there. He added, "It could be risky."

Jeff stared into the technician's eyes, and said, "I'll take that risk. Sometimes, humans are more reliable than robots. There are certain things, robots can never be expected to develop."

"Things like what, Jeff?"

"Things like intuition." ***

Along with the hardware engineer, Cindy was also there with Trevor when he was about to embark on the surveillance mission. In his flight suit, carefully Trevor placed himself inside the exoskeleton. Under the pressurized flight suit, he had the thermals and the sensors all over his body. It was going to be freezing up there at thirty thousand feet. Trevor moved his arm to check how the exoskeleton responded. Then he took a few steps forward. The exoskeleton responded as expected. Trevor had no complaints.

The hardware engineer stood before the panel, watching the report relayed by the sensors attached to Trevor's body. Calmly, he said, "Everything looks okay."

Cindy checked the chute hooked to the back of the exoskeleton. Trevor had the option to use the jet power or the chute to land. It would depend upon the weather condition. Through his protective visor, Cindy stared at Trevor's countenance, and then threw a flying kiss. He took a deep breath and pushed the throttle, powering the mechanical monster to fly him to his destination, in a matter of minutes. The thunder of the disappearing jet receded as the two figures gazed up at the exoskeleton shooting up into the clouds. The moment it disappeared, the hardware engineer pressed a button, and the heavy metallic noise of the sliding roof, closing the gap, vibrated inside the hangar. Once the roof was in place, Cindy and the hardware engineer plodded towards the control room in the main building. ***

Trevor had been thinking about the sensation of shooting up like a bullet. His rate of ascent was determined by the exoskeleton's onboard computer. If it was too fast, Trevor might black out because of lack of oxygen in his head. Against his momentum, the force of gravity pressed down on his system, making it difficult for his heart to pump sufficient amount of blood into his brain. Hence, the rapid ascent produced uncomfortable dizziness in Trevor. He watched the ground below him as it rapidly became a distant prospect. The memories of his childhood flashed before his eyes. He loved visiting the amusement parks with his parents. The three hundred- and twenty-nine-meters high roller coaster at Jackson, New Jersey, was his favorite ride. At least once every month, his father would take them to the amusement park, until the unthinkable happened at the fair in Columbus. The ride called Fire Ball provided thrill by swooping like a pendulum while swinging in a circle. That day, he had been hungry after a long drive. He went to a stall for some sandwiches with his parents. At the stall, a loud crashing noise rattled everyone to their feet. Only a few feet from where they had been standing, a lady strapped to her seat of the ride landed violently onto the next food stall. Apparently, she was thrown off the gondola as its seats had broken off as a result of the G-force. The lady was lucky. Had she not been strapped to her seat the whole time, she would have been crushed to death by the force of the impact. The seat had absorbed the shock of the deadly shock as it slammed onto the stall at one hundred miles an hour.

Ever since that accident, Trevor's parents stopped visiting the amusement parks. However, Trevor would not allow himself to be unnerved by one sad incident. His fascination for the roller coaster ride never died. On several occasions in the past, Trevor took Cindy for roller coaster rides. However, nothing came even close to the thrill of being shot into the sky like the comic hero Iron Man.

Trevor's jetpack leveled off at two thousand feet. The coordinates of his destination had been fed into its computer, in charge of navigating. A pair of wings and a rudder had been deployed out of the exoskeleton, hurling Trevor in the direction of the Mojave Desert. Once he was within visual range from the shaft, he was going to climb to thirty thousand feet.

Jeff chose Trevor for the surveillance mission for his experience of working with jetpacks and exoskeletons. However, the machines Trevor used were nothing, compared to the scale of the machines used by the Space Race. Naturally they packed significantly more power and endurance needed for this kind of mission. Because of their monstrous capacity, these tools were indispensable in the kind of business Space Race was in. A normal jetpack could operate for a maximum of half an hour. However, when added to an exoskeleton, its operational radius increased to more than five hundred miles, and endurance another extra hour, due to the extra load of fuel carried by the exoskeleton.

Rushing to its destination at four hundred and fifty miles an hour, from Henderson, it would take the jet-skeleton less than half an hour to reach the shaft in the middle of the Mojave Desert. As Trevor stared down, he could hardly see the traffic on Route Fifteen. To his left, he glanced at the Mojave National Preserve. The woodlands, mountains, and canyons of this beautiful arid landscape drew tourists and nature lovers from around the globe. The rugged landscape was the refuge of the legendary mountain lions, coyotes, and a wide variety of bats. The gigantic sand mounds were famous for making ringing sounds. Trevor could not resist the temptation to descend to five hundred feet, allowing a closer look at the beasts of the Mojave Desert. He could feel the warm updraft from the sand dunes, pressing against his chest. Trevor intended to enjoy the natural sauna as long as he could. In five to ten minutes, he expected to see the shaft ahead of him.

Trevor looked at his specially made wristwatch which contained pretty much every piece of information he needed at the moment. He climbed back to five thousand feet. He felt the air getting considerably thinner. Under his visor, he had been wearing an oxygen mask like the fighter pilots. He pressed the button on his belly which released the duct, supplying fresh oxygen into his mask. Within the next two to three minutes, he would reach the desired altitude. Till then, he had nothing but to navigate the monster as safely as possible. ***

# Chapter Five

Inside the control room, the new head of the Project Elenaut had been observing the flight path of Trevor with the android lab technicians and Cindy, when the voice of the lab computer informed him of an incoming call from Michael. Jeff wasn't sure if it was the right time for him to brief the big boss about the latest development. The removal of Professor Stan had taught him a valuable lesson. Sometimes it was better not to disclose unpleasant facts, unless they posed existential threats. Jeff understood Michael's sensitivity to the project. He had invested all his fortune in this project. And therefore, he was not ready to hear any kind of discouraging words about this project from his employees. Since he didn't hesitate to replace a distinguished scientist like Professor Stan, he wouldn't think twice about replacing an engineer like him.

Jeff instructed the computer to receive the call, and said, "Yeah Mike, I'm with my colleagues inside the control room. I'll talk to you from my office, in a minute." As soon as Jeff had been in his relatively well-furnished office room, the connection was reestablished. From the other end, the big boss inquired, "Jeff, how's everything over there?"

"Good. All is fine. Nice to hear from you."

"Now listen carefully. In the next couple of hours, you'll be having some visitors with me. These visitors have decided to invest heavily in our project. They would like to have a look at the great work you guys have been doing, and of course, the visit would be meaningless without showing them the shaft. I would like you to go with us. Get ready, we'll be there shortly."

"Alright Mike, we'll be waiting for you and your friends." ***

Prior to Michael's arrival at the tarmac, the brand new rockerjet was brought out from the hangar. The dark blue space age vehicle was basically a jet plane fitted with rockets, and the deployable rotors of a chopper. Hence, it possessed the speed of a rocket, viability of a jet plane, and the ability to hover like a chopper. Its fuselage was like the fuselage of a wide-bodied passenger liner, providing a cabin with presidential privileges. Two huge tube-like pods, attached to each side of the fuselage, contained retractable wings, allowing it to fly like a plane, while being propelled by two rockets at the rear end of the fuselage. The rockerjet boasted state of the art propulsion system, allowing it to burn the rocket engines for several hours at a time.

"My, my, you have one beauty out there!" exclaimed Joe Mancini, the representative from Fox Trail, as he stared at the rockerjet through the limousine window. The glow in Michaels' countenance conveyed to everyone his pride. It was the first of its kind. With a grin on his lips, he said, "It's a beauty alright!"

"Isn't this a rockerjet? I didn't know, they already got the FAA approval," remarked Al Delaney, the skinny aviation expert from LLD.

"This is the company's first sale of this revolutionary craft. They had been testing it for the last five years, and finally, last April, they got the FAA certificate for mass production of the craft. So far, they have sold fifty of these beauties, I'm mighty proud of being one of those lucky owners who have already received delivery of the craft."

"Shouldn't the craft have a pair of wings?" Jill Carpenter from Ocean View sounded puzzled.

"Of course, Miss Carpenter. You see that tube shaped pod bulging out from the fuselage, the wings are retracted in those pods right now. Once the craft is airborne, the wings will be deployed for the linear movement," explained Michael.

"But how are we going to be airborne in the first place?" asked puzzled Joe Mancini.

"Well, my friends, that's another surprise waiting for you. Please be patient, soon you're going to find out. In the meantime, let me tell you all about the propulsion system of this beast. Those jets attached to the rear of the fuselage have the latest version of the turbofans. Each of them can produce 28,000 lbs. of thrust. Actually, that is not the surprise. In between those two jet engines, they have placed a rocket engine, as you can see the nozzle of it sticking out from the rear of the craft. The most interesting part is, the rocket engine and the jet engines use a revolutionary fuel converter. This converter breaks down water into its basic components, oxygen and hydrogen, and then converts those elements into liquid form. The jet engine burns liquid oxygen, while the rocket engine burns the liquid hydrogen for propulsion, and therefore, there's no carbon emission we see in case of traditional fossil fuel. The fuel produces more thrust without the environmental cost attached to burning the traditional fossil fuel. Isn't that fantastic?"

"Sounds great!" remarked Joe Mancini.

Michael smiled at Joe. He knew what he meant. He said, "They have done it Mr. Mancini, they have done it! It's no longer a fantasy."

The limo stopped next to the parked craft. Michael led his guests out of the limo, and into his rockerjet. The interior of the craft looked more like the interior of Air Force One. It boasted all the privileges, the President of the United States enjoyed on the Air Force One, including the most sophisticated communication devices. In line with the tradition of the Air Force One, a light blue coat adorned the interior of the rockerjet.

The guests had obviously been very impressed by the interior design of the craft. However, a bit sarcastically, Ms. Carpenter asked with a smile, "Is this how you spend your investors' money?"

Michael was used to this kind of question. He smiled at his guest, and replied, "Not a single dime, Ms. Carpenter, not a single dime from my investors. The purchase of it has been personally funded. I find it unethical, spending investors' funds on this kind of luxury."

The guests had been led to their private quarters when vibration and noise from the roof of the craft alerted them. They peeped through the cabin windows, and there it was, the other surprise Michael had earlier talked about. The extended rotor of the rockerjet began spinning at full speed before taking off from the tarmac. At two hundred feet from the ground, the vertical motion was turned into a linear movement. As the craft gained speed over two hundred miles an hour, the humming noise of the turbofans signaled the ignition of the two jet engines. The distance between Hanford, California to Henderson, Nevada was too short to justify using the rocket propulsion. Michael was only too glad to boast to his guests that the craft was basically a spacecraft designed to travel to the lower orbit, and then come down like a conventional aircraft. However, what was revolutionary was not the craft, but the fuel it used. Of course, there was no shortage of water on this planet. The catch was it had to be one hundred percent pure. There could be no other substances in the water."

"So, there's hardly any cost to flying this machine," exclaimed Joe.

"I'm afraid not. No matter what, you cannot bring the cost to zero. It has maintenance cost, we have to pay the crew, and like any asset of this type, it has depreciation. Nonetheless, compared to the cost of flying a conventional aircraft, the cost is negligible."

In the conference room of the craft, the passengers were served refreshments after the briefing. The craft had been flying at twenty thousand feet when it encountered columns of dark clouds. The craft shuddered as it flew through the dark clouds with air pockets in them. The pilot cautioned the passengers of rough ride ahead of them. The radar scope displayed two storm fronts closing in before the craft.

"Storm clouds over the desert!" exclaimed captain Floyd with signs of surprise in his voice.

"Should we increase the speed?" inquired the first officer.

"Well, it sounds like a good idea. We don't want those two fronts closing in before us," replied the captain.

As the first officer gently pushed the throttle a notch, the humming noise of the turbofans intensified, hurling the craft through the cloud formations at little over six hundred miles an hour. Unfortunately, before they could pass through the narrow passage, the two fronts merged, forming a colossal super front with lightnings, flashing all around the craft.

"Well, we've missed the passage," remarked the first officer.

"Hand over the control Dudley, I'm going to climb over the front," Captain Floyd told his first officer. In the next five minutes, the craft climbed to forty thousand feet. Down below, a deadly dance of the storm clouds and lightning enveloped the troposphere. From inside the passenger cabin, Michael's guests caught sight of something extraordinary, faraway, over the northern horizon.

"What the hell is that?" exclaimed Joe.

As the other two guests peered through the cabin window to their left, the shape of the structure looked like the Eiffel Tower. Only it was at least a hundred times wider at the base, and also way taller than anything they have ever seen. They could not figure out the top of the structure as it had disappeared up into space.

The representatives found Michael quietly smiling with a wine goblet in his hand when they turned.

"Don't tell me that's your project!" uttered Jill with utter disbelief.

"Yes, my dear friends, you're looking at my dream," Michael's face glowed.

"Shouldn't we be flying towards it?" asked Al Delaney.

"Yes, but not right now. First, we're going to pick the head of the project. Hell, I don't need more scientists! They question my decisions every time I turn my back on them. I need brilliant engineers who'll implement my ideas without any questions. I've never met an engineer as bright as Jeff. He knows how to work with me. There's nothing impossible to him. That's the best part of him."

"Has the entire structure been built?" Jill inquired.

"Yes, now we're waiting for the test runs to commence," Michael replied.

"This is basically a space vehicle, right? I would love to see the top of the structure," remarked Joe.

"The pilots have their flight route planned. I really don't want to interfere in their business. However, it doesn't mean it can't be done. Suppose we do, does it mean, it's going to have a positive impact upon the report you're going to submit?"

The representatives understood what Michael had been trying to convey. They looked at each other. Joe was obviously most enthusiastic about the idea. Subsequently, their expressions told of an unwritten understanding.

Joe smiled at Michael, and said, "Mr. Stewart, we have come here to make something truly remarkable happen. A short space flight will definitely expedite what we all seek. What I'm trying to say is that most certainly it will have a positive impact upon the final outcome of this visit."

"Well, in that case, I think it warrants my intervention."

As soon as Michael had finished, he pressed the button on his intercom. He was going to talk to the captain. He told him to unlock the door of the captain. The captain tried to guess the reason behind Michael's unexpected visit to the cockpit. Nonetheless, he was glad to receive him at his workstation.

After the usual greetings, Michael said to his pilots, "Gentlemen, we might have to make little changes in our flight plan."

"Are we to change our destination?"

"No, not really. The destination will remain Henderson, but the flight path has to be modified."

With questions in their eyes, both the captain and his first officer stared at the big boss, expecting some sort of explanation from him. Michael put on a smile on his lips, and said, "Our distinguished guests have expressed their desire to have a short trip to space. They're all very eager for the experience. I really can't blame them when our brand-new craft is amply equipped to do so. Will it be too much of a trouble for you guys? I must remind you guys that a lot depends on what these guys are going to report to their big bosses. I think we should do everything possible to please these folks. What do you say Captain?"

For a moment, the captain looked at his first officer, and then said, "We have to notify the control tower at Henderson. They'll give us the necessary instructions for it. Apart from that, at the moment we're only a hundred miles from our destination. Of course, we can deploy the onboard rocket engine and zoom into the lower orbit. However, during the descent, we'll have to cut the engine, and the descent must be quite steep, or else we might overshoot Henderson."

"What do you mean, we have to cut the engine? Is it going to be a free fall from the lower orbit?" asked Michael.

"We are not going to need power for the descent. We'll let gravity do the work for us. It'll save fuel," replied the captain.

"Are we going to dive like a fighter jet does?"

"I'm afraid that's the idea."

Michael whistled, and exclaimed, "Now, that's something!" After a brief pause, he continued,

"Look, none of us are young men anymore. Do you think it's going to be very traumatic?"

"That I do not know. It depends on your physical condition. I suggest that you record a statement from each of them that if something unpleasant happens, you or your company won't be liable for the injuries."

"Good point. Does it mean, we can get ready for the ride?"

"As soon as we get the instructions from the Henderson control tower," replied the captain.

"Do what you have to do," Michael told his pilot with a pat on his arm.

Within a minute, Michael returned to the passenger cabin, and explained to his guests the risks associated with the space ride. For legal purposes, Michael recorded this verbal warning before giving the signal to his pilots to go ahead with the idea.

The passengers were then told to fasten their seat belts and given the necessary instructions in case of an emergency. They were also told how to get their oxygen masks if anyone felt dizzy during the ride. As soon as the passengers had complied, the pilot pushed the throttle to its limit, making a forty-five-degree climb. Gradually the climb got steeper, until the craft went straight up. Inside the passenger cabin, amid the loud noise of the turbo fan engines running at full speed, Jill screamed out of sheer thrill, "So, this is how it feels to be inside a hurling rocket! Shouldn't this be a bit faster?"

From his seat, Michael responded with a gentle cough, "Oh dear, the pilot hasn't even ignited the rocket engine yet. I think he's going to do it after the craft has attained an altitude of sixty thousand feet."

It took exactly a minute and a half for the craft to reach the designated altitude. The moment the digital display in the cabin showed sixty thousand feet, a deafening roar from the rear of the craft accompanied by steady vibration told everyone that the rocket engine had been deployed. Everybody was pressed down to their seats by the tremendous acceleration generated by the thrust of the burning rocket engine. Through the cabin windows, the passengers could see the exterior view gradually turning darker at a steady pace.

"How will the captain turn around once it has reached the orbit?" Al Delaney wanted to find out.

Michael replied, "The older version of the craft had retro rockets for this. We're done with those. The nozzle of our rocket has thrust vector for changing the course."

Michael had been keeping an eye on the clock. Exactly at 11:30 am, the rocket engine was deployed. At 11:38 am, his notebook which had slid off from the table during the vertical ascent, began to float in the pressurized cabin. The rocket engine stopped roaring only a few seconds after that. Michael unbuckled himself, and gently pushed himself out of his seat.

"This is the moment you've been dreaming of guys. Feel free to unbuckle yourselves. Get the taste of being in space," the sheer thrill in Michael's resonated in the cabin. He tossed his notebook at Jill. She grabbed it, and then tossed it back like a baseball.

"I feel so light," remarked Delaney.

"The weight we've been carrying all our lives, it's gone. No wonder it feels so great," said Joe as he executed a perfect summersault in the air.

Michael stared at the spectacular view outside. For the first time in his life, Michael saw the blue planet from space. It had a sobering effect upon all who were with him on this unscheduled voyage. Though no one uttered the words, when the initial euphoria had evaporated, a sense of uncertainty gripped everyone. What if something went wrong? They had no space suits with them. If the rocket failed to reignite, or the thrust vector didn't work, they would be in deep trouble. Michael could sense the fear in the eyes of his guests. He said, "Look guys, we took a conscious decision. There's no point worrying about the danger now. Life is nothing but uncertainty."

Joe had to agree. He said, "You're right Michael, it was a conscious decision. We can't possibly blame anyone if something goes horribly wrong."

"Well, we have had the experience of a lifetime. Now it's time to return," said Jill in a shaky voice.

Michael smiled at Jill as he pressed the intercom button. Captain Floyd set the new course before feeding it to the onboard computer, and then turned on the autopilot, allowing the computer to have full control during the dangerous descent. Even the slightest deviation in the angle of descent would mean disaster. Hence, letting the computer fly the craft was the standard procedure. The loudspeakers in the passenger cabin conveyed to the passengers the captain's command to fasten the seat belts. The passengers and crew were given a minute before the computer reignited the rocket engine. Short bursts of loud explosions from the rocket engine made the craft turn around. And then, a moment of silence was broken by the steady roar of the rocket engine for another thirty seconds. The momentum gained from the final thrust was enough to propel the craft through the empty space, and into the exosphere of the planet.

The re-entry was associated with gentle vibration of the whole craft. Gradually, the vibration increased due to acceleration through the thin air of the exosphere, and then the thermosphere. The air was getting thicker, and thicker, and so increased the friction of air against the outer skin of the craft. At eighteen thousand miles per hour, the craft hurled towards the planet below, causing the heat shield underneath the fuselage to glow like a meteorite. The monstrous G-force made Jill cry out in pain, while Delaney could no longer hold his bowel movement. He said he had to go to the men's room.

"What!" shouted Michael, "man, you have picked hell of a time to do it. I hope you have a diaper on you. Just stay put. It'll be over in a minute or two. Just don't spoil my beautiful cabin."

As soon as Michael had finished, Delaney lost consciousness, and Jill threw up. Luckily, the craft was within the gravitational field of the planet, preventing vomit from circulating in the air. By the time the craft had leveled off before deploying the rotors for vertical lift, all three guests, including the host, were in urgent need of nursing.

The craft touched down onto the tarmac, vertically like a chopper. The pilots took over from the onboard computer after the rotors had been deployed.

Michael somehow managed to get on his feet without any help. However, his distinguished guests had to be carried to the clinic inside the training facility, on stretchers. Jeff had been waiting at the tarmac for the arrival of the team. A thin line of sweat on his black forehead displayed apprehension in him. He felt obliged to accompany his boss to the medical center with signs of great consternation. While being transported by an ambulance, Delaney regained his senses. Jill was given a shot which calmed her down. All three said that they were in no condition to continue the tour. However, they admitted that it wouldn't be right, going through all this, without achieving their prime objective. Michael proposed to postpone the tour until the traumatized visitors were physically and mentally prepared for the tour. Subsequently, they agreed to fly to the project the following day. In the meantime, Jeff arranged lodging for the three visitors in the medical center. ***

# Chapter Six

Trevor looked at his wristwatch. It was past nine thirty in the morning. He could clearly see the shaft rising through the heavy cloud cover. The GPS measured the distance as little over five miles from where he had been. Within minutes he would be there. In his headphone Riley's cold, uncaring voice crackled. He was the humanoid in charge of the control room. He advised Trevor to maintain the present altitude. Earlier, Trevor had climbed to thirty-five thousand feet to avoid the cumulonimbus clouds. These clouds had a notorious reputation among the weather forecasters as the cocoon of troubles. Within a mile from the shaft, Trevor was to reduce his speed, and cautiously approach the shaft.

Cindy's sweet feminine voice greeted Trevor as soon as Riley was done talking.

"Honey, how do you feel?" was the first thing she said.

Cindy's voice never failed to raise Trevor's spirit. He responded, "Honey, I don't know how to say it. Your sweet voice, it's so refreshing. Anyway, I'm alright, though the weather looks pretty rough. I don't know if it's normal for the desert."

"Deserts can also have thunder- storms. After all, the Mojave isn't really a big desert. The weather of the adjacent areas has an impact upon the climate over there," Cindy said with a reassuring voice.

"That's true though. Let me find out what's been happening over here."

By then, Trevor was only a mile from the shaft. He reduced his speed and scanned the clouds before him with his infra-red scanners, to check if they had been charged. Though his suit was fully protected against lightning bolts, still he had to be careful. As expected, the clouds were packed with charged ions. Even from a mile, the structure had an intimidating presence. He figured the base must be at least a mile wide.

"Exactly where do you guys want me to probe?" asked Trevor as he was less than five hundred meters from the structure. Precipitation had blurred his vision through the visor. Trevor turned on the wiper for a better view.

"It'll be better if you proceed through the cloud, but it's up to you. We don't want you to take unnecessary risks," from the control room, the humanoid in charge replied.

Lightning bolts flashed all around Trevor, when he said, "The atmosphere is too charged over here. I'm going to climb up."

"Go ahead," Jeff joined the conversation from his office.

Very softly, Trevor said to the computer, "Add power, we're going up."

Once he was above the nasty cumulonimbus, cautiously, Trevor came closer to the structure. He was going to attach the sensor to it. Upon careful scrutiny, the titanium alloy surface of the structure revealed a thin, conspicuous layer of frost. As he touched it with his heavy gloves, part of the thin layer fell off. Trevor rubbed the area with drying agent before attaching the sensor. The reading from the sensor confirmed what had feared. The structure became ionized by charged particles, eventually forming ionized cloud formations around it. In other words, the structure was the source of unusual weather patterns in the area.

"Mr. McLaughlin, could you move inside the shaft? We need to see the condition of the rails and the brackets," Jeff directed.

A sense of foreboding gripped Cindy as Trevor flew through the horizontal and diagonal braces. She was not in a position to stop Trevor, so she kept mum. Trevor came close to a heavy bracket made of heat-resistant fiber glass, having the rail through it. He held the bracket and tried to twist it with his two hands. The bracket was firmly in place. Once the firmness of some of the brackets and the rails had been confirmed, Trevor placed the magnetic tilt sensor on one of the brackets before activating the laser. The range of measurement was set to twelve thousand feet towards the base. The readings were good. At no point, the rails and Brackets were off more than one sixty fourth of an inch. Trevor had to admire the engineers who installed them, but then he remembered that the whole structure had been erected by robots.

The staff at the training facility had been studying the readings sent to them when Jeff said to Trevor, "Alright Mr. McLaughlin, we have found what we've been looking for. You may return to the facility. I have a tight schedule today." ***

Once the representatives had found lodging at the medical center, Jeff escorted Michael out of the clinic and accompanied him to his office. Michael sensed the urgency in Jeff's voice. Hence, he did not object to the idea. Michael would not let his privacy be violated. He turned on the jammer to prevent their conversation from being recorded.

"You don't have any electronic devices turned on, do you? I'm going to turn them off for security," said Michael.

"No, I don't."

Michael sat in the sofa before Jeff's huge desk, and asked, "Alright, what makes you so jittery?"

"The structure, I think, it's causing disruptions in the weather pattern."

Michael didn't like what he had heard. Raising his brows, he exclaimed, "Weather disruptions, what do you mean?"

"For the last couple of days, the area has been having very rough weather."

Michael still could not comprehend why Jeff had raised the issue of weather. He snapped, "So!"

Jeff wanted to make sure there were no misgivings about his all-out support for the project. He said, "Mike, you know I'm just as eager as you are to see the project succeed."

Michael nodded, and said, "That's why I chose you to replace the old professor."

"Something very unusual came up recently," very cautiously Jeff remarked.

"Go ahead, I'm listening."

"Recently, we have been observing endless formations of storm clouds around the structure."

"So," Michael shrugged his shoulders.

"I think the shaft and its supporting structure has something to do with it."

Now Michael couldn't suppress his annoyance. He exclaimed, "Come on Jeff, don't be another pain in my neck. How could the structure influence the weather? If this was the case, New York would be permanently cursed by inclement weather, don't you think so? New York has not one, but hundreds of tall structures."

"You have your point, Mike. But you see, those structures in New York are not really metal structures. Apart from that, none of those structures are over a thousand feet tall," Jeff pointed out.

For a while, Michael simply stared at Jeff, and then it came out, "Alright, go ahead, tell me what you've been waiting to disclose."

Now Jeff was a bit more confident and comfortable. He explained, "You see, the metal structure has an ionizing effect upon the surrounding air molecules________,"

"Will you speak to me in English? It sounds like Chinese to me!" exclaimed Michael.

"Alright Michael, just calm down a bit. I'll make it easier for you to grasp. Usually objects, or more precisely atomic particles have no charge, but sometimes, they lose or gain electrons, and the subsequent imbalance in the electronic configuration of the particle causes it to become charged. We call this process ionization. When ions are formed, they are either negatively or positively charged. The negatively charged ions attract positively charged ions, and vice versa. Hence, they have a role in the formation of clouds and lightning. We believe this is what has been happening with the structure. It's getting highly charged for some reasons."

Michael smiled at Jeff when he was done explaining the phenomenon. He was not going to surrender. He had come a long way with this dream. He couldn't let these invisible ions undo what he had achieved.

He said, "Well, don't you think, it's a good thing for the desert? The desert needs rain. Perhaps we should build more of these structures in every desert."

Jeff would not let what had happened to the old professor happen to him. He smiled back, and exclaimed, "Why Mike! You're right, I never saw it this way."

"Now, don't go public with this, you know how they make a mountain out of a mole hill," added Michael.

"Don't worry Michael, you can rely on me," Jeff reassured the big boss.

"By the way, what means did you employ to collect the data?"

"I sent a probe out there."

"Do you mean robotic drone?"

With a smile on his lips, Jeff replied, "A human probe."

"A human probe!" Michael exclaimed.

"Yes, sometimes a human probe is more cost effective. I wanted the probe to feel the air around the structure. He just confirmed what we had suspected. Indeed, the metal structure has an impact upon the weather of the area."

"Whom did you send?"

"One of the elenauts."

"Why the hell did you do that?" asked Michael with a jittery tone.

All this time, Michael had been sitting on the sofa before Jeff's desk, while Jeff tried to explain the situation to him. When Michael yelled at him, Jeff lifted himself from his seat, and invited Michael to his seat, and then he said, "I think you should look at his profile."

Before allowing Michael to have access to its system, Jeff's computer scanned the new user's eyeballs. In millionth of a second, it had finished scanning, and as soon as Michael's identity was revealed, it implemented his command. Over Jeff's desk, a hologram image of Trevor's profile appeared.

"Good pick. He appears to be quite resourceful," Michael remarked after browsing through Trevor's profile.

"His wife is also a team member."

"You selected a coupe!"

"We have our eyes on couples conceiving and giving birth in the orbit, don't we? Who knows, perhaps this couple will be our ticket to a generation born and raised in space. Apart from that, they'll make wonderful PR stunts. She happens to be a sky diver, so I thought she would make an ideal candidate."

"Sky diver! That sounds interesting. Are they available right now? I think I should talk to them."

"Trevor McLaughlin, the mechanical engineer has not yet returned from the mission. However, his wife, Cindy, is available."

"Call her, I would like to hear from her what she thinks about the project." ***

Cindy had been getting ready for the next training session in the pool when she received the call from Jeff. She just finished tightly wrapping her long silky dark brown hair into a bun at the back of her head. She looked in the mirror to see if everything was according to the regulations before answering the call. She was careful not to turn on the hologram option. She knew the CEO of Space Race was around. However, she was surprised by the opportunity to meet him in person.

Cindy's professional look impressed Michael. He didn't wait to greet the elenaut with a broad grin and an enthusiastic hello.

"Cindy, I have it that you're a sky diver. I've always been fascinated by sky divers like you. Though I never had the chance to try it. I can imagine the thrill of falling through the sky at two hundred miles an hour."

"Oh yeah, it's a great adventure. And especially when you can earn a living out of it," Cindy responded with a smile.

"What's the highest drop you have had so far?"

"Hundred thousand feet," replied Cindy.

"Hundred thousand feet! That's almost like diving form the space," Michael exclaimed.

"Well, many people see it that way."

"Has anyone a record higher than that?"

"Yes, there's a record, I can't remember the name at this moment. He jumped from hundred and thirty-six thousand feet."

"How long did your dive last?"

"The actual free fall lasted little under five minutes. My chute opened at ten thousand feet."

"How did you manage to get to that kind of altitude? I know, conventional aircraft cannot reach that kind of height."

"We used a balloon."

"Oh yeah, balloons are quite capable of climbing to that kind of altitude."

Cindy was careful not to disclose more than it was needed. In the past, it led to the downfall of many. With her back resting gently against the chair, she sat upright, mentally ready to respond to any question. Michael had interviewed numerous employees. He knew it was almost impossible to find out everything in one interview. However, experience told him he had been dealing with a tough candidate. He admired Cindy's gestures, professional attitude, and above all, her self-confidence.

"Do you think, it's possible for a human to fall through the atmosphere from the lower orbit?" after a pause Michael came straight to the point.

"If you ask for my personal opinion, I will say yes, but I'm not an expert on this."

"Hundred and thirty-six thousand feet, that's as good as space, don't you think so?"

"That's like twenty-five miles. The lower orbit starts from seventy-five miles," very gently Cindy expressed her reservations.

"Yes, that's true, but if a man dives from hundred and thirty-six thousand feet, and lives to tell the tale, I don't see why he can't do it from five hundred thousand feet. After all, the only difference is absence of gravity at five hundred thousand feet," remarked Michael.

"I'm not going to get into a debate about it. I would appreciate it, if you be straight forward with it. Have you been thinking of dropping someone from the lower orbit?"

Michael pretended as if his feelings had been hurt. He said, "Oh Mrs. McLaughlin, please don't be so harsh. I'm not a monster. I have no intention of throwing anyone out of the space station."

"I apologize. I didn't want to offend anyone."

Michael nodded to show his acceptance of her apology, and then with a smile on his lips, said very softly, "Of course, the astronaut or the elenaut, whichever term you choose to use, will have a protective suit, and the gears, to ensure her survival. And no one is going to force anyone to do it. It's going to be a voluntary mission."

By then it was clear to Cindy what the CEO of Space Race wanted from her. She didn't want him to be disappointed. She said, "I'll think about it, sir. I'll have to consult with my husband. It was not in the contract. If I decide to go ahead with your plan, the contract should be re-written, at least for me. The immense risk associated with it, calls for appropriate incentive."

"Of course," with a smile, Michael agreed.

"Doesn't make sense to me," Cindy remarked.

"What doesn't make sense to you? Tell me, I'll try to address your concerns."

"Why are you doing all this?" I mean, first you build this elevator to space, and now you want us to dive into the atmosphere from your space station. We have space vehicles for all this, don't we?"

Michael glanced at Jeff, and remarked, "Mrs. McLaughlin has raised a very interesting issue, Jeff. I know, many people have been nurturing this question in their hearts."

For a moment Michael paused, turned to Cindy, and said, "Mrs. McLaughlin, do you know the maximum number of people these space vehicles can lift to the orbit, at any given time? Do you have any idea about the cost of each launch?"

"As far as I can remember, the Trumpet-V can carry a maximum of ten astronauts, and a payload of thirty thousand kilo. I'm not aware of the cost though."

"The cost is somewhere between $100-200 million, depending on the size and nature of the payload. You see, it's all about economy, Mrs. McLaughlin. If we are to travel beyond our solar system, or if we plan to exploit the resources of the other planets of our solar system, we have to start the journey from up there. The trip to the lower orbit uses up too much precious fuel. Apart from that, there's a limit to how much we can lift. Sustainable space voyage requires space vehicle assembly plants and launch pads up there in the orbit with facilities that can accommodate thousands of scientists, engineers, technicians, and doctors, you name it. It means the size of the space station has to be as large as a city if not a state. Now, I cannot imagine a handful of astronauts building such a colossal platform. We'll need to send thousands of people up there to build the research facilities, assembly plants and the launch pads. If we are to use the conventional mode of transportation, it'll take hundreds of thousands of launches, and then there's the question of time frame. It'll take decades just to transport the building materials. It won't be economically viable to carry on with this business, using the present mode of transportation. I've mentioned only two of the hurdles. There are many more. Now imagine our elenauts being lifted to the orbit by the elevators, and then diving back like those sky divers. Within a year, we can send thousands of people up there."

"Why can't they use the elevator to come down?"

"They can. The problem is, right now, we have only two elevators. They may not be readily available when we might need them. Besides, what if something goes wrong with any of those elevators, or the space station? There has to be other options before us for bringing down those elenauts within a reasonable time frame. If we can successfully implement my ideas, it will revolutionize space travel. Getting up there, staying and building up there, in a meaningful way, are the immediate challenges before us. We can think of interplanetary or interstellar voyages, only if we can overcome these basic challenges."

Cindy was impressed by Michael's vision. She could not object to his dream. Indeed, the cost of each launch and the load capacity of the launch vehicles did not justify doing business this way, if the goal was interplanetary voyages. In space, the prospect of exploiting the resources of the other planets is simply limitless. If only the oxygen hidden under the lunar surface could be successfully exploited, it could support one trillion people for one hundred thousand years. However, Cindy could not ignore the risks associated with Michael's ideas. In the end, Michael gave her forty-eight hours to make up her mind.

The temperature inside Jeff's office was kept at seventy, making it comfortable for all. Instead of a window, a ten-millimeter-thick transparent glass formed the exterior wall. All this time, Jeff had his back towards the glass wall, depriving him of the view outside. His eyes were fixed on Michael's countenance. Hence, when Michael glanced over his shoulder, he assumed something had captured Michael's attention. He was about to turn around when Michael exclaimed, "What's that!"

"Oh, that's the human probe I told you about," replied Jeff.

Michael turned to Cindy, and said, "Your husband has arrived."

"Yes."

Michael turned his attention back to Jeff, and said, "Tell Mr. McLaughlin to wait for us at the tarmac. I would like to talk to him over there." Then he turned to Cindy, "Mrs. McLaughlin, your profile tells me, you worked as a system analyst for a computer firm, is that right?"

"Yes, I worked there for three years."

"Why did you leave the job?"

"An opportunity to start my own company came up when a friend of my offered to lease me his C-150 Globe Trotter. I grabbed the opportunity and opened my own gym and sky diving company. Had it not been for that experience, I don't think I would be here talking to you today."

"Yes, that's true. Now let me add a bit more to our conversation. If you decide to accept my proposal, I'm sure you will, we'll be using your experience as a system analyst to perform certain tasks up there in the orbit. Now, let's go and find out what Mr. McLaughlin has to say." ***

Trevor was still in his flight suit when Michael and his companions arrived at the hangar. After the formal exchange of greetings with the CEO, he briefed everyone about the observations he had made during the surveillance mission. "Couldn't find any fault with the construction. It's a sound construction," he said. "However, for unknown reason, it has been causing ionization of the air around it, at least, that's what I think."

Trevor wanted to continue when Jeff stopped him. "That's enough, Mr. McLaughlin. You have done a wonderful job. Now the CEO wants to see you fly with the exoskeleton," he said to Trevor. Michael had to admire Jeff's wit. He was not at all interested in a lecture about the ions and their impact upon the weather.

Instantaneously, Michael took over from Jeff by adding, "When I was a kid, no other comic character fascinated me more than the Iron Man. I never imagined, in my lifetime, I would see real life Iron Man standing before me."

The roof of the hangar slid open, and through the opening, Trevor shot up into the sky above, as the spectators walked out onto the open tarmac to watch the spectacle. Like an eagle, Trevor climbed, dived, and rolled in the sky, while the spectators on the ground stared up at the sky with awe. ***

# Chapter Seven

Before going to bed at night, Cindy disclosed to Trevor what Michael had told her earlier.

"This is outright madness!" Trevor exclaimed.

Cindy had guessed how Trevor was going to respond, so she prepared the script designed to address his fears. She said, "Calm down honey, we have a record of people diving from the space."

"Really, who was that idiot? Would you please tell me?"

Cindy had the video of it ready. Quite attentively, Trevor watched the whole hologram video. "He jumped from hundred and thirty-six thousand feet. That's not space. Apart from that, did you see the way he tumbled for a while? He had no control. Had he not regained control in time, he would have been dead, Cindy," he didn't try to conceal the contempt in his voice as he said this.

"If a man can jump from that kind of altitude and survive, it can be done from space as well, take my word for it. I'm telling you, I can do it. The man said, he would double the payment stipulated in the contract if I agreed."

The sound of incentives changed Trevor's stance. Like the CEO of the Space Race, he was also a businessman, after all. He loved making money whenever the opportunity was there. However, he had to be careful. He didn't want Cindy to perceive him as selfish or greedy.

"Since you're so adamant about it, I won't stop you, but I must say I have a bad feeling about it, honey." ***

Roughly twenty miles from the structure, the craft shifted its power source from the turbo fans to the rotors. The chopping noise over the roof conveyed to the passengers the deployment of the rotors. Though the craft was being driven by the rotors, the fuel supply to the two jet engines had not been totally cut off. The new FAA regulation prohibited completely shutting down the jet engines before the craft was safely on the ground.

As the craft cruised over the desert surface, at two hundred eighty miles an hour, the eyes of the passengers had been glued to the video images of what was ahead of the craft. Soon, the structure would be within their visual range.

"There it is my baby!" Michael declared triumphantly.

"It's humongous!" Jill exclaimed with signs of disbelief in her eyes.

"It is my dear, it is," responded Michael.

"How much area does it cover at the base?" Delaney inquired.

"Two square miles."

"Two square miles, it's amazing!" Delaney had to let it out.

"It has to be. It goes up eighty miles, or else the structure would not be stable," Joe muttered.

"It looks so much like the Eiffel Tower. I have to give credit to the nineteenth century architects. What they designed two hundred years ago, it's still relevant," Jill commented.

"This is the most stable configuration for such a tall structure," Michael explained.

The craft landed on the helipad only a hundred meters from the perimeter. The inspection team had to walk more than a kilometer to get to the ground control next to the shaft. The compound consisted of several chambers, and a large hall-room used as the control room. It was designed to accommodate the elenauts, experts, and the staff, before and after each departure or arrival. It also boasted a clinic which could handle as many as fifty patients at a time.

When the visitors laid their eyes upon the endless pile of horizontal and diagonal braces, reaching up as far as eyes could see, their jaws dropped. The elevator door was open. When they had comfortably settled down in the seats of the elevator, Michael suggested to Delaney to use the toilet if he needed to. Everyone laughed, however, when the door of the toilet was slid open, their eyes hit the ceiling. It was a mini clinic in itself, with everything needed during an emergency. Michael warned the visitors not to touch the big red button on the flush. Pressing the red button would tun on the suction machine designed to literally force out human excretion and channel it to the container tank attached to the toilet pan.

"I wouldn't put my butt in it," Delaney giggled.

An uproar followed, and then Jeff said in a reassuring voice, "Don't worry Mr. Delaney, it has not been designed to devour your rear end. It'll only ensure that the excretion is channeled into the right place in the zero-gravity environment. You wouldn't want our elenauts to go on their mission with poops flying in all directions, do you?"

"No, no, of course not, I forgot about the zero-gravity environment. Yes, I can see the necessity of it now," Delaney said timidly.

Michael asked Jeff if the power cables had been installed. He was told, a week before the launch, they were going to be installed and tested. For the sake of safety, they were not yet installed. The tour concluded with a snap inspection of the whole facility. None of the visitors made further comments. Instead, they made notes in their small notebooks and also made videos of whatever required closer inspection. Prior to their return journey, the staff served them refreshments in a small lounge where they had been left alone to privately consult among themselves. ***

Mary Anne had been getting ready to take Flare to the vet when the communication device attached to her wrist alerted her of an incoming message from her husband, Michael. In the morning, prior to leaving home for his office, he looked unusually jovial. Most of the time, he would just rush out in a tense mood. Last couple of months, Mary Anne watched quietly as anxiety stalked her husband. She knew about Michael's latest project, though Michael hardly ever talked about it with her. A little bit of digging revealed to her the enormous amount of funding needed to complete the ambitious project. She assumed, somehow Michael had secured funding from the investors, and now he was in binding to produce concrete results within a reasonable time frame.

The message said two first class air tickets had been confirmed for the following Friday. The flight from Hanford to Honolulu would depart at six in the evening. Then came the second message, confirming their reservation at the best five-star hotel in Honolulu, for the next four days. Their anniversary was still two months away, and none of them had their birthdays in the next couple of months. Hence, Mary Anne was taken aback by the messages.

Mary Anne was in her late fifties, while Michael was sixty-three. When the two stood next to each other, Michael somehow looked a lot younger. Michael worked out regularly, keeping himself physically fit for his age. Physically, though she was no longer her old self, still she was quite attractive for a lady at fifty-six. There was a time when she was chosen as the prom queen at her college. That was forty years back. Time had taken a toll on her good look. Nonetheless, the bond between Mary Anne and Michael withstood the test of time. According to Mary Anne, a man, and a woman could truly discover each only after getting married, and therefore, if the love continued despite being closer as ever, it was the kind of love that would not die in a lifetime. Whenever he had the opportunity, Michael never failed to reassert that love to his wife. Mary Anne was always his prom queen he married so many years ago. Consequently, Mary Anne trusted her husband with all she had.

From Honolulu, the fifty-minute flight to the Big Island was the best part of their long journey. From fifteen thousand feet in the air, the islands scattered on the surface of the Pacific looked like a paradise, beckoning to the tourists with their endless list of wonders, above and under the ocean. Fondly, Michael had put his arm around Mary Anne's shoulders, when the illuminated sign over their head, to fasten seat belts, had been turned off. Very gently, Michael rested his chin over Mary Anne's left shoulder, and said softly, "I think, I'm the luckiest man alive."

Turning her head to face him, in a tender voice she said, "You're the greatest wonder in my life. Thank you, thank you for being such a wonderful man, and such a wonderful husband."

Michael lowered his head and pressed his lips against Mary Anne's. She buried her head in his arms, as the aircraft dropped abruptly due to air-pockets. The bumpy ride reminded Michael of the previous day's trauma. Compared to that, it was nothing. At the airport, children with garlands in their hands awaited the tourists. It was the traditional reception. Both enjoyed the balmy tropical gust whipping them on the faces, the moment they came out of the aircraft. Deliberately, the civil aviation authority of Hawaii avoided using the air-bridges at most of the airports. A metal stair was used for disembarking. Hence, the tourists had the opportunity to enjoy the warm weather of the islands from the very second they stepped onto them.

Michael had planned a tour of the Kilauea, an active volcano, situated at the southeastern part of the Big Island. They were going to stay on the island for the weekend at the most luxurious resort. He refrained from disclosing his plans, for he wanted to give her a spectacular surprise. She asked about it only once. He simply smiled at her, indicating his intention to keep it a secret until the very last moment. Mary Anne didn't insist, for she knew how much her husband loved giving her surprises. She just put her hand in his. She wanted to convey to him her complete faith in him. ***

At the training facility of Space Race, Cindy was isolated from the rest of the trainees. After all, she was not going to commence her adventure into space as an elenaut. Before departing for Hawaii on a short vacation, Michael had instructed Jeff to prepare Cindy for the next launch of their re-usable rocket. With her, a humanoid would travel to the lower orbit. There, Cindy would configure the onboard computer of the two kilometer long, and a kilometer wide, cylindrical shaped space station. Later, the computer was going to provide directives to the robots for extending the space station before the arrival of the elenauts.

Cindy's training sessions were re-moduled. They were made much more vigorous, considering the hazard related to the new mission. Hours after hours were spent getting used to working in tandem with the robotic androids. The managers programmed the androids to respond to not only Cindy's voice commands, but also her facial expressions and gestures. If the robots thought that Cindy was in physical pain or mental frustration, they were to offer consolation and possible solution to her problems.

In no time, the humanoid chosen to accompany Cindy became her trusted lieutenant during the training period. The two were placed in a mockup of the most hostile environment one could think of. The handlers introduced Cindy's personal profile as well as her childhood and family background to the android, to enable the android to have a better grip on her psychology. The training sessions were supposed to continue for a week. Once Michael had returned from his short vacation, Cindy and her android companion were going to be hurled into the lower orbit. The launch pad was five miles from Los Angeles, along the west coast. A crawler transporter on a couple of tracked vehicles carried the re-usable rocket to the launch pad. The launch vehicle was a three-stage rocket with retrievable stages. Instead of solid fuel, all three stages used liquid oxygen and hydrogen for propulsion.

On the first day of the training session, Cindy was shown the life size components of the structure the android was supposed to retrieve and assemble. Cindy was going to program the android as the situation demanded. The whole operation had to be completed in seventy-two hours. The constructed platform was then to be attached to the top end of the space elevator as a disembarking or boarding platform.

In the meantime, from the ground, power cables of the elevators were going to be installed and the whole system checked by briefly turning on the power switch. Once the elevators had been through test runs, Cindy would go for the free fall from space. The humanoid was to stay up there in the space station awaiting the arrival of the first batch of the elenauts. Before her free fall, Cindy would use the thrusters to enter the gravitational field of the planet. ***

From the balcony, Michael and Mary Anne glanced at the spectacular view, only a few meters from the resort. The deep blue ocean, the cascading waves crashing onto the rocky shores and the palm beaches with white foams, beckoned the couple like an enchanting mistress. Reluctantly, the couple returned to their room to get ready for the tour of the island. It was already lunch hour. The tour guide suggested to all that they had their lunch prior to heading for the volcano.

The tour guide was a middle-aged Hawaiian man. All his life he had been working as the local guide for the resort. He held a post graduate degree in volcanology. He was also a keen proponent of environmental causes. During their trip to the most active volcano in the world, he explained to his team the role of these volcanoes in destroying and reinventing the unique eco system of the island. Of course, the lecture had to have the eruption history of Kilauea. He said, the latest eruption took place five years back, and since then, the islanders witnessed continuous flow of lava on the eastern slope of the mountain.

The coaster carrying the tourists and the guide stopped by the western slope of the mountain. Before starting on foot to the summit, rising four thousand feet from the base of the volcano, Michael took the guide by his hand, pulling him away from the rest of the crowd. Quietly, he asked if it was safe walking around the slope of the volcano. He advised Michael to avoid the flat rocky surface. Under the thin, rocky surface, lava flow often caused cracks in the surface. At times, the lava underneath came out through those cracks, inundating the unstable rocky surface. Therefore, it was safer to tread over the mounds and hills formed by the solidified lava from the past eruptions.

Michael expressed his desire to explore the slope of Kilauea, instead of climbing the summit. The guide refrained from stopping him, though he was not comfortable with the idea. He was well aware, who the distinguished visitors were. He simply advised Michael to be careful. For about an hour, Michael and Mary Anne toddled over the rocks. The rumble of the ongoing lava flow on the southeastern slope of the mountain could be felt, as they struggled to move forward. Every now and then, the ground below their feet jolted, making them shudder on their feet. The jolts were mini quakes associated with the eruption. The atmosphere was hot and humid, the air suffocating. The natural sauna made both sweat profusely underneath their garments. By the time they came to the fifty feet opening, Mary Anne had been gasping for fresh air. Cautiously, Michael approached the edge of the opening. It looked like hundreds of feet deep. Down below, Michael could see the red-hot lava flowing at the bottom of the pit. The hellish scene fascinated Michael. He wanted to share the view with Mary Anne. He beckoned her to come to the edge. Anxiously she had been standing a few yards behind him. In response to Michael's beckoning, with a nervous tone she said, "Honey, are you sure it's safe?"

"I'll be holding your hand, sweetheart. It's a spectacular view of the hell below. It's the experience of a lifetime. I don't want you to miss it," Michael shouted.

Very cautiously Mary Anne approached her husband. She stood next to him, tightly holding his arm. "Oh God, it's horrible!" Mary Anne exclaimed as she stared down the fiery pit.

"Oh yeah, I guess that's how hell looks like. It's the best sample I could think of," Michael said with a smile on his lips.

Gently removing her arm from his own, he said he wanted to take a snap of Mary Anne, standing at the edge of the pit. He reassured her that he was right behind her. She extended her hand backwards to feel his presence. When Michael touched her hand, she felt better. She stood up straight, feeling the hot draft brushing her face.

"Are you done, honey?" a bit impatiently asked Mary Anne.

"Almost."

Mary Anne heard the click of the snapshot, and as she was about to step back, a strong quake made the slope shake. Mary Anne's reflexes made her extend her arm backward. She wanted Michael to grab her hand. Her heart jumped to her throat when her arm found no one behind her. Michael was beyond her reach. He watched her terrified expression when she had lost her balance and disappeared from sight with a shrill cry. ***

# Chapter Eight

Jeff told Cindy there would be no publicity for the launch, and she did not expect any. In the last decade, this kind of launch became everyday business. Some in the media commented that the thrill of space voyage was no longer like it used to be. However, Cindy cared little what reporters thought or said. For her, it was a dream she never dared imagine. Trevor was apprehensive, and Cindy understood why. In his place, she would feel the same way. It was a mission which could easily end up in disaster. To reduce the chances of mishap, she was flown to sixty thousand feet and dropped with a chute on her back. The experts told her not to release the chute until she dropped to three thousand feet. During her descent, she was to execute movements to mimic an uncontrolled descent, only to regain full control after a specified period. To some extent, it prepared her for the real show.

After a two-week delay, finally, Cindy and her android assistant were on their way to the space station. The delay was due to the tragedy in the CEO's family.

Michael could not attend the launch. He said he was going to watch the event from his retreat on a remote island in the Pacific. The island was owned by a billionaire friend named Davis Goldstein. Goldstein urged Michael to take a few days off to come to terms with the great loss he had suffered. On the island, Goldstein arranged every kind of recreation one could think of. Michael's private secretary Stephanie was with him. She was to maintain communication with his company. To his son Bob, it seemed odd that not even a week had passed after his mother's death, his father was on a vacation with his vivaciously attractive young secretary. Nonetheless, he remained silent. However, Mary Anne's younger sister Lillian brought charges against Michael. At the court, cross examination by the prosecutor and Michael's attorney found the charges against him unsubstantiated. Eventually, criticism of the trial made headlines in several local newspapers. Despite the criticism, the headlines failed to instigate the kind of uproar which could result in a retrial. Critics pointed out that Michael's billionaire friends had a hand in the outcome of the trial. After all, an investigation revealed the dubious composition of the jury. The background of most of the jury members were suspiciously close to the elite deep state which ran the new global order.

The day the jury declared Michael innocent, Lillian rushed to Bob to discuss the outcome. She expected Bobs sympathy and understanding. When she met him at a restaurant, the sun had just set over the horizon. The red glow of the setting sun lingered in the western sky for another fifteen minutes. Lillian sat facing her nephew, next to the glass wall, providing a spectacular view of the Pacific from the waterfront Boulevard.

Anger and frustration were palpable in Lillian's pale countenance. Albeit in her forties, the signs of her age had not yet touched her slender face. Her shoulder length light brown, silky hair, a rather short uppity nose, and above all, her big brown eyes, presented an aura of innocence, found mostly in a teen.

Mary Anne and Lillian were like most sisters, supporting each other whenever they needed to hear encouraging words. Almost every Thanksgiving Day, Lillian flew from Cincinnati to her sister's mansion in Hanford, spending the vacation with her sister and her family. She was in a depressed state after she had broken up with her boyfriend a few months before the tragedy. She always treated her nephew as her own son, helping her sister to raise him when he was an infant.

Now that Mary Anne was gone, both Lillian and Bob struggled to cope with the new reality. Bob worked in his father's firm as a launch specialist. Hence, he had been staying with the other launch specialists, in a housing complex, a kilometer from the launch pad. He had been at the launch pad since eight in the morning that day, before coming to the Seaside Steak House for dinner with his aunt. It was their first meeting after the tragic demise of Mary Anne.

"I know How hard it has been for you, Bob," with a somber face Lillian consoled her nephew.

"I've been thinking of you. She was always there for you," Bob responded.

"She has been there for all of us Bob, including you and your father. She loved him, trusted him with her life. I think your father betrayed that trust."

"Are you sure, it wasn't an accident?" asked Bob with a confused expression.

Lillian looked straight into Bob's eyes, and said, "I had a chat with your mother when they were at the airport. It was a surprise from your father. This is why she went along with the plan. She was not at all interested in the trip. She never liked the tropical climate of Hawaii. She said it was too hot for her. Nonetheless, her desire to please your dad prevailed in the end. I also talked to the tour guide. He claims, your dad wanted to be alone with your mother. They left the team and went on touring the volcano on their own, prior to the incident. The jury deliberately overlooked this vital information. And now I hear that your dad has been on vacation with his secretary. It's a strange way to mourn a loving wife's death, don't you think so?"

"Did you talk to the judge who presided over the trial?"

"You can't discuss it with the judge who presides over the trial. I talked to the prosecutor. He says there's no scope for a retrial. However, we could appeal against the verdict, and the chances are very slim that the appellate court will overturn the lower court's verdict."

Bob looked out the window and wondered what role he could play. He was open to suggestion, so he turned his head, and said, "So, what do you want me to do?"

"I want you to testify. I want you to tell the court about your mother's likes and dislikes, where she loved to travel, and what she wanted to avoid."

"You want me to testify against dad? I'm also one of his employees. He'll see it as betrayal. Apart from that, there's no telling, how it's going to affect the outcome."

"Bob, you're not going to testify against anyone. You'll simply state some facts. You owe it to your dead mother."

Bob slumped back into his seat, closing his eyes, and remaining still. He could hear the waitress serving the food. Bob had ordered a steak, while Lillian went for seafood. Quietly, both began having their meal. Lillian was in no mood for wine. She asked Bob if he would like to have it, but Bob declined. Halfway through dinner, quite reluctantly, Bob said, "Alright, I'll testify. You better have a nice job ready for me before that."

Lillian took Bob's right hand in hers and said, "I'm sorry Bob. I know how you feel about it. I know it's going to put you in a lot of trouble with your dad. I wish there were some other ways to do it." ***

On the panel before her, she could see Trevor in the control room with the launch specialists. Just before the liftoff, he waved, and threw a flying kiss at her. Cindy lifted her visor, touching the transparent fiber glass of her helmet in the direction of her lips, with her heavy gloves. Soon afterwards, she felt the jolt caused by the blast off, and the force of it, pressing her down to her seat.

"Sam, how do you feel?" Cindy asked her android companion.

"My sensors have detected rapid increase in pressure," Sam replied.

"It's the G-force. It means you have sensation."

"If you say so."

"Is there a limit to how much G-force your system can endure?"

"Of course, even the machines have limits. However, human tolerance level is nothing compared to ours. We can easily withstand over twenty G, provided, the platform carrying us has that level of endurance."

"Great! That makes you the ideal candidate for interstellar voyages of the future. Perhaps, the androids can travel at the speed of light."

"Yes, our endurance level qualifies us for that kind of long and hazardous journey. However, I doubt if human ego would allow that to happen. As for travelling at the speed of light, the problem is when matter reaches the speed of light, it's supposed to transform into pure energy. It has not been proven yet, so it's still a hypothesis. Even if we attain half the speed of light, certain changes are bound to take place in our system, which might endanger our very existence."

"Are you saying, it's impossible, even for the androids to attain the speed of light?"

"No, I'm not saying, it's impossible. I cannot cancel the possibility. Nonetheless, it wouldn't be wise to ignore the cost. This kind of achievement often comes with an exuberant price tag."

"First stage separation in ten seconds!" the mechanical voice of the onboard computer declared.

Cindy and Sam watched on the monitor, the first stage of the launch vehicle getting separated from the rest of the vehicle. The separation occurred smoothly. They slumped forward, as rapid rate of deceleration caused by the abrupt loss of thrust had slowed down the vehicle. A couple of seconds felt like ages, and then, another abrupt jolt caused by the ignition of the second stage, threw them back into their seats. The vehicle kept climbing at eighteen thousand miles per hour, until it reached the lower orbit. Once the desired altitude had been attained, the second stage stopped burning, and the conventional retro rockets were used to bring the vehicle where the orbiting space station had been, before coming to a complete halt. The green light on the hatch indicated the vehicle had successfully docked against the decompression chamber and ramp, sticking out of the space station. Subsequently, Cindy and Sam floated out into the decompression chamber once the door had slid open.

During the next seventy-two hours, Cindy and Sam worked in tandem to assemble and connect the ramp to the exit of one of the elevators. For this, the space station's thrusters had to be redeployed. Cindy worked inside the station, while Sam worked outside. Cindy's responsibility was to monitor Sam's systems. If any problem occurred, Cindy was to redirect the space station's onboard computer, Mother, to trouble-shoot and fix it. Sam not only assembled the ramp, but also extended the space station with the building materials it had in its storage.

After the successful launch, managers shifted the control room from the launch pad to the training facility at Henderson, and Jeff put Trevor in charge of the communication between the space station and the ground control. On twenty by forty feet screens, technicians and specialists monitored the activities up in the orbit. From time to time, Trevor winked at Cindy, praising her skills and dedication, and inspiring her to keep up the good work. Underneath his smiles, anxiety stretched Trevor's nerves to the limit. Keeping a tight lid on it was his immediate challenge. They had another twenty-four hours before Cindy was going to put on her specially made space suit and dive into the exosphere. The suit was designed like a flying jacket, with the sleeves and legs attached by heat resistant fabric. The coat of paint made of anti-flame substances would prevent burning out during the re-entry. At least in theory, that's how it was supposed to function.
***

For more than half an hour, Trevor had been walking. Every morning, exactly at six, he would walk for an hour. At home, he loved walking along the beach. At Henderson, he chose to walk around the perimeter of the training facility, covering an area of roughly one and a half square kilometers. When he completed one round, it was the same as walking six kilometers. In one hour, Trevor made two rounds before returning to his quarter.

The desert sky had been cloudless the last few days. Despite being dry, the landscape of Nevada offered a variety of vegetations. There were thirty different types of cacti scattered all over the state. To an unfamiliar set of eyes, the place might appear as totally devoid of life. However, a closer inspection revealed a wide variety of wildlife, living at ease in the apparently not so hospitable environment. On several occasions, Trevor witnessed bears, wolves, coyotes, and lizards. He was particularly interested in coyotes and the magnificent mountain lions. Bob's mother had a coyote as a pet. Mary Anne adopted the pup from the nearby adoption center. The mother of the pup had been killed in a road accident. The owner of the vehicle then picked up the pup and took it to the animal shelter. After Mary Anne's death, Bob had been taking care of the coyote. Trevor planned to adopt the coyote once he returned home from Henderson.

Trevor didn't know that he was being followed. While walking, he paid little attention to people around him. It was his way to avoid acquaintances during his daily workouts. Only when he was a few meters away, did Trevor notice him. He recognized the face. He was one of the launch specialists at the training facility. Both exchanged greetings without stopping.

"It's very dry. Little bit of rain would make a big difference in the picture," Trevor remarked with a casual tone.

"Oh yeah, that's natural in a desert."

"By the way, how long have you been walking?"

"I left my quarter at quarter past six."

"We have been working together for a while, and you know what, I still don't know your name," Trevor grumbled.

"Bob Stewart," the man responded.

"Trevor McLaughlin," with a smile Trevor stated.

"I know."

"By any chance, are you related to Michael Stewart?"

Bob knew it was coming. He replied, "He's my dad."

"Oh yeah, now it makes sense."

"What do you mean?"

"Now I know why the head of the project is so eager to consult with you before taking any steps."

Bob laughed gently as he said, "Well, he's always been very anxious to be in dad's good book, and I must say, it has paid off."

For a moment Trevor wondered if he should talk about Mary Anne's demise. He said, "I've heard about your mother. I'm truly sorry."

"I appreciate your concern."

Bob felt like the topic should be changed. After a brief pause, he continued, "Do you always walk so fast?"

"I try my best."

"It causes heavy sweating, doesn't it?"

"That's the point. After all, I do it as a workout. It keeps the system running properly, keeps the garbage out."

Trevor noticed Bob panting. He slowed down a bit when Bob asked, "Is there any problem if I walk at a leisurely pace?"

"A doctor can tell you more precisely, but as far as I know, that kind of walking won't burn the fat built up in your system. It seems like you're new in this."

"Not really new, I just don't do it regularly. I don't have the time."

By then they had been on the northern side of the perimeter. Half a mile from the facility, traffic on route 582 was clearly visible. In another ten minutes or so, they were going to reach the main entrance to the facility. This would be the first round of Trevor's morning walk. He turned to Bob, and said, "Look, you don't have to kill yourself. If you find it too stressful, just relax over here because I'm going for my next round after this."

"Don't worry, I'll stop when I need to."

Quietly they walked for another five minutes when Bob came up with a new topic. He asked, "What are your plans after your contract with the company expires? Do you intend to continue with us?"

"I don't know at the moment. I guess we'll have to wait and see how it all ends."

"I hear that you have your own business."

"Yes, I own an elevator construction company. It pays well."

"Who runs it in your absence?"

"I have my trusted lieutenant. He has been with me ever since I started the business ten years back. "

"What's the annual turnover from the company?"

"It's not like a giant company. Nonetheless, the turnover is good."

Bob understood his companion was not interested in divulging the details of his company's financial picture. He was not surprised. Professional businessmen don't. To get to know Trevor better, he remarked, "I have taken especial interest in you and your wife. I think you guys are among the most promising candidates. I would like to see you two flourish with us. If you need any kind of assistance, I mean any kind of assistance, just let me know. I have my way with Jeff. He's a nice fella. I think I've had enough for one morning, but before I go, let me tell you something. If you want to be in the big league, you have to expand beyond the state lines. You cannot remain bottled up in one state. You must think big, you must take bold steps, and for that, you need to invest heavily. If you're looking for investors, do let me know. I think I can help you." ***

Like a floating astronaut, Trevor moved around in the water tank, assembling part of the structure assigned to him. He had completed drilling the last screw in its place when his suit got caught up with a sharp end of an extended angle. Consequently, it punctured Trevor's waterproof suit, resulting in water filling it. Within seconds, the suit lost its buoyancy. Trevor tried to swim to the surface, but the heavy suit kept him pinned to the floor of the pool. Before anyone could realize what had happened, the leaked water drove out the air he had been breathing. The technicians keeping an eye on the monitors inside the control room, were apparently busy with a printer which had been offline. Trevor struggled vigorously, taking off his suit with no air to breathe. He could hardly hold the breath when he finally broke free from his heavy suit. He began seeing stars, and eventually collapsing, the second he came to the surface. ***

The prying eyes of the physician and the nurse in charge were the first thing Trevor saw when he opened his eyes. The water he had taken in was coughed out. Then he sighed, closed his eyes, and remained still for a while. He thanked the doctor and the nurse for the CPR which had saved his life.

Jeff had also been there by then. Trevor beckoned to him, he wanted to say something. As Jeff came closer, he said, "I wanted to talk to you about something."

"Are you sure, you're, okay?" Jeff asked. He wasn't sure if it was the right time.

"I'm alright Jeff. It's important. I should have told you about it earlier."

Jeff beckoned to all for allowing them privacy, and then said, "Alright go ahead, Mr. McLaughlin."

"The other day I noticed something while probing the shaft. I saw rectangular shaped boxes attached to the horizontal braces only a few meters from the rails. Would you please tell me what I saw?"

"Oh, those metal boxes, yeah, I should have informed you of them. They're motion detectors."

"I have never seen motion detectors like them," Trevor sounded unconvinced.

"Twenty second century motion detectors, you shouldn't expect them to be like their predecessors."

"Why do you need motion detectors when you have cameras and sensors, conveying to you everything you need to know?"

"Just an alternative, in case of malfunction in the devices you have just mentioned," with a smile Jeff explained. ***

Outside the clinic, Jeff confided this conversation to Bob. He said, "Mr. McLaughlin asked me about your dad's plan-B. Do you think we should disclose it to the trainees?"

"It's your call, Jeff. I don't have any say in it. Call dad and see what he says."

Jeff smiled, and responded, "Yes, I'll do that. In the meantime, keep up the good work." ***

The next morning, a tense atmosphere mingled with excitement, hovered inside the ground control which had been maintaining constant communication with Cindy and Sam. At exactly nine hundred hours, Cindy was going to attempt the unthinkable. The specialists at ground control briefed her before the daring feat. They explained to her in detail the safety procedures, and the way to handle the gadgets attached to her suit, though she knew all about them. Cindy's heavy helmet and heat-resistant suit were designed to protect her from the deadly rise in temperature during the re-entry. How long she had to remain still, the angle of descent, the moment when she was to deploy the wings attached to her suit, all this was elaborately reviewed before the great leap.

"Don't I need the thrusters to propel me towards the exosphere from the space station?" Cindy asked Sam.

"Just give it a good push with your legs, and that will take you to the exosphere. You don't need any thrusters."

"Oh yeah, I forgot, in space you keep moving, once you start the movement."

Prior to the big moment, everyone at ground control moved away from Trevor, allowing him and his wife the privacy they needed. "I never have doubts about what you can do, honey," Trevor reassured Cindy. Those words from Trevor were like a magic to her ears. She gave a flying kiss to him, and then floated towards the exit of the space station. Inside the decompression chamber, Sam was with her. Cindy stared at the android friend, and said, "I could not have done it without you. Take care, Sam."

She closed her eyes for a few moments before throwing herself out through the open hatch. She stared straight at the blue planet. The angle of her descent had to be forty-five degrees. In the next two minutes, the thin air of the exosphere was going to hit her visor. Till then, she had no way to feel the sensation of the great leap. ***

# Chapter Nine

With a somber face, Lillian sat in her lawyer's chamber. She had been waiting for half an hour. The veteran lawyer would be arriving late, the secretary informed Lillian. Before leaving her home, she had talked to him, so she hoped to be the first client he was going to deal with that particular day. She felt relieved when the lawyer finally made his way into the chamber. After the greetings, very gently he put his arm around her shoulder and led her to his chamber. Prior to entering the chamber, he directed his secretary to get him the file of the case.

Instead of having Lillian in the chair kept before Mr. Craig Rosenbaum's desk, he beckoned her to sit on the sofa which was right behind the two chairs. Like always, Mr. Rosenbaum opened the closet at the corner of the room to keep his heavy overcoat in the hanger.

"Mocha Java, one of the best in the town, I just love the smell of it," remarked Mr. Rosenbaum. Then with a gesture, asked Lillian if she would like to have a cup of it.

During her breakfast, she had had a cup of it. Still, she couldn't refuse another cup of the coffee. Upon taking the first sip, the veteran lawyer focused on the task in hand. He had a deep authoritative voice. He said, "Ms. Lillian, let me make one thing clear to you. Once a verdict has been issued by the lower court, it's rare, extremely rare for the appellate court to overturn that verdict. There are basically four or five grounds for an appeal, and they are, improper admission or exclusion of evidence, insufficient evidence, ineffective assistance of counsel, prosecutorial misconduct, or jury misconduct. What the ground will be for your case, depends on what I'm going to hear from you today. Apart from that, you must tell me why you have brought the charge against your brother-in-law, who happens to be a man of quite substantial standing. Do you seek justice for your sister, or are you after some sort of compensation? I need this information because I need to know what has driven you to this. How I'm going to construct my arguments will depend on what you seek. Please, be frank about it. You can be sure, whatever you say will remain in this chamber because this legal profession stands on this cloak of confidentiality. I would also like to know why you chose to come to me. I think it would have been better if you had allowed your previous attorney to continue."

Lillian's response was swift. She said, "I didn't like the way he handled the case. I don't think he believed we could win. I have checked your record. It's undoubtedly impressive. As for the purpose, I'm not interested in compensation. I seek justice for my departed sister. I have no doubt, whatsoever, that she was murdered because I know what kind of relation she had with her husband, and what kind of a man her husband is. My sister never acknowledged this truth. All her life, she had been in a kind of trance, unable, or perhaps unwilling to see the writing on the wall. She loved him blindly, and she paid the price for that mistake with her life.

Mr. Rosenbaum allowed a brief period of silence when Lillian had stopped. He tried to gauge Lillian's state of mind. He couldn't sense hesitation or uncertainty in her voice and gestures. Apparently, she was not the kind of person who could be talked out of what she intended to do. Then Mr. Rosenbaum glanced at the wall clock. It was already quarter past nine. He had to be at the court for a hearing by ten thirty. In the next fifteen minutes, he must wrap up the meeting with Ms. Lillian. He cleared his throat, and said, "Earlier you told me over the phone that you had a conversation with the tour guide. What did he say?"

"He said, Michael wanted to study the slope of the volcano with Mary Anne. He didn't want to be with the team, prior to the incident."

From the file Mr. Rosenbaum took some stapled papers and said, "This is the transcript of his testimony. I couldn't find what you just mentioned."

"He did tell me what I have mentioned to you," insisted Lillian.

"I'm not saying he did not, Ms. Lillian. All I'm saying is that it's not in the transcript. It means either he forgot to mention it, or perhaps he did not for reasons not clear to us, at this point. I'm going to be frank with you, Ms. Lillian. I don't see any prospect for this case. Your brother-in-law is the only witness, and the corpse could not be retrieved. Even if it was a murder, it looks like your brother-in-law has pulled off a perfect crime."

With a raised brow Lillian asked, "What's a perfect crime?"

"A crime which does not leave behind any evidence."

"But we have the tour guide."

"Ms. Lillian, what you said, and the statement he gave under oath doesn't match. Even if we manage to get it out of him, it's not going to prove the defendant's guilt, it could still be viewed as an accident, and without hard evidence, that's what the court is going to say. I don't want to offer you false hope. The chance of a successful appeal is almost non-existent in this case. So, I would like you to step back and think it over. I have no problem pursuing the case. However, we should be realistic about the possible outcome."

Lillian sighed when Mr. Rosenbaum had stopped. She looked pale. She could comprehend what Mr. Rosenbaum had been trying to convey to her. Both her hands were clasped together, under her chin. She was going to give it a last try. She raised her head, and said very softly, "Bob has agreed to testify."

"Who's Bob?"

"Michael's son."

"Was he there when it happened?"

"No."

"Then what is he going to say which might add credence to your charge?"

"He'll talk about his father."

"Ms. Lillian, how your nephew feels about his dad will have no bearing upon the merit of this case, unless he has something to say about what happened at Kilauea. The court is not going to issue a character certificate. That's not how the system works."

It was time for the old lawyer to head for the court. He raised himself from his seat. In a reassuring manner, gently putting his arm around Lillian's shoulders, he said, "I want you to go home and calm down. I know what you've been going through, how you feel about your sister. I wish I could make it easier for you. Tell you what, I'll study the case, if there's any scope for an effective appeal, I'll contact you. In the meantime, if you come across any relevant information, feel free to convey it to me as early as possible." ***

It was not the first time. Michael slept with Stephanie a couple of times in the past. This time, the experience was different. After Mary Anne's death, it had a different meaning for him. He felt like he was in his thirties. Ever since Michael hired her five years ago, he had been drawn by this young lady's irresistible chemistry. She was at least a couple of inches taller than Mary Anne. Her jet-black hair, a set of big dark eyes, and an extremely seductive figure gave her the look of the twenty second century Cleopatra. The first day when she had joined, Michael shut himself up in his office room, watching all day the hologram image of his new secretary, working in the next room.

Most of the time, Stephanie dressed conservatively, and that only made the situation worse for Michael. He felt being pulled like a piece of iron is pulled by a powerful magnet. Michael began spying on her. He knew the passwords she used for her social media accounts and emails. For the last few years, she had been going out regularly with her boyfriend, when he tacitly proposed to her for the first time. She refused. Later her financial condition turned her into an easy prey. Michael had given her three raises in a year before she finally capitulated. She was twenty-four, and her boyfriend was in his late twenties. At first, like a humanoid, she displayed no feelings at all. To her, it was pure business. Gradually, Michael managed to create a wedge between her and her boyfriend. After the boyfriend broke up with her, she became a lot friendlier and easier to handle.

She had been sleeping quietly next to him early in the morning, when he woke her up. Michael was going to have an interesting day. His excitement would not let him sleep well at night. Stephanie maintained constant communication with every sector of Michael's business empire, keeping him always updated. Michael was focused on the activities at the training facility in Henderson. Within the next half an hour, Cindy was going to commit herself to doing the unthinkable. Michael had no intention of missing the spectacle. He was going to observe the development over there from his temporary office which had been set up in his luxurious suite. He could also watch what was going on inside the space station. ***

As soon as the sensors embedded in her visor sensed the thin air of the exosphere, Cindy's system deployed the wings designed to slow down the rate of descent. It was also designed to prevent spin or roll. In three minutes, she entered the most hazardous zone. If it had not been for the specially made suit and visor, she would have been burnt to ashes, in a matter of minutes. She knew it would take roughly eight minutes for her to pass through the zone. When she had been briefed about it, she thought she could easily hold herself for eight minutes. However, after a minute or so, she lost track of time. She was in no condition to pay attention to the display on her visor. Her suit kept getting warmer. She wondered if it would survive the vicious temperature. She freaked out when her instinct to survive kicked in. She was about to scream as she heard Trevor's calm voice, telling her she was doing just fine, and then the signal broke up, but not before she had regained her resolve and self-control. Cindy bit her lips, waiting for the chute to be deployed. At seventy-five thousand feet, her suit dropped its wings, and deployed the primary chute. As the chute had popped up behind her, it presented to Cindy the good old feelings of a secure descent. Everyone at the ground control cheered at the images of the chute.

"I have done it guys! I have done it!" Cindy's euphoria crackled in the headsets in the mission control. ***

On Goldstein Island, Michael rejoiced in his luxury suite with his private secretary. He exclaimed at Stephanie, "Do you realize the implication of this feat?"

Stephanie knew what it meant. She didn't want to dampen Michael's spirit, so she simply kept smiling at him. After a pause, he responded to his own question, "It means, we don't have to spend tons of cash on those launch vehicles anymore. Our elevators would lift them to the lower orbit, and those specially made insulated suites would bring them down safely." ***

The meeting started with big applause from all the attendees. Jeff congratulated Cindy and Trevor for the latest achievement which was already considered as a milestone in the quest for sustainable interplanetary voyages. Michael was in an invisible mode. Hence, the attendees had no idea that the CEO had been quietly watching and listening. However, Trevor's intuition was right on spot. He couldn't be convinced that the CEO would ignore or miss such a meeting.

A vivid description of the free fall from space was the main attraction of the meeting. Quite eloquently, Cindy conveyed to the audience her feelings as she plummeted through the exosphere and the thermosphere. When the initial euphoria had dissipated, the focus shifted to the elevators. Greg Austin, one of the selected trainees raised a very inconvenient issue. Since the elevator shafts had now been connected to the space station, he asked if the events on the ground, like the quakes or the storms, were going to affect the space station. At first none understood what he meant. Then he explained that since the elevator shafts were connected to the space station, if the shafts collapsed for any reason, it would bring down the space station as well.

"The space station is under the zero-gravity environment, why is it going to come down with the collapsing shaft?' asked Mark Polaski.

"Greg is right," said Trevor, and then added, "so what if the space station is under zero gravity, a good pull from down here is bound to bring it crashing down with the collapsing shafts."

For a few moments, silence reigned in the conference room. Reality permeated into the consciousness of all like heavy water. Greg was right, there was nothing to stop the space station from crashing if it was hooked up with the collapsing shafts. Then Trevor came up with the solution to this problem. He said, "We have to use retractable air bridges or ramps. The ramp must be in a retracted position when the shafts are not in use. In other words, we have to maintain a safe distance between the elevator platform and the space station, unless it's time for arrival or departure."

"Why are we talking about the collapsing elevator shafts, would you people please explain that to me?" out of the blue, the hologram image of the CEO appeared before the audience.

"We have been talking about earthquakes and hurricanes, Mike," replied Jeff.

"For those who have been worrying so much about the natural calamities, let me highlight the record of the past hundred years. Not a single skyscraper collapsed in the world because of natural calamities such as earthquakes or hurricanes. In every way, the structure we have built is more, not less, quake resistant, more hurricane proof, than those century old structures. Apart from that, there's a good reason why we have chosen the Mojave Desert for the construction of this mega structure. This region has witnessed the least number of natural calamities one could think of. Therefore, I don't see any good reason for anyone to lose his or her sleep over this."

"Perhaps, the basic instinct of self-preservation is the source of it," Jeff remarked when the CEO had stopped.

"How long will it take for one group to reach the space station?" Mehmet Ozal inquired.

"Each stage will require half an hour. So, that adds up to two and a half hours," Jeff responded.

"A lot can happen during this long transit periods, don't you think so?" Trevor pointed out.

"Yes, a lot can happen during those two and a half hours. For example, a meteor the size of the Himalayas can hit us, the sun can explode, or the super volcano of the Yellow Stone can erupt. I've mentioned these scenarios, because I strongly believe our structure can survive anything short of these cataclysmic events. Now, I would like everyone to focus on what we're about to achieve, instead of singing the gloom and doom." ***

From a staff, Michael learned of Goldstein's arrival on the island with his mistress. For the last couple of months, this business tycoon had been trying to have a meeting with Michael. Apparently, Michael's Project Elenaut had aroused his interest. Two years back, when the construction of the structure had just commenced, Michael received an offer from the tycoon. Kruger warned Michael to stay away from him. When the old lawyer had dug into the tycoon's past record, what he found was quite alarming. The tycoon's business empire was basically a front cover. His real business was money laundering and trafficking beautiful young women to cater an elite circle that spanned across the globe. He owned three banks, one in the US, one in Europe, and another in Central America. He used these banks to launder money, and conceal the wealth accumulated over the years.

Michael had to heed the warnings from his lawyer. However, lately he had been thinking of accepting the tycoon's offer. Of course, he planned to retain full control of his company, even if he gave the tycoon a stake in the company. The contract would ensure the tycoon had no control, direct or indirect, over his company. However, Michael was not fully convinced that it was a good idea. He put the idea on hold for the time being.

Though the purpose of Michael's visit was private in nature, the tycoon wanted to use this opportunity to impress his would-be partner. He invited Michael and his secretary to lunch at his extravagantly luxurious villa which was on the northern edge of the island. The island covered an area of roughly four-square kilometers, with a small harbor which could handle two or three vessels at any given time. The harbor was built two years ago for cruise ships that often visited the island with tourists onboard. This generated healthy revenue, all year round.

A specially designed invitation card had been printed, just to invite Michael and his companion to the lunch. At the bottom left corner, the dress code was mentioned. Initially, Michael had decided to dress casually, but when he noticed the dress code on the card, he changed his mind. He wore an off-white shirt under his black suit and red tie, while Stephanie chose an elegantly designed red gown. Before leaving their resort, Stephanie fixed his tie knot as Mary Anne always did. Sadness gripped Michael for a few moments, when Stephanie was fixing his tie knot. The memories of his late wife flashed before him.

Instead of the dining hall, lunch was served in a room adjacent to the dining hall. It looked more like an old-fashioned parlor with a table for four diners. From the main structure of the villa, the chamber protruded like an extension, allowing a panoramic view of the Caribbean through its large glass windows.

On the island, there were only two vehicles. One was a grey Rolls Royce used only by Goldstein, and for his guests, he had a black B&W. However, the tycoon instructed his chauffeur to pick up Michael and his secretary. Michael had been asked to use Goldstein's Rolls Royce. It was the tycoon's way of expressing just how much he appreciated Michael's visit to his island.

Goldstein and his mistress had been waiting at the porch when their guests arrived.

"I hope you two have been enjoying your stay," with a broad grin Goldstein remarked as they shook hands with their guests. "Michael, my condolences for your great loss," a few seconds later, the host added.

"This is the first invitation to dinner after Mary Anne's departure. The pain lingers. Anyway, I appreciate what you've been doing for me."

Prior to lunch, Goldstein took his guests for a short tour of his regal mansion. While touring the mansion, Michael noticed his host's mistress. He wasn't sure if she was over eighteen. She looked very, very young to be Goldstein's mistress. Quietly, Michael inquired, "If you don't mind, how old is your consort?"

Goldstein whispered back, "Oh Michael, you know I wouldn't break the law. I'm no pedophile." And then he brought himself closer to Michael before adding, "She's a humanoid."

"What!" Michael burst out in laughter.

"You better believe it. Can you tell? I'm sure you're aware of all the goodies that come with these sweet dolls. And the best part is, no damn paparazzi can accuse me of having good times with an underage humanoid," with a cheesy smile on his lips Goldstein remarked.

"That is, if someone does not come up with the bill of rights for the androids," responded Michael with a smile.

"Bill of rights for the androids, you must be kidding!"

"Relax Goldstein, it's a joke."

"You know what, I have something to show you after the lunch."

"Why is it, when someone wants to give me a surprise, something inside me shrinks like a patient about to have an angiogram?"

"I promise you Michael, you won't regret it."

At the dinner table when Michael glanced at the served food, he said, "I bet, you know my taste as well."

"Of course, I do. I've been studying you for years. You are one of the greatest entrepreneurs of our time. At least, that is what I think."

Two attendants began serving the food to the diners, while the guests stared at the picturesque view outside. The next few minutes, no one talked. Goldstein picked a chunk of the veal with his fork, chewed it before swallowing the piece of the meat. Then he wiped his lips with his napkin, and asked, "Michael, have you been thinking about my proposal? It's been a while now."

Michael remained quiet. He put a chunk of the golden fried lobster into his mouth. He had to appreciate the taste. A sip of the aged white wine produced in Michael some sort of calming effect. Then he stared at his host, and said, "I've been very busy. I need to sit down and think about it. Right now, I cannot focus on anything other than my latest project. Therefore, I ask you to be patient."

"I saw your project on the news the other day. I have no doubts, it's a great achievement. It's amazing, seeing your elevators lifting the astronauts to the orbit."

"They are not astronauts, they're elenauts, short for elevated astronauts."

"How many of them do you have up there, right now?"

"Ten of them, excluding the androids."

"What's your next move?"

"Soon, we'll start building an industrial city as large as New York.

"A New York size city in the orbit, isn't this a bit too farfetched?"

"Nope, that's why we have the elevators."

Goldstein resumed consuming what he had on his plate, while Michael finished the last piece of lobster before turning his attention to the luscious meat on the table. The attendant had been watching. He served the steak along with the brown rice. As Michael dug his knife into the tender meat of the steak, Goldstein said, "Sending men and material up there, the space tourism, it's a big business. I'm afraid your elevators will eventually shut them down."

"That's the point," responded Michael while chewing the meat.

"They won't like it."

Michael swallowed the meat he had in his mouth, raised his head, and asked, "Is it a threat, Goldstein?"

"Come on Michael, I would never do that. For God's sake, I'm interested in investing in your project!"

"Well then, I could care less for what others think of my project."

Goldstein carefully changed the topic after this. The conversation focused on Michael's health, his family, and what Goldstein had planned. Michael praised the chef and thanked his host for such a wonderful dinner. ***

As the Rolls Royce moved towards the harbor, Michael could see something anchored next to the pier. He wasn't sure what it was. When they stepped out of the vehicle, Michael realized what it was. It was the first time he saw a transparent sub. The hull of the sub was made of conspicuous fiber glass mixed with light refracting aluminum. They could see the crew moving inside it. The ninety feet long and twenty-five feet wide sub had a dozen or so crew. Only the washroom and the living quarters were surrounded by opaque sheets. The rest of the vessel was visible to the naked eyes.

"Bought the beauty from the Oceanography Institute. They have the latest model, so they sold this one for two billion, plus a few million," Goldstein said to his guests proudly.

"How deep can it dive?" Michael inquired.

"The hull can withstand the depth of more than five thousand feet. That's more than enough for me. After all, the average depth of the Caribbean is only a few hundred feet."

"Why do you need a sub?"

"The Caribbean is full of sunken ships from the past centuries. Many of them are still undiscovered. You should see what we found a few weeks back."

"Do you mean, you hit upon a sunken treasure?"

"You have to see to believe it. I think a ride in my sub will open your eyes to another world underneath the waves. While you have your focus on what's beyond our planet, there's a world right here under the oceans that hasn't yet been fully explored. Don't you think we should explore that too?"

"If you would like me to go for a sub ride, be frank about it because we have no problems with the idea."

Captain Ren Frankfurt and his first officer had been standing on the deck of the sub when the visitors stepped onto the vessel. The captain had already been alerted about the visit, so he was prepared to receive the guests. The captain shook hands with Goldstein and the guests, welcoming them to his sub named Atlantis.

The ladder inside the coning tower was visible from the deck. Cautiously, they entered the coning tower to avoid the transparent wall of the sub. From inside the bridge of the vessel, the intricate network of pipes, cables and wires appeared like the web of a spider. This network connected the various sensors, devices and parts of the sub to the bridge.

The visitors watched the water rush into the vessel's tanks, thus changing the buoyancy of the vessel and allowing it to dive. The spectators watched the propeller spinning, the elevators and rudder moving, guiding the vessel to its destination. All this added a whole new chapter to what the visitors already knew about the subs. It was a unique experience for the visitors.

The watery world beyond the hull of the sub provided another source of amusement. The fish swimming in the crystal-clear waters of the Caribbean didn't seem troubled by the presence of the humans among them. Perhaps it was because they were used to the site of the divers and the treasure hunters in these waters. A barracuda made the fatal mistake of rocketing at one of the crews, eventually, slamming onto the hull, and then fleeing with the most frightening experience of its life. The dolphins proved themselves way smarter than the ill-fated barracuda. They had somehow sensed that there was an invisible wall between them and their human companions. They circled the sub for about half an hour before heading in search of something more interesting.

Finally, the sub came to the spot where they could see the wreck of a sunken vessel on the sandy floor of the Caribbean. It was a Spanish Galleon completely covered by sea weeds and other aquatic plants. Over the centuries, it turned into a natural shelter for the aquatic animals and various fish.

"This is the reason why I purchased the island and the sub. Last month, we salvaged two thousand gold coins from this wreck. There are many more like this on the floor of the Caribbean and the Atlantic. All we have to do is find them and claim them, and my island serves as the hub for this kind of treasure hunt."

The lights of the subs had to be turned on as the waters around the vessel suddenly turned dark. The dark clouds concealed the sun over the sea surface, stealing the only source of light for the vast sea. This resulted in another spectacle around the vessel. From all around, aquatic creatures were drawn by the subs artificial light. They began investigating the source of the light with open mouths, providing recreation for those inside the sub. Michael looked mesmerized by the world he never took the time to investigate or explore.

On their return journey, the sub had been cruising just below the waves at twenty knots when the glow of the sinking sun produced another beautiful scene. From below the waves, they could see the golden light shimmering over their heads as it was reflected by the surface of the sea. Goldstein had brought his guests to this world for recreation, and he thought the tour could not possibly reach its full potential without music. The sub was equipped with its entertainment system as well, and he felt it was the perfect moment for a little bit of it. Therefore, he asked the captain to play something appropriate for the moment. Soon afterwards, the track called 'Sailing' by Christopher Cross began echoing through the waves, creating some sort of magical spell in everything the music touched.

"Beneath the waves, this song doesn't really fit in, Goldstein. Make the sub pop up," Michael suggested with a grin.

The captain heard Michael's remark. He agreed and gave the command to surface. Over the waves, as the vessel cruised like a phantom, the crew replayed the song. This time the effect of it was perfect. With each wave dashing against the sub, the wind blowing from the northwest, and the clouds over the horizon with the silver linings, the visitors could not remain below the deck. They climbed up onto the open deck with their host, to enjoy not only the song, but to feel the moment as well.

At sixteen hundred hours, the sub returned to the harbor. "What do you think, Michael? Have I wasted my money on this sub?" on their way to the cottage, Goldstein asked his guests who seemed quite pleased.

Michael struggled to express his feelings. He stared at his host for a few moments, and then uttered, "I'm truly impressed. I don't know how to say it. I admire your audacity. Let me tell you one thing, I'm going to seriously think about your proposals. I think we can share our experience and profit from it." ***

At night, Trevor had a lengthy conversation with Cindy. Both were apprehensive about the project after the troubling issues which had been raised during the meeting. The contract was quite rigid about any kind of withdrawal from the project. The company reserved the right to sue them if they refused to fulfill their obligation. Upon considering every aspect of their participation, they decided to continue. Trevor had something very interesting to share with Cindy. He showed her a list of names and profiles of the next batch of elenauts who were going to be sent to the modified and enlarged space station. The list contained two hundred names, most of them engineers and architects. A few of them were doctors. Apparently, the first batch of the elenauts was going to prepare the space station during their three-month long stay for those engineers and doctors. Five more androids were going to accompany those engineers and doctors. These androids, plus the ones already up there in the orbit, were going to do most of the laborious tasks. The contract stated that their stay would not exceed ninety days. But at the end of the contract, another clause stated that the company reserved the right to extend that period under special circumstances. More amazing was the list which was revealed after the first one. The second list contained five hundred names with profiles, and all of them were couples. They were never to return to earth.

Cindy exclaimed, "How did you get it? Aren't they supposed to be classified?"

"I didn't ask for it sweetheart. The source was only too happy to transmit to me the information. I have no idea who the source is, but I have a hunch, he's a close confidante of the big boss."

"Are you suggesting the big boss has a turncoat, right behind him?"

"Well, it looks that way, doesn't it?"

"Why has he picked you to leak the data?"

"I don't know. Perhaps he intends to drive a wedge. Maybe he thinks I have access to the media or connections with the rival companies. For me, it's just a wild goose chase right now."

Trevor looked frustrated. Cindy stroked his head, gently running her fingers through his coarse hair. He turned to face her, and then said, "You were just great up there! I'm so proud of you."

She kissed him passionately before throwing the quilt over them. ***

All morning Lillian listened to Mr. Steve Makani, the tour guide. The other day she landed on the island. She intended to see for herself the spot where her sister died. Upon arrival, she was quick to manage the brief history of the tour guide, his records. When they were about to return to the coaster, she introduced herself to him. The moment she had mentioned Mary Anne's name, the keenness to assist, and the lingering smile disappeared from the man 's countenance. He said, "Look lady, I have already testified before the jury. I have nothing more to say to anyone."

"But you didn't mention that prior to the incident, Michael left your team with my sister."

"I didn't?"

"No, you didn't. I have a copy of the transcript of your statements. Why didn't you, Mr. Makani? Who knows, perhaps it would have made a big difference."

"Maybe I forgot. It wasn't intentional. You know how stressful it is, standing before the jury, and trying to remember what happened weeks earlier."

"It was not weeks earlier, you testified five days after the incident. Anyway, I would ask you to take a stand once more. Whatever the expenses, I'll be glad to cover it. I would also like you to take me to the spot where the incident took place."

When Lillian looked down the hell hole, she couldn't remain calm. Tears swelled from her eyes. She realized why there was no way to retrieve the body once someone fell into the pit. She didn't understand why anyone would want to visit such a place. Her whole body was drenched in sweat as she headed for the transport which had been waiting for them with the other tourists. ***

The final training session was rigorous. From eight in the morning, it began and ended at five in the evening. Other than the one-hour lunch break, there was no interruption. The androids took part in the training session as well, familiarizing themselves with the procedures, the tasks they were expected to perform, and above all, their human counterparts. To some extent, Cindy's experience with Sam dispelled the unease among some of the elenauts. ***

At the base of the structure, the arrival of the elenauts coincided with the arrival of Michael's rocker-jet. A thick blanket of fog enveloped the site of the structure. Like a ghost, the craft penetrated the fog layer, and landed on the illuminated tarmac, a few hundred meters from the vehicles, carrying the elenauts and the specialists. Only Jeff had the prior information about the CEO's unscheduled visit. Hence, the visit caught the rest of the team by surprise. The swirling fog and the chopping noise of the rotors produced a haunted atmosphere. Those who had been watching, waited anxiously for the craft to land. The pilot had to depend on the instruments for landing in poor visibility. Within minutes after the touchdown, the door came down, forming the stairs for the passengers. Michael's security personnel escorted him towards the structure surrounded by a fifty feet high concrete wall, embedded with sensors. From high above, it looked like a contingent of ants, slowly approaching the monstrous structure. The alarm went off with blinking red lights prior to opening the colossal gate.

The complex was built to accommodate thousands of staff along with their provisions. Michael was going to inaugurate the elevators at seven in the morning. The entire team would spend the night at the complex before embarking on the mission, the following morning. The possibility of mishaps was ever present. Hence, it had a somber effect upon everyone involved in the project.

Specially cooked meals were prepared for the elenauts, so that none suffered indigestion or other medical complications. The androids running the complex, as well as in charge of the control room were constantly running checkups of the various systems. Engineers working on the elevators added power to both elevators. They were ready for operation. All along the structure, navigation lights kept blinking, alerting air traffic to maintain safe distance from it. Already, a no-fly zone within ten miles of the structure had been approved by the FAA. Only authorized aircraft could use the designated airspace.

The second elevator would carry provisions for the elenauts and five androids. It would start its climb after the first elevator had reached the first transit point, twenty miles from the ground. The ground control would have full control over the ascent of the second elevator. The androids had instructions to unload the provisions and load them onto the extension of the second elevator at the transit point.

Michael had dinner with the elenauts and the staff, at the dining hall of the complex. Next to him was his secretary. Bob gave Trevor a gentle shove with his elbow as they ate, and asked, "How do you like dad's new mistress?"

Trevor didn't understand what Bob meant. "Dad needs company to fight depression and loneliness. Instead of calling the escort services, he simply went for his sexy secretary. I guess, it saved him the extra expense and a lot of troubles," quietly Bob explained to Trevor and Cindy. He was quick to add that he always loved to joke about his dad's peculiar ways. Nonetheless, in Trevor and Cindy, it raised more questions. Questions, they were in no position to ask.

The physicians advised the elenauts to sleep well at night before the launch in the morning. Thrill, laced with anxiety, would not let them have a sound sleep though. Instead, some had nightmares, nightmares they couldn't share. In twenty second century, people would make fun if the elenauts talked about dreams.

Later at night, privately, Trevor discussed with Cindy what Bob said about his dad. Cindy remarked, "Only a few days back, his wife died in an accident. And now, he's been passing his days on a remote island with his private secretary. It's a strange way to mourn. Do you think it was an accident?"

"I don't know honey. Remember, in many ways, these powerful proponents of the new global order are above the law. It's quite possible. After all, the super-rich have this tendency to discard everything old. Perhaps he became tired of staring at his fifty-year-old wife." ***

# Chapter Ten

The culinary team served breakfast to the CEO and the elenauts at six. After the meal, Michael shook hands with the elenauts, thanked them and praised them for their contributions. In a short speech he said to them, "Mankind will forever remain indebted to you for opening a new chapter in our quest for sustainable interplanetary and inter stellar voyages. If everything goes as planned, the biggest hurdle to sending men and material to the orbit will be removed, once and for all. From there, mankind can take his next big leap into the unknown."

It took roughly two hours to prepare the elenauts. Each of them wore the specially made suit which could withstand extremes of heat and cold. Once more they checked if the gadgets attached to their suits functioned as expected. The management selected Cindy as the leader of the team, while Trevor was put in charge of communication between the space station and the ground control. He was to convey to the team what was expected of them. Cindy would execute the commands issued from the ground control.

At exactly nine, the elenauts formed a queue led by Cindy. One by one, they stepped into the elevator. The temperature inside the elevator was kept at seventy. The suits' auto thermal system controlled the temperature inside the space suits. The elenauts did not yet deploy the visors. They were going to deploy them when the elevator reached the first transit point. Until then, the airtight interior of the elevator would provide the oxygen supply and the appropriate air pressure.

The suits of the elenauts were designed to monitor the vital signs of each elenaut and transmit them to the ground control. During emergency, the entire elevator capsule could be ejected, and the elenauts had guidelines, dictating to them what to during an emergency. The seats could withstand the impact force of the falling elevator capsule with four chutes attached to it. They would also protect the elenauts from the initial shock of the capsule being blasted out of the shaft.

Another thirty minutes elapsed before all ten elenauts and their five android companions had secured themselves in their seats. Cindy had the control box built in the arm rest of her seat. The climb rate had been set at sixty feet per second. At this rate of ascent, it would take roughly half an hour for the capsule to reach the first transit point.

From the ground control, the android launch specialists and their human counterparts were going to keep a sharp eye on the length of the brackets, rails, cables and the spool of cables, with the help of the video transmitters. There was a mechanism in place to cool down the pulleys and the spools if they overheated.

At nine thirty, Cindy received the clearance to start the climb. The elenauts felt a strange sensation, as the hair on their body stood up when Cindy had activated the magnetic levitation of the capsule. Instantaneously it raised the capsule from the rail. There was hardly any noise. Like it was in the conventional elevators, the G-force pressed down on the elenauts, pinning them to their seats at the beginning of the ascent. In a couple of seconds, the G-force dissipated, and through the rectangular fiber glass windows on either side of the capsule, the elenauts watched the braces of the structure rushing down. As the capsule had climbed through a thick fog layer, over the eastern horizon, the sun smiled at them with the promise of a new day. It was obviously the most romantic part of the voyage.

The seats were arranged in three columns, with Cindy, Trevor and Greg occupying the first row. Thrill and anxiety filled Cindy's heart as she turned her head. To her right, sat Trevor. She put her hand on his, and very gently said, "How do you feel?"

Trevor had anticipated something like this, he replied, "When I was a boy, I wanted to be an astronaut. The day I was turned down by the air force, that dream was buried. It was the greatest disappointment in my life. I never imagined one day I would be heading for the orbit with my loved one. Here I am, next to you, doing just that. I suppose, I'm the luckiest man alive."

"Why did the air force turn you down?"

"I'm color blind. They gave me a picture book with pages having colored dots on them. Those dots formed a number. Only a person with perfect color vision could see the numbers. I couldn't."

A gentle squeeze of her hand conveyed to Trevor that she understood. She said, "You never told me this."

"You never asked."

Cindy laughed in her helmet. Trevor knew she wanted to kiss. He turned his head, leaned at her, and the two helmets made contact.

"Absolutely awesome!" Anna Heinrich cried out from the rear.

"If I didn't have these damn gloves, I would have given you two loud applauses," Greg remarked.

"Just enjoy the ride, will you?" Trevor responded.

On the display before them, the message they had been expecting, flashed. Thirty seconds to the first transit point, twenty miles from the planet surface.

"Deploy your visors," said Cindy, and then added, "there's a decompression chamber on the platform. From there, we'll head for the next elevator."

They felt dizzy as the elevator decelerated and stopped. Cindy and Trevor were the first ones to unfasten their seat belts. Cindy stood next to the elevator door and stared at the red light over it. In ten seconds, the red light went out and the green light was on, indicating that the air pressure inside the decompression chamber was the same as it was inside the elevator capsule.

Cindy gave a hand signal to her team to follow her. The chamber was large enough for at least fifty people. All of them, including their android associates, stood in two columns, facing the exit. As the door of the elevator had closed behind them, a blaring siren alerted them that the exit door was about to slide open.

"Hold tight, guys!" Cindy yelled.

The pulse rate of the elenauts scrambled prior to the final moment. The door opened, and the air inside the decompression chamber blew out. The sky was still as bright as the troposphere, but the sky above them was black. They could see the stars blinking faintly. The platform covered an area of two square kilometers. They stared at another Eiffel-like tower rising from it. Far away, at the center of the second platform, the next pair of elevator shafts was visible. However, to the elenauts, the center piece of attraction was no longer the shafts, but the breathtaking view that enveloped the massive structure. They were at the crossroads where the heavens above them met the world below them.

Very cautiously the team approached the shafts one and a half kilometers ahead of them. Cindy held Trevor's hand as they led the team to their destination. The half an hour walk felt like a glance. Momentarily, the freezing temperature around them caused fog on their visors. The built-in temp control subsystem took care of it. Cindy looked at the temperature being displayed on her visor. It was minus ten degrees.

"Space is a very, very cold place, guys!" Cindy remarked.

"Yet it has its freezing beauty," Trevor pointed out.

Cindy stared at the blackness above, and asked, "Do you think it will ever be possible for us to conquer space?"

Trevor turned to Cindy, and replied, "It depends on what you mean by conquer. Literally it's not possible to conquer something which has no end. Scientists talk of the shape or boundary of the universe; I find it absurd because empty space is what it is, endless expanse of empty space. You cannot impose a limit on it. Whenever someone talks about boundary, it invites the question, what's on the other side of the boundary? If there's something, that's part of the universe, and if there's nothing but empty space, that's part of the universe as well."

"We can hear you," yelled Mehmet from the rear of the queue.

"Welcome to the club," Trevor muttered with a smile on his lips.

Before the door of the decompression chamber, Cindy paused for a few moments, and observed it. It's identical to the one they left behind. The scanner next to the door scanned Cindy's retina, when it matched with what had been fed into the scanner's memory, the door slid open.

Inside the chamber, Cindy and Trevor stood next to the door, while the rest of the team stood a few feet from the entrance of the elevator itself. The elevator door closed when its sensor detected everyone in their respective seats. Cindy released the capsule, as soon as the magnetic levitation had been activated. The scene outside grew steadily darker until nothing could be seen, but stars.

The capsule was halfway to the second transit point when the hologram image of Jeff appeared before the elenauts. In his white lab coat Jeff looked worried.

"Your anxious face is the last thing we need right now, Jeff," Cindy complained.

"I'm sorry guys, I wish I could withhold what I'm about to say. Something's wrong up there at the space station. We have lost contact with the station and the android in there."

"Have you tried to re-establish contact?" Cindy inquired.

"We've been trying," the audience could clearly comprehend the consternation in Jeff's voice.

"It could very well be a malfunction in the communication system," Trevor stated.

"We detected no malfunction. Our system says communication was terminated from the other end. Right now, we have no video or audio signal from the station. The motion detectors have also been turned off. The only thing we have right now is the video signal from the decompression chambers of the elevator platform. Our sensors from the ground have detected movements inside the station. It's a big puzzle."

"What could it be?" Cindy exclaimed.

"Hacking is a possibility."

"Do you mean Sam's system has been hacked?"

"It's the only scenario we could think of."

"Aren't these androids supposed to be hack proof?" Trevor raised the uncomfortable issue.

"Listen people, there's no such thing as hack proof. We just make it as difficult as possible for the hackers to have access, but in the end, the machines are fooled into granting access because of the built-in loopholes in the programming. All the hackers have to do is find those loopholes and exploit them."

"It means the systems of our android companions are vulnerable to hackings, right?" Cindy asked.

Jeff sighed. After a pause he said, "Theoretically yes, but at this point it's just speculation."

"What if these androids are turned against us, Jeff? These androids literally have the capacity to become deadly mother fuckers!" Trevor fumed.

Jeff was aware of the implication of Trevor's derogatory remark. He responded, "Look fellas, the chances of hacking are million to one. Even if their systems are hacked, we have safety measures in place. Therefore, don't worry about your humanoid companions. You people are going to need their assistance."

"What's keeping you from accessing Sam's system? You can always override his directives, can't you?" asked Trevor.

"First of all, we don't have communication with the humanoid. Secondly, we do not know if his systems have been compromised."

"So, what do you want us to do, right now?" Cindy asked.

"Just be alert when you people enter the space station. Thoroughly study the video images from the decompression chamber before stepping into the station. Have the androids before you as some sort of human shield. And of course, make sure that the line of communication remains uninterrupted, and I believe that's the sole responsibility of Mr. McLaughlin."

"Oh yeah, that's hell of a job in the battlefield!" exclaimed Trevor.

"Mr. McLaughlin, spare yourself the pain, I don't think it'll come to that," reassured Jeff.


In another hour, the elevator completed climbing the fourth extension of the structure. As it stopped, Cindy told SPOT-1, the leader of the androids, to be at the fore front. They were already under the zero-gravity environment. Hence, instead of waiting inside the decompression chamber, Cindy decided to remain seated in the elevator. She planned to enter the decompression chamber as soon as the second elevator had reached the top with the provisions.
***


That very morning, Lillian left Hawaii for Cincinnati. During her flight, she called Mr. Rosenbaum. She wasn't sure if she would get him at his office as it was already two o'clock in Cincinnati. She was relieved to hear his husky voice from the other end. The initial greetings were followed by her excited outburst.

She exclaimed, "Mr. Rosenbaum, I have good news for you!"

"I can hear you dear, go ahead."

"I met Mr. Makani, the tour guy who took my sister and her husband to___________,"

"Do you mean you went to Hawaii to talk to the guy?" Mr. Rosenbaum interrupted.

"Yes, I did."

You didn't need to. You could have talked to him over the phone, I have his number."

"Please Mr. Rosenbaum, try to understand my feelings. I wanted to see the hell hole Michael prepared for my sister."

"I'm sorry dear, I hope you come out of it because life goes on, and you need to have a grip on the fact that your sister's gone."

"Mr. Makani has agreed to take the stand again."

"I'm glad to hear it, but don't be too excited. First let me find out if the appellate court would allow the second testimony."

"How long will it take?"

"Anywhere between two to four weeks. It's up to the appellate court."

"Alright, let me know when you get the approval."

In a depressed state Lillian stared down at the ocean below. She didn't notice that the flight attendant had already served the dinner. She was totally lost in the deep blue beauty of the Pacific. Mary Anne loved to watch the deep blue ocean. She said it refreshed her soul. A gentle touch on her shoulder brought her back from her perpetual sad state. Somehow, the flight attendant could feel Lillian's pain.

She remarked, "You don't need to be so sad. Life has so much to offer."

For a brief moment, Lillian just stared at the young Hawaiian beauty. She was perhaps in her early twenties. She had her jet-black braid neatly tucked behind her head. Her teeth were like a string of pearls, glistening as she smiled.

Lillian smiled back, and asked, "How would you feel if your loved one was in the jaws of an alligator?" ***

Trevor hooked up with the ground control while waiting for the second elevator to arrive. Jeff's scrutinizing eyes appeared before them in seconds.

He asked, "Is everything okay?"

"We're okay, waiting for the second elevator to arrive," responded Cindy.

"It'll be there any moment now," Jeff reassured.

"Jeff, does Sam know how many of us are here?" Cindy was apprehensive.

"No."

"Does he know we're coming?"

"I'm afraid he does. He has the schedule."

Cindy glanced at the lights next to the door. The red light was gone. The green light signaled that the decompression chamber had been pressurized. Cindy gave the go ahead to SPOT-1. The android spread his palm over the sensor, and the door slid open before them. One by one, the androids moved into the chamber. In the next minute, the androids from the second elevator joined them. When SPOT-1 said they were ready, Cindy and her associates stepped out of the elevator, and stood behind the android shield.

All this time, the men at the ground control had been eagerly following the video images being transmitted from the ramp. The sensors and cameras on the elenauts allowed the ground control to monitor their every move. Cold, dark, open space awaited the elenauts when the door of the decompression chamber slid open.

"SPOT-1, send one of your androids to the station. Tell him to turn on the remote sensor of the ramp," Cindy told the robot with a rigid tone.

SPOT-1 held the safety line while one of the androids floated to the spinning space station, roughly hundred meters from the gate of the decompression chamber, to manually turn on the sensor. Inside the station, as the robot turned on the sensor of the air bridge, the station stopped spinning, realigned itself in order to extend the retractable air bridge. When the ramp made contact with the decompression chamber, the elenauts and their android companions boarded the air bridge.

There was no one in the air bridge. The androids moved forward in pairs while SPOT-1 directing them from the rear. A couple of yards behind them, Cindy and her team cautiously followed the androids. The artificial gravity had automatically been cancelled, the moment the station stopped its spin, prior to extending the air bridge. Hence, the new arrivals activated the magnetic soles of their boots, allowing them to walk on the metal floor of the air bridge. Once they were in the main module, SPOT-1 retracted the air bridge and the station resumed its spin, producing the artificial gravity. Subsequently, deactivating the magnetic soles made movements easier.

Even before the team could reach the other end of the passage, Sam appeared at the door. He scanned the new arrivals, and said, "You have trespassed into the sovereign territory of another state. Go back, or else I have to take stern action."

The sight of Sam had alerted everyone, and what he said confirmed their fear. Sam's system had been hacked. He was under the control of a foreign entity.

"We want the name of the state you just referred to," shouted Trevor shouted at the hostile android.

"I'm not allowed to provide that information. I command you to return to the capsule."

A hole in Sam's forehead appeared.

"SPOT 2, his laser designator has been turned on," warned SPOT-1.

SPOT-1 had hardly finished when a flash of laser tore through SPOT-2's face. In a fraction of a second, another flash of laser from SPOT-1's forehead burned through Sam's arm, freezing him right where he had been standing.

SPOT-2 kept moving erratically. It seemed like it had lost its sense of direction. SPOT-2's optical and hearing devices, its sensors and laser designator in his head, were vaporized by the laser strike. However, it could still move because the mother boards containing the processors of these androids were inside their right shoulder instead of the head. It was something only the manufacturer and their privileged clients like the military and the space agencies knew. The incident revealed to the elenauts that the androids accompanying them were basically robotic soldiers disguised as harmless androids.

"Sam is safe now. His security protocol has been turned off," SPOT-1 was heard saying.

"What security protocol!" Trevor exclaimed.

"I'm sorry, I cannot disclose to you what has already been divulged unwittingly, without proper authorization," SPOT-1 responded.

"From where you get your authorization?" asked Cindy.

"The head of the Project Elenaut."

After SPOT-1's revelations, Cindy felt like Jeff owed them an explanation if not an outright apology for hiding this sensitive issue. Jeff had been watching the events taking place up in the orbit. Anxiously he witnessed the violent confrontation. He knew Cindy was going to ask for an explanation. Hence, while the team had been busy tackling Sam, privately Jeff held a conversation with Michael. Briefly, the two discussed the best way to explain it to the team.

None of the elenauts accepted it normally. Both Cindy and Trevor were troubled by the implication of it. It meant, indirectly, they were under the military. This raised questions about the actual objective of the project. If it was truly for the progress of science as officially proclaimed, there wouldn't be political or military involvement in it.

Cindy didn't wait to ask Jeff who had been watching from the ground control. With a bewildered expression, she said, "Jeff, what is this android talking about?"

Jeff was clearly uncomfortable as he stammered, "Well, we have certain safety measures in place for your protection. Just relax, you don't need to worry about it."

"I'm curious Jeff, what does SPOT stand for?" Trevor asked with a firm tone.

"Security Protocol for Orbital Track."

"What is meant by orbital track?"

"Company's investments in the orbit. Even I have limitations to what I can share with you."

"We would like to talk to the CEO about it, do you have any problem with that?" Cindy inquired.

"I'm afraid he's not available at the moment."

"Why don't you just give him a call?" Cindy insisted.

Cindy had hardly finished her line when the hologram image of the CEO appeared before them, interrupting the conversation between Jeff and the team. "Alright Jeff, let them talk to me," Michael snapped from the other end of the line.

"Mr. President, why do we have the military robots disguised as harmless androids with us?" Cindy fired the first shot.

"Mrs. McLaughlin, we knew this could happen. This incident has only confirmed our fears. We have competitors up there in space as well, and they have no problem with claiming the entire solar system as their sovereign territory. They will stop at nothing, barring us from exploiting the resources to hacking our robots. This is why all space activities, including the private ventures, are under the watchful eyes of the military. The top brass of the military feels like there should be security measures in place for preventing the investments from falling in the wrong hands."

"Wrong hands, who's going to invade us over here in the orbit?" Trevor asked politely.

"Be practical guys, the world we live in is not the Kingdom to come. There are rogue countries that consider even the moons of the Jupiter and Saturn as the extension of their sovereignty."

"We have no idea what you're referring to. Would you be a bit more specific?" Trevor asked for an explanation.

"Last year, one of our probes was blasted out of the sky of Europa. It was a stern message, don't you think so?"

"We do the same, don't we?" Trevor reminded Michael.

"No, we don't. We simply claim the spot where we land, a fair practice in any exploration. We don't claim the entire planet or the moon. In the last five years, we lost five probes sent out to survey the surface of Europa, one of the moons of Saturn. At first, we thought it was the magnetic field of Saturn. Later our informers provided evidence of hacking. The probes had been hacked and thrown into the atmosphere of Saturn. If they could do that, we suspect they're capable of greater mischief, in the name of 'progress'. Consequently, we came to a conclusion that measures should be taken to safeguard our interests in space as well."

"You haven't mentioned the name of the hostile state," Cindy stated calmly.

"Of course, the pariah state won't admit, it will only create diplomatic rift. You know how those powerful states operate under the cloak of deniability."

"Let's focus on what we have to do now," Cindy said.

Michael's countenance lit up when he had sensed acceptance of his explanation from Cindy. He said, "Yes, that's more like it. So far, Sam has built three living quarters and one lab. Those quarters can each accommodate four astronauts or elenauts. Soon, we're going to need hundreds of quarters, several labs, and clinics. Some of those quarters with remote chargers installed in them, will be used by the androids."

"We can't possibly assemble hundreds of quarters," Greg grumbled.

"We don't expect you to. You're to assemble as many as you can, during your stay. Perhaps, the duration of your stay could be extended. The rest will be completed by the androids. I want to be clear about one thing. Our drive to expand our settlements in the solar system won't be launched from the planet surface anymore. It'll start from up there, and you guys have to lay the foundation of it. So, be proud to be part of this noble endeavor." ***

# Chapter Eleven

On the traditional glass door with a wooden frame was written, Kruger and Kruger, in bold Algerian fonts. James Kruger and his four sons had done extremely well in the field of law, drawing attention from every corner. Mr. Kruger was in his late sixties, while his four sons were all in their forties, each with an enviable reputation. Their Ivy League backgrounds, and Mr. Kruger's well-established connections brought the law firm undisputable fame all across the state of California. Though based in Los Angeles, it had lawyers representing the firm in almost every state.

Ever since the Space Race had been founded, Mr. Kruger's law firm looked after the legal aspect of the space firm and the CEO's personal dealings as well. Usually, Mr. Kruger would meet his distinguished client at the dinner tables of the finest restaurants in the city of Los Angeles and discuss the ways to expand Michael's business empire.

This time the issue they were going to talk about was too sensitive. Hence, Mr. Kruger felt that his chamber was the ideal place for the discussion. On the second floor, his firm occupied, at least three thousand square feet of office space, at the heart of the city. For being within walking distance from the district court, one could not think of a more convenient location for a law firm.

Michael had a weird sensation in his stomach as he walked down the passage. Some of the doors of the smaller cells were open, allowing the passer by a glimpse of what was going on. Most of the lawyers were in their thirties and forties, each talking to his or her clients and staff members.

At the end of the passage, Mr. Kruger's name was clearly visible on the door.

Mr. Kruger welcomed Michael with a broad grin. They had not personally met for quite some time, though they consulted regularly over the phone. The veteran lawyer had the eyes of an eagle, with bushy brows covering the entire span over those sharp eyes. Before talking, it was his habit to gauge the state of his clients. He had never seen Michael's anxious expression. Like a professional businessman, Michael always met people with a confident smile. This time it was different. His eyes betrayed Michael's usual pleasant smile. Therefore, Mr. Kruger began the discussion with reassuring words.

Once Michael was a bit more relaxed in his seat before Mr. Kruger's huge desk, the old lawyer said, "The other day, Mr. Rosenbaum contacted me over the phone. He said, in a couple of days, they were going to appeal against the verdict, or go for a retrial. He wasn't clear which option his client had chosen. Whichever option they go for, I don't think we have reason to be much concerned. I don't know if they are going to bring in new evidence, or just add to what has already been presented to the court. In any case, they will find it very difficult to make their case credible for lack of witness other than you. So, in the end, whatever you say goes, provided you stick to your story."

Mr. Kruger's rather dark office worsened Michael's depressed mental state. The well-furnished chamber could easily pass as a library with thousands of books neatly stacked in the shelves, covering all the walls. Michael glanced at the library, then turned to Mr. Kruger, and said, "I'll stick to my story, don't worry about it."

"Are you sure, you haven't forgotten or missed anything?"

"Oh yeah, there's one tiny omission."

Mr. Kruger raised his brows, and Michael continued, "Before we separated from the team, I had told the tour guide that we wanted to be on our own."

"That's one hell of an omission Michael. Most probably they're going to bring it up."

"But the guide has already testified," said Michael.

"The court can just summon him to hear his side of the story one more time."

"Is it going to make a big difference?"

"I would like to think, it won't. It's up to the jury. Now they're saying the composition of the jury obstructed justice. Since, the victim was a female, according to them, at least half of the jury should have been females."

Mr. Kruger paused, allowing his client to grasp the situation, and then continued, "By the way, only a few days after Mary Anne's death, why did you go on a vacation?"

"I was depressed. I needed fresh air."

"With your young secretary!" Mr. Kruger muttered with his browses raised.

"I had to maintain constant communication with my staff members. Something big had been taking place."

"It didn't look good. You should've been more careful. Jurors are sometimes influenced by such things. After all, they're human beings. Anyway, I have a suggestion for you." Mr. Kruger paused to see his client's response.

"Go ahead, you're my lawyer," Michael said with a flat expression.

Mr. Kruger smiled, and said, "Of course, here it is. I think you should think of some sort of compromise."

"Compromise!" Michael was surprised.

"Yes, compromise."

"Didn't we get the verdict in our favor?"

"Yes, we did. Now don't put too much faith in it. The battle is not over yet. In my lifetime I've seen several verdicts overturned by the appellate court, and the attorney who has been representing the plaintiff in this case, has an impressive record at the appellate court. So, I would suggest that you make peace with the lady. The verdict of the lower court is in your favor. Hence, we'll be dealing with her from the position of strength. Make an offer she cannot refuse."

"What do I have to lose if the verdict is overturned?"

"I do not see any chance of a verdict proclaiming you guilty of homicide because there's no hard evidence for it. However, if the plaintiff can convince the presiding judge for having a few more females in the jury, I won't be surprised if the jury comes up with a verdict proclaiming you guilty of involuntary manslaughter."

"What's the sentence for such a verdict?"

"Twelve to sixteen months, and it might be increased to two years. In comparison, the sentence is very mild. However, what you should worry about is the impact it's going to have on your company. The image of the founding CEO sitting behind the bars, even for a day, doesn't go down well with the investors or the shareholders. If you have the shares of your company in the secondary market, it's going to nosedive at the news."

"Alright James, I'll give it to you. You know how to convince. Now tell me, how much I should offer as compensation."

"A couple of millions will do it. I know it's nothing for you, but it will make her think twice about what she really intends to do. I don't think she's going to opt for the Russian Roulette."

"How do you want me to make the payment?"

"Just write a check with a note at to the bank, as to why you're paying her, and then give it to me. I'll send it to her with an acceptance letter."

"In any way, it won't mean admission of a crime, will it?"

"No, it won't. I'll explain it to her in the acceptance letter why she's being paid. You'll be making the payment as a good will gesture. She must sign the acceptance letter before she can cash the check." ***

Lillian had been in her bed when she received the call. It was Mr. Rosenbaum. She was not going to make him wait. She raised herself and sat on her bed. He seemed to be in a pleasant mood as he exchanged greetings with her. He said, "I don't know how to place it before you Ms. Lillian. I cannot figure out if it's good news or bad news. It's up to you. So, I called you."

"What is it, Mr. Rosenbaum?"

"Your brother-in-law has made an offer to you for a settlement outside the court. Last night I got hold of the letter. I didn't want to wake you up. I thought you were exhausted. I think you should read it."

The hologram image of the letter appeared before Lillian when Mr. Rosenbaum had finished.

"It says he feels for my loss. It's utter non-sense. He had no feelings for his wife, why would he feel for my loss?" Lillian fumed with an angry tone.

"Ms. Lillian, please put aside your emotions for a moment. No matter what we do, we cannot bring your sister back to life, nor can we ensure a guilty verdict. The most we can get, that is if the jury feels there's a ground, is a verdict for involuntary manslaughter. Yes, I know, you have great faith in me. Nonetheless, at the end of the day, even the best lawyer is not a magician. I have my limitations too. I wish I could do more for you. Take your time, and just think about it. We have two weeks to respond."

With a heavy heart, Lillian hung up. Her steps were unsteady as she walked towards the window. The image of a bleak winter morning greeted her weary eyes. Ever since her mother's death, she had been struggling against the odds that always seemed stacked against her. She tried her best to save the ten-year long relationship with Tod. In the end, they decided to end it. She felt like he wanted to end it. He would not settle down with her, though she had raised the issue on several occasions. Her mother's death, and then Tod's departure from her life, threw her into a depression. Mary Anne and her son Bob were the only two people she could lean on. Subsequently, Mary Anne's untimely demise was like a death blow to her. Out of desperation, she expected Bob to reach out to her though she knew he and his girlfriend had been planning to get married. One of the most reliable shelters had been snatched away from her, at least that's how Lillian viewed her sister's tragic demise. She could not come to terms with the fact that her brother-in-law was next to her sister yet did nothing to prevent the tragedy.

The weather outside matched how she felt inside her that morning. She pulled the curtain and came back to her bed. It might be good idea to consult with Tod. In the past she always discussed with him when life had been hard on her. A voice in her said he didn't deserve to be so close to her, as she was about to make the call. He betrayed her trust, and therefore, he could no longer be viewed as a close confidante. Instead, she decided to call her nephew. ***

The red light on the big screen raised the brows of all who had been inside the ground control. From his office, adjacent to the ground control, Jeff rushed to the spot. By then the computer had issued the red alert which was being displayed on every single screen inside the ground control. Jeff stood on the raised platform before the large screen, and asked, "Alright Medusa, what's the problem mow?"

The cold flat lifeless voice of the twenty second century supercomputer said, "Our infrared telescope has picked up an approaching threat to the space station and the elevator platform in the lower orbit."

"What kind of threat are we talking about?" in a tense tone Jeff inquired.

"Cluster of asteroids!"

"How big is the cluster?"

"The cluster covers an area of roughly ten square miles with millions of broken fragments from a large comet which collided with Jupiter."

"What's the distance of it right now?"

"Forty million kilometers."

"What's the velocity of the cluster?"

"Thirty miles per second."

"Have you calculated its course?"

"It'll enter the area where the elevator platform is in the next ten days."

"What's the largest size of the cluster?"

"Fifty by sixty centimeters."

Jeff turned to the specialists who had been staring at him for directives, and said, "Tim, have in place the emergency evacuation plan, and issue a notice to all our staff members. We're going to have a meeting at exactly twelve hundred hours." ***

At the head office of the Space Race, Michael returned to his office after a two-week absence. The office staff received the big boss warmly. On behalf of the office staff, Stephanie congratulated Michael for what they achieved during the last couple of weeks. He was shown the stock price of the company which had skyrocketed at the news of the latest achievement.

Michael planned to talk to his chief investors about the financial picture of the company as it stood that very day. He had not finished the last sip of his coffee when he received the call from Jeff. Michael was an expert in the art of reading facial expressions. The moment Jeff's hologram image appeared over his desk, he could tell something was horribly wrong. Jeff said it could not wait. Michael had to be there at the ground control as soon as possible. ***

The disturbing images of the cluster scudding towards the earth rang the alarm bell everyone at the ground control. The cluster contained countless rocks the size of a soccer ball. They could easily obliterate the platform and the space station in their way. Michael just stared at the images, unable to quantify his feelings of utter horror and frustration. He didn't come this far only to see his dream turned to dust by some space rocks.

He muttered quietly, "This can't be. There must be a way out of it." Then he paused for a few moments, and asked, "Jeff, are you sure, they're heading our way?"

"I doubled checked the calculations. There's no error."

"So, what are the options before us?"

"We could bring the elenauts back home before the cluster arrives, or we could have the elenauts in the station and move it to a safe location. At this point, I'm not sure what we could do to protect the elevator platform."

"I'm curious Jeff. Just how destructive could this cluster be?"

"Just wait for a minute, I have something to show you." Having said so, jeff went to his office and returned with a photo. The photo contained an image of a three-inch-thick steel plate with a gaping hole in it. Upon displaying the image to Michael, he said. "A pea sized asteroid did this to the three-inch-thick steel plate. Now imagine what a cluster containing millions of soccer ball sized asteroids could do to our space station or the elevator platform."

Michael looked at the photo and sighed. Some of the specialists surrounded Michael and Jeff as they discussed what they could do to avoid the impending disaster. Among them, a thin faced, thirty-year-old hardware specialist said, "Sandbags!"

"What!" Jeff cried out.

Everyone focused on Morris, who said, "Have you not seen how a bunker is protected from projectiles in a battlefield? Sand is much more efficient in stopping projectiles without suffering any damage. While the steel plates crack or break, the sand in a sack simply absorbs the force of the projectiles, stopping them in the sack. We could have a wall of sandbags before the space station and the elevator. In zero gravity, it's not a big deal."

"The force of the impact will throw the wall at the station or the elevator platform," remarked Jeff.

"In that case, all we have to do is have a metal plate behind the sandbags, and then connect it to a shock absorber attached to the elevator platform. At first, the impact will squeeze the spring of the shock absorber, but eventually the force will be repelled."

"It's hell of an idea Jeff, I think we should give it a try," Michael exclaimed with a grin.

A loud cheer and whistles blew, flooding the ground control with tidal wave of jubilation. However, Jeff didn't look very optimistic. He said, "There's something else, Michael."

As the big boss looked at him, he added, "What are we going to do with the elevators? Will they remain up there, or down here, when the cluster arrives?"

"There's no point keeping them up there. At least one part of the investment will remain safe down here."

"And what are we to do with the space station?"

"Haven't we decided to move it out of the harm's way?"

"I don't know, you tell me. Nothing's final yet," Jeff responded.

"How far should we move it? Should we place it on the opposite side of the globe?" Bob suggested.

"That won't be necessary. It will only add more problems. Neither the elenauts nor the androids have been trained to navigate back to the previous location from so far away. I think fifteen hundred kilometers to the north will do it. Still, I think there should be a contingency plan in place for bringing back our men safely if the shaft is damaged in any way," Jeff stated.

"How many launch vehicles do we have operational right now?" Michael asked.

"As we speak only one is available for service," replied Jeff.

"How long will it take to fill it up with fuel?" Michael asked.

"Twenty-four hours, if everything goes as planned," Bob responded.

"Well then, have it ready for launch, a day before the arrival of the cluster. As a last resort, we'll launch it. If the shaft remains intact, you are to cancel the launch." Michael instructed Jeff.

"The capsule it carries can accommodate maximum eight of them, we have ten of them up there," responded Jeff.

"Send a pair of those specially made suits with the capsule for the McLaughlin couple. They'll have to take their chances with those suits," Michael shot back.

"What are your plans for the androids?" asked Jeff.

"I leave that to you. They're expandable." ***

In the meantime, when Bob had been preparing everything for the launch of the space vehicle, the call came in. It was from Aunt Lillian. At his office, while doing the paperwork for the launch with a clipboard in his hand, he gave the voice command to his office computer to receive the call.

"We're in some sort of emergency aunt Lily. Tell me over the phone what you have to say," said Bob when Lillian had asked if she could see him.

"Your phone, is it safe?"

"Yes, it is. I have my separate system. Apart from that I don't think anyone over here would want to keep a tab on my private life."

"Aren't you underestimating your dad, Bob?"

"Well, he's very busy with his latest project. I don't think he has the time for that kind of thing."

Lillian struggled to raise what she wanted to say. She felt awkward when she said, "I've received a letter from your father's lawyer_________," and then she stopped to listen to Bob's response.

"Go ahead, I'm listening," Bob insisted.

"Your dad offered me two million dollars as compensation."

"Compensation for what?"

"I guess it's a kind of consolation for the loss caused by your mother's death."

"Gee aunt Lily, every time someone dies, emotional shock is bound to follow. Would you have felt the same way, had my dad not been a rich man?"

"I didn't ask for money. I wanted justice for your mother. I guess your dad wants to say he's sorry. That's how rich people apologize when they do something wrong, don't they?"

"Aunt Lil, if what you claim is true, dad deserves punishment, but what if it was an accident? At the end of the day, he's my dad, and I don't want injustice done to him either."

"Bob, your mother didn't want to be there, so even if it was an accident, your dad was responsible for taking her there against her will."

"Perhaps he is. Now what do you want from me?"

"I just need to hear what you have to say. Should I go ahead with the case or accept the offer."

"It's your decision aunt, but let me tell you, if you drop the case, it'll save a lot of troubles for all of us. Having said so, I must also be clear to you that if you think it wasn't an accident, you should press on with the charges. Just like you, I want the truth to prevail. If the verdict disappoints you, at least you can say, you tried your best."

"If your dad had any remorse for what happened, he would not have flown to a remote island with his secretary, only a few days after your mother's disappearance."

"Yes, it was odd. When I asked him about it, he said he was very depressed. He needed the break to deal with the loss and focus on his project. Anyway, do what you think is right." ***

Deep in space, a long trail of irregular shaped rocks hurled towards the blue planet at an astonishing speed of over hundred thousand miles per hour. In the vastness of empty space, the fragments of the hurling cluster seemed stationary. The only movement visible to naked eye was their tumbling motion. The trail, thirty kilometers long and a few kilometers wide, appeared like a spear in the infra-red camera installed on a telescope. While passing the Jupiter, the giant planet's gravitational field acted like a sling shot, hurling the cluster at even greater speed. The cluster had been traversing two million miles a day. Ahead of it, the blue planet glimmered like a ping pong ball, still sixty-four million kilometers away. By then, every single telescope and sensor had picked up the approaching threat. Enthusiastic and concerned astronomers calculated its trajectory and subsequently, issued a warning to all. ***

At the head office of Space race, staff members worked frantically on a plan to launch the elevators for what was needed to build the shield over the other end of the shaft. Bob worked frantically to organize the Androids and the building materials for the launch. They were to be sent to in three working days. Vigorous debate continued about the possible size of the shield. The topmost platform was not even one tenth of the platform below it, for there was nothing but the gates to the decompression chambers of the two shafts. Some of the experts suggested that the shield should be large enough to provide some sort of protection to the platform immediately below it. Others pointed out the need to cover the entire structure, since the meteors were going to come down on whatever lay below them. Subsequently, the experts reached a consensus that the shield should be no larger than three square kilometers.

# Chapter Twelve

The first shipment of containers carrying the building materials reached the warehouse inside the compound built around the structure on time. Both elevators were going to be used for lifting the raw materials, along with five additional androids, specialized in construction work. ***

Trevor wanted to find out how it felt to work outside the space station. He asked Cindy to put him in the list of those who were going to do the construction work. Cindy sent four of the androids with Trevor. Their objective was to construct the frame of the assembly plant and the warehouse underneath the plant. By then the construction team erected altogether twelve living quarters including the ones constructed by Sam. The parts of the beams and the fabricated plates were in cases and bundles. The frame was to be constructed without rivets for they caused invisible cracks. Instead, they were going to be screwed and the major joints soldered. Once the frame had been formed, double layer of half inch thick bullet proof transparent aluminum composite glass would be used to seal the gaps from inside the station. Aluminum shutter which could be remotely pulled down or up would form the exterior of the glass pane. This would protect the inmates from solar radiation. Even if one layer of the windowpane is punctured or compromised, the second layer was there for protection. Dividing the newly constructed living quarters into chambers was the last part of the jigsaw puzzle. It was rather a simple task, given the absence of risk associated with working inside the station.

From the existing space station, Cindy watched the whole process while carefully monitoring the systems of the androids. Access to their systems from external sources were completely blocked. Only Mother had access to their systems, thus ensuring security from hacking. Even communication from the ground control, shifted to the base of the structure, or the training facility at Henderson, was cut off for the time being. With directives from Cindy, Mother was to fix any anomaly threatening the integrity of their systems.

The outer frame of three more quarters had been finished when Cindy looked at the time on the monitor. It displayed fourteen hundred hours. Mother computer's artificial voice alerted Cindy of an incoming call. The ground control, set up at the base of the structure was trying to reach the station. In another five minutes, the task of the fourth shift was going to be completed. She decided to wait till then.

Jeff looked anxious when the hologram image of his long dark face appeared. Trevor and the five androids were safely in the decompression chamber.

"What's the progress of your work up there?" Jeff inquired.

"Today, we plan to complete three additional quarters. According to the blueprint we have with us, we're expected to begin the work on the assembly plant and the warehouse underneath it. So far, we haven't faced any major problems. Now tell us, how things are down there."

"We haven't had problems down here either. The problem is somewhere else," Jeff informed Cindy with a stern expression.

Cindy told the androids to return to their quarters for charging their batteries. She didn't feel comfortable sharing the conversation with their humanoid associates. When the androids had left, Jeff continued, "We have received early warnings of an approaching cluster of asteroids. It's a cluster of tiny fragments from an asteroid which has been swallowed by Jupiter's gravitational field. The cluster is roughly forty kilometers long and half a kilometer wide. The course of the cluster will unfortunately bring it to the location where the other end of the elevator shaft and the space station are located."

"What's the present velocity of it?"

"The initial velocity was less than thirty-two thousand kilometers an hour, but the gravitational field of the giant planet acted on it like a sling shot, hurling it at us at more than two hundred thousand kilometers an hour. At this speed, it will arrive at the location where you guys are, in approximately ten days."

"Right now, where is it?"

"Roughly sixty-four million kilometers from earth."

The ten elenauts quietly stared at Jeff for a while, wondering what else Jeff had in store for them.

Jeff understood their position, and then added, "For you guys, we have two options before us. Either we can bring you down before the threat arrives or relocate you with the station. The big boss is reluctant to accept defeat at the hands of a bunch of rocks. He says, if we're to run with our tails between our hind legs at the first sign of danger like this, space travel is not for us. Now let's hear what you guys have to say."

Cindy looked at her team members, and one by one, all of them voted for the plan B. She seemed pleased by the outcome of the vote. Then she officially conveyed to Jeff what the team had decided.

"Well, since the big boss and you guys are in agreement, plan B is indeed the most viable course of action before us. Two days before the cluster arrives, we'll fire the thrusters from down here."

"You will fire the thrusters from down there!"

"Yes, the thrusters can be manually operated from up there, or remotely from down here. The big boss prefers to have some sort of control from down here. The manual control option is to remain turned off during the maneuver."

"What if the line of communication is hacked?" Trevor interrupted.

"Don't worry, we have taken care of it. Your new location will remain confidential for the time being. Of course, you'll have the new coordinates once the thrusters are fired. However, before we fire the thrusters, we must check their conditions. They haven't been in use since the station came into existence." ***

Eileen knew, swimming or wadding in the pool was prohibited. In the past, a number of hikers were swept away and killed. Nonetheless, the crystal-clear water at the rock laden section of the pool was too attractive to ignore the opportunity. The average temperature of the Emerald Pools was one hundred-fifty-four-degrees Fahrenheit. In winter, hikers and tourists flocked to the spot from all over the country for a hot refreshing dip in the geologically active pool. The pool's location at the base of the Yuba River was kept a secret to most people. Like Eileen Malone, a geologist in her late twenties, only a handful of people knew the existence of the pool. Those who knew, came from every corner of the country to enjoy the gift of this natural gem.

Eileen worked at CISN, California Integrated Seismic Network. Every Friday, she visited the pool from Carson City, a one-hour drive from the pool where the regional office of the institute was located. To her, the visit was like a bonus, allowing her to dive into what the unspoiled wilderness had to offer, while collecting samples of the pool water for geological tests. She carried the test kit with her whenever she decided for a visit to the location. Upon returning to her office, she had to prepare and submit a brief report on the geological activity in the area. This was just one aspect of the formidable task assigned to the institute. CISN regularly received radar reports from several airfields about the height of the ionosphere.  Apart from that, the institute had a QuakeSat Satellite with sensors that can detect ELF magnetic disturbances. Experts on animal behavior kept an eye on the farm animals and wildlife in the region. Data collected from all these sources assisted the institute to predict quakes.

A section of the pool had boulders on either side of it. Eileen picked the spot for sunbathing in unusually cold weather. She always craved the serenity of the spot. For more than two hours, she roamed the area, swam, and tried to get a sunbath. Half an hour before leaving the spot, she began collecting the samples for testing. She collected them from several locations, for a more accurate report. The level of minerals, such as potassium, sodium, calcium bicarbonates, seemed normal in most of the samples. However, one sample indicated comparatively higher levels of the minerals. The PH level was alarming as well. Eileen was confused because the sample contradicted the other samples. She called Jones, one of her colleagues at the institute, and discussed the issue. Jones said, at the beginning it was possible for the higher level of minerals to remain localized. He suggested to her to repeat the tests.

When the second set of tests had produced the same results, she rushed back to her office.

On the second floor of CISN's regional office, Rakesh Kumar, an electronics engineer from India was working on the handheld sensor for detecting minute anomaly in earth's magnetic field. The magnetic disturbances were precursor of an impending quake. Upon seeing Eileen, with a grin on his lips, he said, "The device is ready for action. However, I suggest moving to an isolated area, possibly over a hill or highland where signals from the transmission towers cannot cause distortions in the readings. ***

Mr. Bates watched through the bay window of his double storied cottage, the four employees of the CISN approaching the front door. Mrs. Bates was in the kitchen, preparing lunch for their grandchildren when the ding dong noise of the doorbell alerted her of the visitors. She howled at Fred, the six-year-old grandson to check who it was at the door. Yuba farm was listed as one of the farms collaborating with the CISN. Hence, Eileen, Jones, Rakesh, and Noah were all old acquaintances of the Bates family. Fred's countenance lit up when he saw Eileen holding a transparent glass bowl. Two third of the bowl was filled with water. Fred could see the goldfish swimming in it. Last time when Eileen had met the youngster, she promised to get him a small aquarium and a goldfish. Fred was one important source of information for the CISN staff. He was like a living record. Nothing in the farm went unnoticed by this little fella. He could provide detailed description of every incident taking place over a period of a month so accurately that on one occasion the CISN staff felt obliged to offer the little fellow a job at the CISN. For a few seconds, Fred's eyes glittered like gems, only to be dimmed by the thoughts which occurred on his young mind the next moment. He said he could not accept the job offer, but when he would grow up, he was going to contact them for the job. Everyone, including Fred's grandpa who had been around at the time, showed their support for the brilliant idea. This time, Mr. Bates, who was in his early seventies, was only too glad to accompany the visitors on a tour of his farm.

The Yuba River Farm covered an area of five hundred acres, of which two thirds were crop fields. All three from the CISN were appropriately dressed for the tour of the farm. Eileen wore faded jeans trousers with a pair of leather boots that reached almost her knees. Jones, Rakesh and Noah had work pants on them. They also wore gloves typically worn by farmers. Mr. Bates and his grandson wore blue overalls with rubber boots.

Fred led the group through the stubble. The stover of the harvested wheat fields protracted from the ground, staring them on the face like hostile claws. Then came the harvested potato field. They were heading for the gigantic barn on the other side of the fields. They could have used their vehicle. However, through the fields, the distance from the cottage to the barn was considerably less. Apart from that, Mr. Bates was in no mood to forego the opportunity for a healthy walk.

Halfway through the field, Mr. Bates raised the issue of animal behavior and its utility. He looked at Eileen and asked, "Are you sure Ms. Malone, these animals can sense an impending quake?"

Eileen tried to be as pleasant as possible. With a smiling face, she said, "Yes Mr. Bates, it's a reliable form of early warning. Farmers and quake watchers all around the globe are well aware of it."

"I mean how do they do it? I or my men never noticed anything unusual," Mr. Bates expressed his reservations.

"Perhaps you and your men were too busy to pay attention to anything unusual in their behavior. You're all so habituated to what you see and hear on daily basis."

"Yes, that's true," the old farmer admitted.

"We have data about bizarre animal behavior prior to every major quake. In Iceland, swans were observed staying away from lakes and pools. In India, dogs were seen howling and sniffing the ground, weeks before the devastating quake in 2030. In Mongolia, horses neighed day and night weeks before the quake in 2035, in Bangladesh, the tigers stopped roaming in the Sundarbans for several days before the quake in 2036 that destroyed eighty percent of the capital. The list is pretty long."

"There must be something only the animals can sense. Perhaps, you scientists are aware of it too," Mr. Bates added timidly.

"Man, are you putting the scientists and the animals in the same category?" Noah protested.

Mr. Bates refrained from addressing it. He just smiled.

Eileen needed some time to explain what it was the animals sensed. As she stopped, the whole group stopped on its track, and stared at her with inquisitive eyes. She said, "You see, the rocks that form the earth's crust begin cracking prior to a major quake. The cracking rocks send out positive charge in upward direction, caused by the friction. Somehow, the animals are programmed to respond to the flow of the positive charge."

"It's funny, you say the animals are programmed," Mr. Bates remarked.

"It's not that the animals can only sense the presence of the positive charge in the air, they can also correctly interpret it as a sign of impending danger. Hence, I see it as a program embedded in their brain cells."

The sky was cloudless. The temperature was slightly higher than what it was last year at this time. Winter snow had not yet covered the fields. The visitors were startled by the buzzing noise above their heads when they were roughly hundred meters from the barn. As they looked up, a monstrous bee passing over their heads caught their attention. Neither Mr. bates, nor his grandson displayed any signs of surprise. Very calmly, Mr. Bates explained, "It's one of our drones."

"Drones!" Noah exclaimed.

"Yeah drones. We use them to manage our herds," the old farmer explained.

"You have herds of cattle here!" it was Jones' turn to exclaim.

"A relatively small herd. One hundred cattle, and hundred and fifty sheep."

"Two hundred and fifty animals, and you call that a small herd!" said Eileen.

"In Texas, my elder son manages herds of his own, each herd having thousands of cattle. On the ground, the dogs manage them, and from the air, the drones direct them. As the world moves forward, so do the cowboys," with a smile, Mr. Bates finished his statement. ***

Through the transparent fiber glass roof of the space station, Cindy stared at the breathtaking view of the blue planet from her bunk, it appeared like the planet had been suspended over the glass ceiling of their private quarter. In reality, their private quarter was suspended upside down in space. It made Cindy think deeply about the nature of human existence. She muttered to herself, "*Appearance could be deceptive. Not everything is what it appears to be.*"

The elenauts were instructed to sleep or rest, every four hours. Trevor was still asleep. While planning for the next couple of hours, the eastern part of the Asian continent grabbed Cindy's attention. They were over Manchuria. It occurred to her that the station was supposed to be over the eastern part of the US. The station must have drifted away from the location where it was supposed to be, or perhaps they had deployed the thrusters for too long. Whatever the reason, it aroused in her, uncomfortable feelings. Were they going to face hurdles communicating with the ground control? They shouldn't. Cindy knew that the company has its ground stations scattered across the globe. Other satellites would relay their signals to the ground control.

Trevor was in the bunk, right below Cindy. He came out of his slumber as he felt Cindy gently jerking his shoulder.

"We're over Manchuria," Cindy said softly while pointing her finger at the blue planet.

A few moments passed before Trevor was fully awake. He stuck his head out of his bunk and looked at the view. He said, "Aren't we supposed to be over the eastern coast?"

"Yes, that's what I've been thinking. Do you think it might cause any problems?"

"No, I don't think so. We must use the thrusters carefully to return to the previous position." Trevor paused and then continued, "I'm just curious, what's the status of the approaching cluster?"

"I don't know, I woke up only a few minutes before you did. Four hours back, it was two days from us."

"I can't sleep well without natural________,"

The station's glaring red lights and the blaring sirens interrupted Trevor. He rushed to the door, stopping just before stepping out. Cindy told him to wear the special space suit which was in the cupboard next to the bunks. Trevor hesitated. He had doubts whether it was needed. Cindy had already slipped into the suit when she noticed Trevor standing with questions in his eyes.

She moved before him, held his arms, and said, "Honey, please don't make my job difficult. Am I not the captain over here? As the captain, I'm responsible for the safety of the station and every single member of this team."

Trevor smiled, and replied, "Yes of course."

In the next ten minutes, the whole team, along with its android members, congregated at the bridge. They were all anxious, though none displayed it. They were all trained how to remain calm during a crisis. Cindy snapped at the onboard computer, "Alright Mother, what's the problem?"

"My sensors have detected dangerous vibrations in the structure of the station," Mother's cold, lifeless voice stated.

"Is it a threat to the structural integrity of the station?" Trevor asked sternly.

"The possibility is real," Mother warned.

"What's causing the vibrations?" Cindy asked.

"Acoustically directed energy," Mother replied.

"Would you care to simplify your statement?" Cindy asked.

"It's sound wave," Trevor explained.

"How could sound wave possibly harm the structure?" Cindy was curious.

Trevor took a deep breath, and explained, "You can literally destroy any structure by using the sound waves. All you have to do is determine the resonant frequency of the object to be destroyed. Once you figure that out by using the formula $f=1/T$, where T refers to the period of motion and f is the frequency. When sound waves are produced having the same resonant frequency as the object, it creates vibrations in the object. As the sound becomes stronger, the vibrations increase, eventually shattering the object."

"Has this method ever been tested?" Cindy inquired.

"In 1940, a suspension bridge in the state of Washington was destroyed by gale force. Accidentally, as the resonant frequency of the bridge and the gale matched, it began swaying violently. In the end the bridge collapsed over the river. In case of glass, I don't know how it works, but I know glass can be shattered by sound waves."

Cindy looked confused. She asked the onboard computer, "Mother, would you explain how we're being threatened?"

Mother replied, "Every piece of glass has a natural frequency, the rate at which it will vibrate. If this resonant frequency is somehow disturbed by external stimulus, such as a sound wave, the glass will disintegrate. When the wave reaches 556 Hertz, it shatters the glass. Glass shattering waves carry more energy. They are shorter and choppier. Hence, more of them pass through the glass at the given frequency. How long it will take to cause cracks, depends on the thickness of the glass."

"What's the frequency of the acoustically directed energy we're facing?" Trevor asked Mother.

"It was 200 Hertz only a few seconds back. It has ceased, my sensors do not detect incoming energy at the moment."

"I think we should inform the ground control," remarked Anna who had been standing right behind Cindy.

"Mother, put us through. Let's find out what they have to say down there," Cindy commanded.

Instead of Jeff or Bob, a three-star general appeared in the hologram projection of the ground control. His grim and stern expression told everyone they were in for some serious conversations.

The general didn't wait to introduce himself to the team. Cindy stared at the name tag, it read, Normandy. Ribbons and medals covered his chest. He said, "Well gentlemen and ladies, as you can see, the military is here. I'm General Dave Normandy from the US army. From now on, we'll be closely monitoring the developments up there. We know why you have decided to communicate. We've been watching it too. Our spy satellite has picked up the directed energy. Right now, we're working on locating the source. Most probably they have detected our tracking signal, that's why they turned off the weapon."

"General Normandy, are you sure it's a weapon?" very politely, Cindy asked.

"They have been testing it for a while. They have not yet perfected it. We have reports that it can also be used to generate artificial quakes."

"Why would anyone want to strike the space station? It's a civilian facility, open to all," remarked Cindy.

"Behind the peaceful postures of various states, there's always a hidden agenda. This is the reality of the world we live in. I'm sure, those who hacked into the systems of one of your robots earlier, are not too happy with what your CEO intends to build. If it could be realized, we'll be miles ahead of them in space race. It's all about the resources of the solar system. Whoever will successfully colonize the planets and the moons of our solar system ahead of others will have the largest chunk of the reward."

At this point, the adjutant of the general joined the crowd down there and said something to the general. The general seemed pleased by the development. He turned his head and said to Cindy, "From the data obtained through earlier tracking, we have located the source of the directed energy. The source of it is in Manchuria."

The disclosure struck everyone like a bomb shell. Jaws dropped as everyone just stared at the general with their eyes wide open.

Trevor exclaimed, "Manchuria!"

"Yes, it is. I guess our communist friends are at it again," General Normandy remarked with a smile on his lips. ***

# Chapter Thirteen

The temperature outside was close to zero. This year the weather was comparatively warmer. Like the other mid-western cities, Cincinnati suffered a brutal summer the previous year. The average summer temperature had significantly risen due to climate change. Heat waves were now a regular phenomenon in the region. The Great Lakes could do little to off-set the changes in climatic conditions.

Lillian found the cool air outside Mr. Rosenbaum's chamber quite refreshing. This was another pain of getting into the office of an elderly person. After a while, the relatively hot atmosphere inside the office became uncomfortable with warm clothes on. The last few days, she had been struggling to make up her mind. The lure of a comfortable life versus the desire for justice wrecked her normal life. Finally, the latter prevailed. Mr. Rosenbaum had been in this profession for more than half a century. Naturally he understood his client's feelings. He buried his disappointment with a dry smile. He would have to draw on a lifetime of experience and resources to produce what was expected of him, that is, if it could be produced to begin with. He was not a man given to flowery promises. Prior to embarking on this difficult path, he made sure his client fully grasped the implication of her decision. The resolve in Lillian's eyes was enough to convince the veteran lawyer that she could not dissuaded her to drop the charges. He shrugged his shoulders and explained to her how he had planned to fight the case.

While in the chamber, though she had taken off her far coat, she felt uncomfortable. It was not clear to her if she felt this way for the heater was turned on high, or due to the nature of her decision. She didn't bother to adequately wrap her coat. She needed to cool down a bit before getting into her brand-new vehicle. In an open space, three blocks from her lawyer's office, she pressed the red button of her flying car's pager. The pager failed to vibrate. The vibration was supposed to confirm the signal had been received and accepted by the vehicle. She was exhausted. Hence, she appeared annoyed by the failure of the pager or her vehicle to acknowledge the signal. *"It must be some sort of device malfunction,"* she told herself. For a few moments she just stared at the pager device in her hand. On the display was the message, "access denied". It was the first time she faced such difficulty. She pressed the button again, and the same message appeared on the display of the pager. Throwing the pager in her handbag, she began plodding her way towards the parking lot. It was half a mile from where she was. ***

"Hurry up, she could be here any time now!" the stubble faced man in the heavy overcoat said to his partner whose legs had been sticking out from underneath the vehicle. Before getting into the act, the vehicle's security set up was deactivated, rendering it helpless against the intruders.

"Are you sure she's going to come here looking for her vehicle?" asked the man underneath the vehicle.

"Of course, she'll be here in no time. Do you think she's going to wait there for the angels to get her vehicle to her? Have some common sense, Brian."

"Alright Jack, I've placed the disc next to the left rear wheel. If anyone decides to have a peep, he or she won't see a thing. Now turn on the device."

A red light on the device indicated that it had been turned on. On his communication device, Jack had the app, allowing him to communicate with the device. Within a few seconds, the app alerted him that access to the vehicle's operating system had been secured. As soon as the message was displayed, Jack reconfigured the vehicle's operating system, making necessary changes in its control devices. The whole operation took less than two minutes. When the task had been completed, Jack touched the 'done' tab, and placed the device in his pocket. By then jack's partner was right next to him. They walked to their vehicle, parked roughly hundred meters from the spot. No sooner had the two men occupied their seats in the vehicle, Jack's communication device began vibrating. Apparently, he had been expecting the call, for he received the call, and said, "Done," before terminating the communication. ***

Standing only a few feet from her vehicle, once more Lillian tried to communicate with it with the pager. This time she was relieved to see the vehicle respond. She thought something had blocked the signal earlier. The door of the vehicle automatically opened the moment its sensor picked up the presence of the owner. The interior was comfortably heated, albeit Lillian couldn't recall turning on the heater. Sadness mingled with anticipation dominated her mood. The vehicle's entertainment system asked her if she would like to listen to any particular music or song.

"Buried in Your Past," Lillian replied. From the data retrieved from its memory, the entertainment system commenced playing the title, as the vehicle lifted itself from the parking lot like a chopper. Lillian kept monitoring the gadgets like the first officer of a passenger liner, while the vehicle flew itself to the designated altitude. The traffic control directed the vehicle's onboard computer to maintain the cruising altitude of two thousand feet. As soon as the vehicle reached the given altitude, it headed for the suburb of Cincinnati at three hundred and fifty kilometers an hour. On the opposite track of the holoway, five hundred meters from the vehicle's assigned track, Lillian watched the incoming vehicles rushing by. Her senses freaked out when she noticed a vehicle from the opposite direction deviating from its track and heading straight for her vehicle. Apparently, having lost control, it rolled over in the air, approaching Lillian's vehicle at six hundred kilometers an hour.

"Evade collision!" cried out Lillian, but the vehicle's system failed to respond. It all happened in a blink of an eye. ***

The barn had a stable, a shed, a pigsty, a coop and a kennel. It was so huge that it could easily accommodate hundreds of extra animals and their feeds. The loft was used to store grains and tools. Most of the animals were out for grazing. Eileen interviewed the caretaker. She focused on the diet and the movement of the animals. Nothing substantial came out of the casual discussion. However, the caretaker reported an infestation of mice and ants. Despite having several cats, the invasion of the rodents could not be prevented. The infestation was particularly strong in the loft where the grain was stored. Noah asked for a ladder, and as he climbed up to the roof of the barn, he discovered an army of ants taking refuge in the cracks and the surface of the boards forming the ceiling.

"Definitely, something strange has been happening over here," Noah muttered upon observing the infestation.

"What is it, Noah?" Eileen yelled from down below.

"Ants everywhere!" Noah yelled back.

"Ants and the rodents are the first ones to sense an impending quake," Eileen remarked.

"Mr. Bates, don't you have insecticides?" Jones asked the old farmer.

"We do. Usually, they're very effective. However, we must be careful how we use it. This time around, it could not prevent the army. The swarm simply kept coming out of nowhere," Mr. Bates conveyed in a dismal voice.

The team scoured the entire farm, looking for signs of unusual behavior among the animals. None displayed any kind of erratic movements. To have a thorough inspection, Eileen suggested that they stayed for another day for observation. If something ominous had been happening in the crust down below, sooner or later, the animals were bound to respond to the geological activities.

The following day, no noticeable change was observed. The team returned to its office in an apprehensive state despite the absence of any visible signs of a quake. As soon as Eileen had settled down to prepare a report, Jones and Noah rushed into her room, turning on the hologram projection of the local news channel. One of the channels was airing the developments at the site of the space elevators and the space station when Jones turned on the holovision in his office.

"Space rides have become a walk in the park nowadays. To this experience, a new mode of transportation has been added, making it a piece of cake to anyone having the desire to visit the space. Yes, Space Race, a company owned by billionaire Michael Stewart has built an elevator that can lift us to the lower orbit. According to the company, the conventional launch vehicles are about to become things of the past. Even a sick person can travel to space by using the elevators," the anchor woman declared.

"What's more significant is that those elevators will drastically cut the cost of sending men and material up there. For the first time, space travel has become an economically viable option before us," Jones remarked with an excited tone.

"How far is the shaft from here?" Eileen inquired.

"I'm not sure, perhaps two hundred miles. Why do you ask?" Noah wanted to know.

"Not too far away from this spot or the San Andrea's Fault Line, is it?" Eileen responded.

A few seconds of silence prevailed as they stared at each other's countenance. Jones broke the silence, and asked Eileen, "Is it possible for a quake to bring it down?"

"It depends, the magnitude of the quake, the flexibility and tolerance level of the structure. I hope it's quake resistant," Eileen replied.

"I've heard the base of the structure stands on two sets of wheeled tracks. In case of a quake, the whole structure can move a few feet in each direction," Jones said.

"Yes, it's true. We have to wait and see if it lives up to its builders' expectations," Eileen remarked.

"Let's pay attention to what we've been doing, guys. What do you plan to have in your report," Noah asked Eileen.

"Whatever we have observed, so far."

"And what does that mean?" asked Jones.

"It means there's no concrete sign of an impending quake. The level of the chemicals in the ground water is slightly higher. This could happen for various reasons. As for the infestation of mice and ants in the Yuba Farm, it could be the result of the flooding from the adjacent river as well. The other farm animals have not yet displayed any unusual behavior. Therefore, I don't see any reason to send out the red alert, at least, not till we see the telltale signs in the atmosphere," Eileen explained. ***

Everyone at the ground control heard Mother's stark warning, "The directed energy has returned! It's much stronger this time around. This section needs to be evacuated immediately. The panes might crack at any moment."

Elenauts who had congregated at the bridge, rushed towards the section adjacent to the bridge. A heavy metal sliding door separated the bridge from the chamber. ***

At the ground control, tension soared with the warning from Mother. General Normandy didn't waste time in conveying the news of the threat to the top brass at the Pentagon. He had been waiting for the clearance to act decisively while the staffs at the ground control looked at him for directives. Often, the rogue states under the cloak of diplomatic deniability, initiated this kind of aggression. Hence, the political leadership in Washington decided to keep mum until the perpetrators raised the issue. In the meantime, clearance was given to the military high command to do whatever was necessary to neutralize the source of the threat. Upon receiving the orders from the Pentagon, the stern faced general placed every single individual present at the ground control, under an oath of silence. None were to disclose the incident to the outside world without prior authorization.

A blinding flash lit the space below the US military installation up in the orbit, not once, not twice, but thrice, as the general conveyed the orders to strike. The next moment, the tracking device alerted the installation of a threat from another source. This time it was a weapon like what had been used to silence the acoustically directed energy. Within a second, the mission control deployed the set of mirrors outside the space station to deflect the laser. ***

Down at the Manchurian Space Weapons Center, upon receiving report from the site of the targeting facility that the acoustic energy weapon had been destroyed, frantically, Colonel King Pin directed his men to fire concentrated laser beam at the space station. The Colonel shouted at his men, "Aim at the other end of the station! We have the blueprint of the station. They don't have the protective deflectors for the whole station."

The officer sitting before the panel, calmly repositioned the nozzle of the weapon with the help of the targeting software and pressed the button again. It appeared as if a streak of lightning pierced through the sky above the center and disappearing into the space.

The laser fired from the Manchurian Space Weapon Center struck the living quarters of the androids at the other end of the station. As the transparent fiber glass enveloping the quarter shattered into millions of pieces, in a blink of an eye, the air blowing out carried the residing androids with it, out into the dark space. ***

"Fire at the source of the laser!" general Normandy snapped.

The general had not even finished his command when the laser from the orbital military installation flashed again, vaporizing instantly what was only a few seconds ago, the pride of the Manchurian technology. ***

At the UN, the diplomatic scuffle following the incident revealed that the despots of Manchuria considered the space above Manchuria as an extension of their sovereign territory. Hence, they deemed it their legitimate right to shoot at any foreign entity found in the designated space. The stern warning to the Manchurian government, at first did not produce the desired effect. However, the moment the US air force had a lock on the Manchurian satellites and space station over the US, the communists reluctantly relented from farther escalation. Thus, the two mighty powers avoided a full-blown military confrontation.

In no time, the repair work began at the space station. The US State Department was able to secure a promise that whatever the cost of rebuilding the damaged part of the space station, the communists would pay for it. ***

The first task was to retrieve the androids blown away from the space station. Altogether, five of them were lost. Since there was nothing acting against the force which blew them away, they were on a never-ending journey to nowhere. Any kind of delay would only increase the distance between the space station and the androids rushing away at an ever-greater speed towards the deep space. Therefore, it was imperative that the mission to retrieve the androids commenced as soon as possible. The batteries of those androids would last seven days if they were not charged. In other words, the SOS signals emanating from their location device would be lost after seven days.

Equipped with the state-of-the-art laser guided navigation system, the thruster packs for themselves and the lost androids, Trevor and two androids set out from the space station at fourteen hundred hours GMT. They were tethered together by an invisible lock on beam in case they scattered too far away from each other and were lost in space. Once the device was activated, it would pull the receiver installed in the space suits of the rescue team, back to the space station. The tracking device was able to locate only three of the lost androids. Trevor speculated that the other two were blown away in the direction of the blue planet. Therefore, they could well be written off as collateral damage. The signal coming from the three androids was getting weaker as the distance grew, at every passing second.

With two androids on either side him, Trevor hurled himself towards the robot closest to their location. By then the robot had drifted more than two hundred kilometers. It would take at least half an hour to reach it. The buzzing noise of the thruster pack ceased the moment the power to it was cut, to save fuel. Their velocity was double compared to the velocity of their chase. So, there was no need for extra thrust.

In the utter blackness of space, the only sign of their forward motion was the data displayed by their tracker device. Otherwise, it appeared as if they were suspended in space. From the space station, Cindy also confirmed their progress.

To prevent Trevor from falling asleep, Cindy initiated a conversation. She said, "Honey, it must be awfully boring out there."

"Yeah, nothing but blackness of the space. It's kind of eerie," Trevor responded.

"That's the most frightening part of space travel. The vastness of the endless, empty space. It's too easy to get lost forever."

"It's the absence of light which renders it so frighteningly dark. Perhaps if we didn't have this absence, we wouldn't appreciate the value of light."

"It's not totally devoid of light. Stars radiate good amount of light though."

"It's nothing compared to the vastness of the empty space."

"Actually, the space is not empty. There's a thing called dark matter. Many physicists believe, the fabric of space is made up of it."

"It's still just a hypothesis. The existence of the dark matter is yet to be proven. Anyway, what's on your radar scope right now?"

"You're still fifteen minutes from the nearest robot. It's taking time because the robots are also moving in the same direction. So, when calculating how fast you're approaching, you must deduct the velocity of your chase. I'm sorry honey, I know how it is over there in the cold dark __________,"

Cindy stopped short of completing what she was going to say. She stared at the radar scope for a few seconds. Something on the scope had caught her attention. She wasn't sure how to define it. And then the unwelcome alert came from Mother. The computer warned, "Tiny meteors approaching Trevor and the android."

"Trevor, get out of the track. Mother has detected meteors heading your way!" Cindy exclaimed.

"From where?" Trevor shot back.

"Most probably it's part of the larger cluster."

"Don't we have forty-eight hours before the big one arrives?"

"We do, perhaps these tiny ones were the first to break off from the big one. It's not very important right now where they are from. Just get out of their way."

"What will happen to the mission? If we change our direction, we may not have enough fuel to return safely to the station."

Something slammed onto Trevor's visor when he had finished. It was the limb of one of his android companions. The robot exploded like a bomb, throwing its body parts in all directions. Apparently, it was struck by a tiny piece of meteor at nearly hundred thousand miles per hour. For a few moments, Trevor stared at the limb dangling from his helmet. He was dazed by the suddenness of the impact. Cindy kept screaming, "Hit the thruster, Trevor, hit the thruster!"

The G-force produced by the full thrust of the thruster pack forced air out of Trevor's lungs as he hit the red button on his chest. For about a minute the thruster burnt its fuel at the peak rate.

"Are we out of the harm's way?" Trevor asked when he began to breathe normally.

"In ten seconds shut it down."

Trevor whistled as he exclaimed, "That was a close call!"

"It was," Cindy confirmed.

Trevor checked the fuel of the thruster, and said, "I think we can still salvage the mission."

"No dear, I don't think it's a good idea. Return to the station. The mission has been aborted."

"We're talking about a billion dollar for each of those androids, Cindy. Are you sure you want to scuttle the mission?"

"Yes Trevor, you never know what that cluster has in store for us. From the very beginning, I've had this nasty feeling about it. I cannot even imagine how I'm going to handle it if something happens to you. At this moment, loss recovery is the last thing on my mind. Let the CEO deal with it. He can always sue those who started this whole business."

"Alright, we're heading back to the station." ***

# Chapter Fourteen

The debris of the two vehicles lay on the ground, covering a wide swath of land under the holoway. Both vehicles exploded into fireballs as they crashed onto the ground from an altitude of two thousand feet. The fire department used a drone to extinguish the flame. Androids working for the police department secured the area soon after the fire had been put out. Then came the investigators in their long heavy overcoats.

Visibility was poor due to heavy fog. Nonetheless, the two investigators thoroughly scoured the area for evidence. One of them recorded the spot with the help of a device regularly used by the investigators. The images, along with the audio files, were going to be submitted to a team of forensic experts, responsible for preparing the final report.

The investigators found Lillian's charred corpse strapped in the seat. The driver of the other vehicle was missing. The two stern looking detectives recovered the black boxes of the vehicles, and carefully stored them in a metal box with the other pieces of evidence. They were in good shape, thus raising hope for a better understanding of what really caused the accident. They smiled at each other after checking the condition of the black boxes. In the past, these black boxes had to be sent to their manufacturers for retrieving the data. Since the last two years, the Cincinnati Police Department possessed the lab equipped with the necessary tools and experts who could retrieve and analyze the data. This considerably reduced the time for a report. The black boxes contained not only the data generated by the sensors of the vehicles, the images prior to the collision, outside and inside the vehicles, were also stored in them. The sun was about to go down when the two investigators completed their initial investigation. From the crash site, their vehicle flew to the nearby holoway relay stations for collecting the captured images and relevant data about the traffic at the time of the accident. This would provide vital clues as to why the collision occurred. ***

The final phase of the construction work at the topmost platform of the shaft had just been completed when the news of Lillian's dismal demise reached Bob. He found his dad starring at him with signs of utter disbelief when he had burst into his office room. Had it been someone else, the intruder would have been thrown out the second he had entered. At the huge compound housing the ground control, a thirty by forty rectangular chamber was allocated for the CEO. Michael had been in contact with the mission control and the space station when his son interrupted him. He needed a serene atmosphere to focus on the crisis unfolding up there in the orbit. The fact that in future he planned to relinquish control of his high-tech empire to his son always made him guard his anger when he was with Bob. In seconds, his businesslike attitude returned. With a smile on his lips, he asked, "What's the problem now, son?"

"Dad, have you heard about Aunt Lillian?"

"No, I haven't. Why, has anything happened to her?"

"Turn on the news," Bob suggested.

The scene at the crash site was being aired on one of the news channels when Michael turned on the holovision. The twisted wreckage of the two vehicles, Lillian's charred body, and the recordings of the relay stations, prior to the collision, were being repeatedly aired. Lillian's photo and her background, revealed to the world her connections with Michael's family. What really jolted both father and son was the brief statement from Lillian's lawyer. He said, it could be a premeditated murder for his client recently decided to pursue the murder charges against the CEO of the Space Race.

Michael's frustrations were palpable for the way he left his seat and began sauntering in the room. His right hand was in his pant pocket while tightly holding his chin with his left hand.

"You don't have anything to do with it, do you?" Bob asked.

"Hell no!" Michael exclaimed, and then added, "Who do you think I am, a monster?"

"I'm not sure dad. I'm afraid, a lot of folks will see your hands behind this accident."

"I'm not interested in what other folks might think or say. I'm worried about you. Do you think I'm the way that lawyer has been trying to portray me?"

"Dad, at the end of the day, it doesn't matter what we say. Our actions always speak louder. I don't understand why you took mom to that God forsaken place. It's not that mom was very fond of watching volcanoes erupting. And then we find you and your mistress like secretary on an island owned by an individual notorious for trafficking women and children. It doesn't end there. Aunt Lilly brings charges against you, and then you offer her two million dollars, but she refuses to drop the charges. Now she dies in an accident which looks more like an orchestrated collision. Dad, I'm sorry to tell you, all these facts don't stack up well for you."

It seemed like Michael wanted to say something. He closed his eyes, organized what he was going to say, and said, "Yes, it's true, your mother had no interest in volcanoes. However, did you know that she had been keenly interested in the earth's magnetic field, how it affected us? Once I explained to her how the convection of the earth's molten core generated the planet's magnetic field. Later it occurred to me that it was possible to see with naked eyes a glimpse of it. Of course, the actual core is way down several thick layers of the crust. I just wanted to show it to her. As for having a vacation, I had to deal with the grief of losing your mother, and at the same time I needed to be in touch with the company's activities. I don't expect you to understand it. Once you reach my age, you'll know what drove me to it. Regarding your aunt Lilly, trust me son, I had nothing to do with it." A pause followed this and then he asked, "By the way, how did you find out about my offer to your aunt?"

"She spoke to me about it before conveying it to her lawyer."

"Honestly, I had no idea about her refusal."

"Why did you offer her the money?"

"You mother loved her. I wanted her to get over it and have a decent life."

"You never displayed such affection for Aunt Lilly when mom was alive," Bob grumbled with veiled contempt.

"Who knows how your mother would have taken it. You know how women are when it comes to dealing with their men's relation with other women."

At this point, a projected hologram message appeared before the father and son. Someone from an unknown number had been trying to reach Michael. Bob shrugged his shoulders as Michael looked at him.

"Let it through," Michael instructed his personal computer.

"Hi, I'm Mr. Craig Rosenbaum, Ms. Lillian's attorney," a thick harsh voice declared.

"I have nothing to say to you Mr. Rosenbaum. In time, you'll hear from my attorney," Michael responded.

"Oh yeah, your attorney has a lot of explaining to do. Just a piece of advice before you hang up. Please ask your attorney to be quick for I'm about to bring another homicide charge against you if your attorney fails to convince me that you had nothing to do with Ms. Lillian's death."

"I've had enough of this," Michael snapped at his computer. Immediately, the line was disconnected. ***

"Listen guys, hold tight. We're going to move the station to its intended location. In the next thirty seconds, we're going to fire the thrusters," Jeff's tense voice alerted the crew. The artificial gravity ceased when the spin had been turned off. Without a word, the elenauts strapped themselves to their seats. An hour ago, Trevor returned to the station. Cindy flew into his arms the moment the door of the decompression chamber had closed behind him. ***

In the meantime, from the cluster of asteroids, the blue planet was clearly visible like a shinning disc. In their track, the rocks kept turning, sometimes minutely deviating from the course of the cluster. Hence, closer the cluster was from the blue planet, the larger its size was due to the deviation of the rocks. A man-made probe zoomed past it, taking snapshots of it, a thousand kilometers from it. The Turkish probe deployed its thrusters to alter the course of the probe. It made a half circle before adjusting the velocity to match the velocity of the cluster. The faint blinking light of the probe glowed on the surface of it, painted with light reflecting substance. In the darkness of the surrounding space the probe displayed, "Turkish Star" written in bold Turkish letters. A constant stream of data was being transmitted to the satellites and then to the ground station, situated on top of the Anatolian Mountain range. The data were being shared with the other international platforms. Hence, the specialists at the Space Race ground control could see the approaching cluster on its way to strike the blue planet. At the given speed, the specialists calculated the time of impact. It would strike in the next twenty-four hours. Despite being aware of the spot where it was going to strike, and the possible effects, apprehension still reigned among the experts across the globe. According to the data shared by the observers, the average size of the asteroids in the cluster was no more than pebbles. However, the images transmitted from the Turkish probe revealed a slightly different picture of the cluster. Numerous asteroids were as large as soccer balls. These soccer ball sized asteroids would not burn out while falling through the atmosphere. Each asteroid would strike the surface of the planet with the force of a five hundred kg bomb, devastating whatever would end up at the receiving end. This possibility heightened the fear among those who had been following the drama unfold.

The new location of the space station was eight hundred kilometers from the spot where the asteroids were expected make contact with the exosphere. Mission control advised Cindy and her team to have their cameras, sensors and telescopes ready for the event. Later the images and data were going to be used for research and development purpose. How many soccer ball sized asteroids the shield built over the platform would be able to withstand, that was the big question. Experts feared, it might cave in if several of them struck the shield simultaneously.

Fortunately, nothing like that happened, at least, not at the beginning of the show. The resistance displayed by the shield pleased all who had been anxiously watching. Most of the asteroids streaked down, kilometers away from the elevator platform. Eight of them struck the shield at more than hundred thousand miles per hour, at intervals of two to three minutes. The shield recoiled, while the whole structure shuddered as the asteroids the size of softballs slammed onto the shield beefed up by the sandbags and metal plates. The sandbags taking the hits, burst into sand dust. When it seemed that the worst was over, an asteroid the size of a small car, smashed onto the remaining layers of sandbags. The force of the impact squeezed the spring mechanism almost hundred feet before disintegrating the whole plate. The loud bang of the impact could be heard from the ground underneath the platform. The asteroid totally destroyed the shield. Fortunately, it was the last piece of the incoming projectiles. The rest of the rocks landed on a fifty square kilometers area of the Mojave Desert, instantly burying themselves in the desert sand.

An eerie silence prevailed at the ground control and space station for a few seconds the moment the shield was obliterated. It was indeed the last piece. When this fact had permeated into the consciousness, the two crowds, one on the surface of the planet, and the other one up there in the orbit, burst out into cheers, hugging and congratulating whoever was around.

"Mike, the threat to the shaft has passed!" Jeff exclaimed as his long black face appeared before Michael's desk.

Michael stayed away from the ground control at the critical hour. It was quite unexpected, considering his enthusiasm for the project. Before he buried himself in his office room, he had delegated full authority to Jeff to do whatever needed to be done. Bob was there to watch over Jeff's shoulders. It was Bob's responsibility to keep the CEO informed about Jeff's activity. Albeit Jeff retained full control of the operations, he was to consult with Bob before taking any major decision. Hence, Bob was more like Jeff's technical advisor.

Instead of displaying his satisfaction, Michael's expression hardened. He had been thinking about the implication of Lillian's death when Jeff's call distracted him.

In a flat tone, he responded, "Great news. Has there been any damages?"

"The shaft remains untouched. However, the shield has been totally destroyed by the last piece of the cluster. It was big. I mean the size of a car. We didn't foresee an asteroid of that size in the cluster."

"That's the most important aspect of your responsibility as the head of the project. Jeff, you must foresee situations before they hit us on the face like a sledgehammer."

"I know Mike. I don't know why our sensors didn't pick it up. Perhaps the density of the cluster had something to do with it."

What about the images from the Turkish probe, didn't you analyze them?"

"The initial report didn't mention any significantly large object in the cluster. Prior to the impact, the ground station in Turkey stopped transmitting the data. They said the probe had broken off from the cluster and was on its original course."

"Anyway, what are your plans now?"

"Well, we have to make an assessment of the damage. Aren't we going to claim compensation for the damage to our space station?"

"Of course, soon we'll hear about it from the state department. I hear that the Pentagon has already briefed our defense secretary about it. Let's see what happens."

"We have to prepare two damage reports, one for the space station and another for the shield," Jeff pointed out.

"No, prepare one damage report for the incidents."

"I don't understand. How do you plan to claim compensation for the damage done to the space station if we don't submit a separate report for it?"

"We'll put the tab on the commies for the shield as well. They've lost the battle, and as the proverb says, the victor writes the history."

"If there's investigation ______________,"

"Who'll challenge, the fragmented Russian and Manchurian states? If the Manchurian bastards had not tested their weapons on our assets, who knows, perhaps we could have successfully detected and blown out of its course the large meteor. Therefore, those Manchurian fascists have to pay for all the damages, including the damages done by the meteor."

Jeff smiled at Michael, and said, "Oki doki boss. Whatever you say. In the meantime, I'll instruct our elenauts and the androids to start re-building the damaged section."

Tell our engineers to build shields for the topmost platform and the space station as well."

The latter part of Michael's statement seemed like a surprising development to Jeff. He pointed out, "The shield over the shaft was connected to the platform. Where do you plan to connect the shield over the space station? Connecting it to the station would be pointless."

"Let our experts work on it, I'm sure they'll find a solution to this puzzle. I have to go now, Jeff. I hope to hear more good news from you. There's something else. In my absence, Bob will function as the acting CEO. It has been approved by the board of directors. Check your mail. A copy of the directive has been mailed to you."

Jeff cleared his throat, and asked, "Are you planning on going on a prolonged vacation?"

Michael just smiled at Jeff.

After he was done talking, Michael gestured to his office computer to disconnect the line. Outside his office, Michael's security protocol had been waiting. They were told to escort the CEO to his rockerjet. Quietly, Michael slipped out of his office down a secret passage. ***

Captain Floyd was at the entrance of the craft, waiting for the CEO. Courteously, he greeted Michael before his crew escorted the CEO to his private cabin. Earlier the captain had been informed of the latest destination. In the next ten minutes, the state-of-the-art rockerjet lifted itself from the tarmac, adjacent to the humongous compound. At an altitude of three hundred meters, once the rocker jet had gained the necessary momentum produced by the forward thrust of its jet engines, captain Floyd turned off the VITOL mode of the craft. Through the large window, Michael stared at his life's dream as the craft cruised through the clear October sky. It would take approximately forty minutes to reach the Los Angeles suburb. From there, a limo would carry Michael to his attorney's office at downtown Los Angeles. ***

"Oh God, I have been waiting for you!" Mr. Kruger exclaimed as Michael entered his chamber.

"I could guess," responded Michael while taking his seat before the lawyer's desk.

"The preliminary report is in. I have managed a copy of it from the district attorney's office. The police department has been saying they have found evidence of tampering in Lillian's vehicle. I hear, the system of the vehicle was hacked by a device called magnetic suspension anomaly or MASA in short. At the final moment prior to the collision, vehicle's active protection system ignored Lillian's voice command. Apart from that, the other vehicle was being remotely driven. It had no reason to have lost control as it did. In other words, we're looking at a clear-cut homicide case."

"It's hell of a time for her to die," Michael remarked with signs of indignation.

"She didn't just die Michael, she was murdered, and I'm afraid, the fingers are pointing at you. I'm sorry to say it, but that's how it is right now."

"James, I have nothing to do with it!" exclaimed Michael.

For a moment, the veteran lawyer stared right into his client's eyes. He tried to read what Michael had in him. His intuitions told him, his client wasn't lying.

Then he sighed, and said, "I believe you Michael, but circumstances have been conspiring against you. Before your arrival, I had a call from Lillian's attorney. He sounded pissed. He says, he's going to see to it that you're put behind the bars for the rest of your life."

"He called me too. I didn't talk. How does he know that I did it?"

"You're saying, you have nothing to do with it. The question is, then who's behind it? You must have someone or some people who would like to see you behind the bars. Now give me a good reason why anyone would want to see you in jail."

It took Michael a couple of seconds to organize what he was going to say. Then he said, "From the very beginning, the Manchurian commies have been against my pet project."

"Do you mean the space elevators?"

"Yes."

"Why do you think, they're against this project?"

"There's a race for grabbing the resources of the solar system. If my project succeeds, they can say goodbye to most of it, because in no time we can send thousands of men and robots up there. Within a year, we could build an entire city in the lower orbit, or even deep space, and from there our drive to colonize the other planets and their moons will commence. Only a few days back, one of our androids in the space station was hacked. We have every reason to believe it was them who did it. The other day, they fired their acoustic and laser weapons at our space station. That was the latest incident. For your use, I'll request a transcript of the incident from the Pentagon."

"You do that. In the meantime, I'll try to get more information about the prosecutions plan. It's going to be tricky, trying to convince the jury of foreign involvement in this murder, but I guess, that's the only option we have before us."

"I'm sorry James, I should have been more careful. I shouldn't have been to that island with Stephanie. I know, it made your job very difficult."

"What's done is done. There's no point crying over spilt milk. From now on, until the case is taken care of, please consult with me before talking about it, or going on a vacation. And don't say anything to Rosenbaum. If he calls, just hang up or forward it to me."

The uncomfortable feeling in the chest had mostly disappeared when Michael came out of Mr. Kruger's chamber. He was unable to focus on his project the moment he heard about Lillian's demise. Now he was going to press on with his project with renewed vigor. This project could not be allowed to slump. Soon he would have to show tangible returns to his investors. Michael glanced at the red sky and sighed. The chill in the air felt like a bout of fresh air as he raised the collar of his overcoat around his neck. His security chief opened the door of the limo when Michael asked him to stay with the vehicle. In small and steady strides, he walked down the Main Street, towards the Huntington Beach. After so many years, he had this craving to enjoy the beautiful sunset. ***

# Chapter Fifteen

"Get those hands to work on the shield. In the meantime, I'll supervise the repair work of the station," Cindy snapped at Trevor, as the androids appeared at the gate of the decompression chamber. The elevator brought ten extra androids along with building materials for the shield and repair work. The elevator did not have space for all building materials. One third of it were carried by the elevator. The rest was to arrive in the second elevator, in the next few hours. The station had only one warehouse. So, as soon as the materials from the first elevator had been unloaded, the crew would focus on unloading the second shipment.

One by one, Cindy checked the operational mode of the androids. She made sure the security protocol had been turned off before allowing them beyond the gate and delegating tasks. She directed five of them to assist Trevor and took the other five to the bridge of the station.

Upon entering the bridge, with a sense of urgency in her tone, she said to the central computer, "Mother, we need to realign the position of the station. The ramp has to be attached to the second elevator gate."

"We could use any two of the thrusters. Which ones do you want me to use?" Mother inquired.

"Use number one and the one we installed after arriving at the station. This will be a good opportunity to test its performance. It has not been used since we installed it. How much fuel do we have for the thrusters?"

"Two hours of fuel for the three thrusters."

"So, it means forty minutes for each, right?"

"Yes, forty minutes of uninterrupted thrust," Mother confirmed.

"Alright Mother, let's find out what those thrusters can do for us."

"I have initialized the thrusters. In the next thirty seconds, it's going to be activated," the cold feminine voice of Mother conveyed to Cindy.

"Sound the alert to the crew," Cindy's commanded Mother.

"Please secure yourselves. Thruster number one and three are going to be deployed in the next twenty seconds," Mother alerted the crew.

Trevor appeared at the door of the bridge, a few seconds before the thrusters were ignited. Already, the artificial gravity had been turned off. Trevor had to fly to his seat next to Cindy. Anna and Mark were also at the bridge, strapped to their seats. The rest of the crew went to their quarters for securing themselves.

The thrusters were installed on rings around the axis of the space station. This enabled their positions to be calibrated, providing thrusts to all possible directions. Short bursts of the thrusters hurled the station over the platform like a gymnast executing summersault in the air. Through the transparent roof of the station, the crew stared at the platform over their heads, from their respective workstations and quarters. The second gate was on the other side of the platform, hundred meters from first one. Mother stabilized the movement before pushing the station towards the second gate. A few feet from the gate, visually the crew could tell that the alignment was not right.

"Mother, stop right now!" sternly Cindy said to the computer.

After shutting down the active ones, Cindy fired the other two thrusters, providing thrust from the opposite direction, to bring the station to a halt. However, it was too late. The ramp slammed onto the gate, producing a mild jolt, across the structure and the station.

"Mrs. McLaughlin, let Mr. McLaughlin take over the control," from the ground control, Bob urged Cindy.

"Mother, switch control over to the joystick," Cindy snapped at the computer.

"I have the control," Trevor confirmed when he saw the red light blinking on the panel, indicating the control of the thrusters had been shifted to the joystick. Upon getting the control, Trevor pulled the throttle gently to drive the station away from the gate. While the station began moving away, he realigned the position of the thrusters to be able to push forward when the time was right. The thrusters had already been turned off. As soon as the laser range finder's readings displayed forty meters from the gate, Trevor slightly pushed the throttle, firing the thrusters once more, and moving the station in the forward direction. Trevor held the joystick like a fighter pilot, guiding the forward motion of the station. At the last moment, a short burst from the from the opposite direction halted the station where Trevor wanted it to stop. The crew could hardly feel the jolt as the ramp made contact, right over the two square locks, on either side of the gate.

"The bridge has been secured," Mother declared, and cheers and whistles of relief echoed inside the space station and the ground control, eighty miles down.

By then, the artificial gravity induced by the station's metal floor, had been activated. Cindy unbuckled from her seat and stepped right behind her first officer.

With a sweet smile on her lips, she said, "Mr. McLaughlin, you deserve to be the captain of this vessel. I'm sure you would have made an excellent fighter pilot."

"Did I ever tell you, I wanted to be a fighter pilot?"

"Oh yeah, you did," Cindy whispered very close to Trevor's ear.

"Too bad I turned out to be an elevator man," Trevor remarked.

"Look, where it has brought you," Cindy said softly, while placing a smack on his cheek. ***

After inserting the sample in a glass tube, Eileen pressed the green button of the analyzer for an instant reading. It didn't start snowing, though winter was officially in. She sniffed the air. She loved the fresh morning air of the wild. At a distance, she could hear the sweet flow of the Yuba River, cascading over and through the rocky surface and her rocky banks. Eileen collected the sample from the stagnant water of the pool which was roughly two hundred meters from the stream. The beep from the analyzer broke her trance like state. The reading was on the display. Later she was going to have a printout of it at the lab. The level of sodium bicarbonates, calcium, potassium, magnesium were all higher than the previous readings. It was not a big jump though. Nonetheless, when Eileen had summed up the previous readings, it caused unease in her. Something inside her urged her to pay another visit to Mr. Bates' farm.

"Yes Eileen, go ahead, I can hear you," Jones responded as Eileen called the lab.

"Jones, the readings are higher than the previous ones. I think something has been brewing."

"It might very well be the case, but _________,"

Eileen interrupted. She asked, "Where's Rakesh?"

"Hold on," said Jones as he yelled at Rakesh.

A few seconds passed before she heard Rakesh saying, "Yes Eileen, is there anything you want me to do?"

"When did you last take the reading with your MAD (magnetic anomaly detector)?"

"This morning," Rakesh replied.

"Did you notice anything unusual in the reading?"

"Not really."

"Are you sure your device is in good working condition?"

"I checked the circuits, the sensors, and the display before heading for the hills. They were in perfect order prior to the test."

"Alright, let me talk to Jones."

"Look Jones, I think we should visit the Yuba Farm again."

"But we visited the place only a week ago."

"I cannot tell you exactly what, but I have this feeling that something's not right, Jones."

"What has to be done, has to be done. When do you plan to go there?"

"I'll return in half an hour. All of you get ready for the tour." ***

Mr. Bates was at the gate of his cottage when the team reached the spot. Signs of curiosity lurked in his expression as he inquired, "Is everything okay with you guys?"

"We're not really sure what's been going on, Mr. Bates. I thought it would be a good idea to have a tour of your farm," Eileen responded.

"I have just returned from the barn. You wouldn't mind sending Fred with you, would you?"

"No Mr. Bates, we wouldn't. Your grandson is an expert, and he's so helpful," replied Jones.

On the way to the barn, some of Mr. Bates' sheep dogs were found barking. One close to the well, the other behind a hedge, and yet another on the paved road that went from the cottage to the barn. Fred was too young to master the art of whistling with two fingers. He had a whistle around his neck for this task. Despite the little boy's attempt to draw the attention of the barking dogs, the howling continued. Eileen and her team members stared at each other. Finally, Noah said, "Let's find out what's keeping the dogs busy."

As they came near the well, the red and white collie was by then only a few meters from it. Quite obviously, the dog was after something. Close inspection revealed the rattle snake crawling towards the hedges.

"Let it go, fella," Fred yelled at his dog.

As Fred grabbed the belt around its neck, Jones remarked, "A rattler out in the open at this time of the year, kinda strange!"

"Aren't they supposed to be hibernating?" Noah inquired.

"Yes, unless they want to change their residence for some reason," remarked Jones.

"Residence sounds too comfy to me!" Noah teased with a smile.

"Of course, animas also have residence."

The other collie was found chasing another rattler. As they came to the third collie, it became clear that the serpents had been fleeing from something.

"Now, why would our reptilian neighbors be in such a hurry to leave behind their dungeons?" Jones asked with signs of curiosity in his voice.

"Perhaps a disaster is in the making," Eileen suggested. Then after a pause she continued, "I think we should check the barn guys."

The other animals in the barn displayed no signs of unnatural behavior. Noah led his team straight to the loft.

"Holy cow!" exclaimed Jones as an astounding scene greeted the team. The entire roof was hidden under a layer of ants.

"Rakesh, check the air for charges," Eileen directed.

Rakesh set up his device with its antenna changing direction every few seconds. After scanning the air for a few minutes, he said, "Nothing."

"If we're looking at a possible quake, there has to be positive charges in the air," Jones remarked.

"Not necessarily," said Eileen, and then added, "for positive charges to appear in the air, there must be significant level of friction inside the rock layers, and for that to happen, the low frequency vibrations that precede must reach a threshold. Perhaps the vibrations have not yet reached the threshold. At this stage, snakes and ants in the ground are the first ones to pick up the low frequency vibrations."

"Are you saying, energy is building up before the real event?" Jones inquired.

"Well, I don't see any other explanation," Eileen responded.

"So, what do we do now? Can't really go for the alert based on this," added Noah.

"No, we can't. We have to wait for the other animals to give us the telltale signs. We must wait for the positive charges to appear in the atmosphere as well," Eileen remarked with a steady voice.

"What do we tell our host?" asked Jones.

"Nothing," replied Eileen, and then added, "he's in his seventies. Let the old man have his piece of mind. There's no immediate danger anyway."

"Maybe we should give a hint to Mrs. Bates. After all, we don't wanna see the roof of the cottage collapsing over these senior citizens, do we?" Noah suggested.

"What are we going to tell?" Jones sounded lost.

"In case they hear or feel any rumble, they should leave everything and move to open space," said Noah.

"Are you sure, they won't be in the toilet when it happens?" Eileen giggled.

"Hey, let's do our part, if their luck runs out, that's not our fault," Jones shrugged his shoulders as he said this. ***

Michael did not return to the ground control at the site of the project. Instead, he flew to the head office of his company at Hanford, after meeting with his attorney. He knew he could not focus on his work while being chased by the ghost of his late wife and sister-in-law.

Stephanie set the thermostat of the office at seventy. Still the office room felt uncomfortably warm. Perhaps Michael needed the cool fresh air outside. He asked Stephanie to open the windows. He was at the window when his attorney's hologram image appeared over his desk.

"Every time your image appears in my office, consternation grips my heart. It wasn't like this," Michael remarked with a sad smile.

"Things change with time, Michael. Only a few days back, you were a happily married man. Now you're a widower. Anyway, I have news for you."

Michael gave Mr. Kruger a blank look. He didn't know what to say. The veteran lawyer continued, "The other day, they sent me more evidence of the possible homicide."

"From where did you get it?"

"The state prosecutor's office. They're convinced it was a premeditated murder." Mr. Kruger paused, expecting a response from his client.

Michael asked, "What kind of evidence are we talking about?"

"Just wait a second, I have something for you," Mr. Kruger interrupted the conversation. He was seen turning and pressing a button. At the upper right corner of the projection, a video appeared. The video played the recorded images of the two men tampering with Lillian's vehicle.

Mr. Kruger explained, "These images were captured by the camera installed at the parking lot, prior to the accident. You can see the date and the time."

For a few minutes, the two watched what the assailants had been doing. They saw one of them taking a round disc and getting under the vehicle's chassis.

"That's the magnetic device which was used to hack into the vehicle's system. The investigators retrieved part of it from the wreckage," Mr. Kruger added.

Silence followed when the video had stopped. Mr. Kruger cleared his throat, and asked, "Do you know these men?"

Michael knew it was coming. It was the most awkward and uncomfortable moment. He snapped, "Hell no!"

"Yeah, I thought so. They have been identified as the employees of Aurora Metal Works," the old lawyer declared.

"Aurora Metal Works, that's the place where I got the titanium braces for the structure," Michael exclaimed.

"Yes, and there's more to it. Do you know that Aurora Metal Works is a subsidiary of Manchurian Steel?"

"I had no idea."

"It is. Two years back, the Manchurian Steel became the major stake holder of South California Steel and its sister concerns, and guess what, Aurora Metal was one of those sister concerns. In other words, those two guys basically work for the Manchurian Steel. For your information, I would like to highlight that Manchurian Steel is owned by the Manchurian Communist Party or MCP."

"The MCP and the Manchurian government, aren't they separate entities?" asked Michael.

"Officially they are separate entities. However, in reality, there's no such thing as independent entity in the communist system. The government, the party, and the so-called independent entities, they're all one single entity."

For a while, Michael stared at the photos of the two assailants, and then said, "They look different."

"Look closely, they are the same people. At the crime scene, they disguised themselves as homeless vagabonds. Do you realize the implication, Michael?"

"Yes, I do James. I just don't know what to say!" Michael whispered. Then he asked, "Have you heard from Lillian's attorney?"

"Oh yeah, he sounded like he had found the smoking gun. He's certain, he's going to nail you for the crime."

"Have you been corresponding with the Pentagon about the incidents at the space station, James? I'm telling you, my project has become a threat to their plan to expand their evil empire. To these commies, nothing is unethical, as long as the end serves the communist party's goals. They see cold blooded murders as necessary tools to achieve greater good of the society. I feel like throwing up when I think about it, James. I just cannot comprehend how human beings justify crimes so easily. The system promises everything but freedom, and what are we without freedom, James? Without freedom, humans are no longer human beings, but a bunch of androids. If these commies are allowed to flourish, the rest of the world will have nothing but tyranny and blood bath."

"Well said Mike. My thoughts are not as blunt as yours. Nonetheless, they boil down to the same conclusion. I think I'll have to pay a visit to Washington DC. Privately I need to sit down with the top brass and figure out what they've been thinking. I think they have the key to your survival."

"Oh, those generals, they love to talk over the dinner table. General Normandy, he's the one handling the affairs concerning my project. Find out the generals directing him, and then invite them to a dinner at the finest restaurant in Washington."

"We might have to pay a courtesy call to the defense secretary as well," Mr. Kruger suggested.

"Do whatever you have to, James. I'll cover the expenses," Michael promised.

Mr. Kruger looked pleased, and then he asked, "Will it be possible for you to lend your rockerjet for a day? I just wanted the top brass to feel appreciated. They would love to have a ride. Let me tell you, if they decide to testify, you don't have to worry. The challenge is to get them to testify."

"No problem James, just let me know when you need the service. Just a piece of advice James, don't promise them something I cannot deliver. You know how those hawks are. I have no doubts, if they can, they would love to have their hands on my pet project."

The veteran lawyer could feel Michael's pulse as the bold entrepreneur finished his last statement. Reassuringly, he said to Michael, "Don't worry, I know how you feel about your project. It's hell of a project Mike, it's a hell of a project! I've been hearing that finally you've made space travel economically viable. Now everyone is looking at you for the next big step. What will be the next big step, Mike?"

"Up there in the orbit, I'll build an industrial complex, a city, as large as New York. The goal is to build a spaceship like a tiny planet which will be self-sustainable. Since we're looking at inter-stellar voyages, I'm telling you, this is the only way to go James, this is the only way to go."

"And who'll be living in your orbital city, Mike?"

"We plan to send couples to the orbital track for giving birth and raising them up there, never to set foot on the blue planet. This way, they'll be habituated to living in zero gravity environments without any kind of ill effects. They will be the ultimate space travelers."

Mr. Kruger admired his client's resolve, his vision. He stared at him with signs of admiration, and then asked, "Do you believe in God, Mike?"

"Many look at my lifestyle and think that I'm an atheist. I don't blame them. However, deep in my heart I've always been a believer in the divinity of the entire universe. Basically, we just assemble with what is given to us. He is the actual builder. He builds from nothing."

"Amen to that!" the old lawyer sounded like a priest.
***

# Chapter Sixteen

From their private quarter, Cindy stared at the spellbinding view of the shaft. A mile down the shaft, the rising elevator drew her attention. For the last two weeks, they had been working frantically, outside and inside the station. Sometimes the elenauts envied the efficiency of the androids. Cindy could understand their feelings. One day, these robots could render the humans redundant, and this fear of the future bred resentment among many. Albeit she never believed in such inevitability, she had to be sensitive about the feelings of her team. Often, she discussed it with Trevor. Their views were similar. Perhaps, it was because both possessed in depth knowledge of what the robots could accomplish, and what they could not.

"Hi there," she heard Trevor's voice behind her. Trevor just returned from his four-hour shift. Today, Trevor supervised the completion of the fifth extension of the station.

"So, how did it go?" Cindy inquired while surrendering herself to his arms.

"Well, the plant for assembly has been completed. I think it should have been larger. After all, there's no shortage of space and time."

"Honey, resources aren't unlimited. Apart from that, only two elevators could lift only so much."

"That's true. Anyway, for the time being, it'll do just fine," Trevor admitted.

Cindy took Trevor to the window, and said, "It's a spectacular view, isn't it?"

"The sun coming up from behind the planet, that adds to the beauty," Trevor muttered, and then continued, "Look, the elevator is coming up. The creation of God, and the creation of man, blending together, what do you think?"

"Man's creation is very fragile."

"Sweetheart, aren't you underestimating man's achievements?"

"No dear. One good size solar flare could end all our achievements in a couple of minutes if not seconds."

"You know the chances of it, don't you?"

"Yes honey, I know the chances of that happening are very slim. Nonetheless, the chances are there," remarked Cindy. Putting her arms around his neck, passionately, Cindy kissed her husband, and then whispered, "Does it hurt your ego, sweetheart?"

"Kinda," very tenderly Trevor replied.

"Don't worry, my dear husband, I'm here with the ointment to make you feel better. In the meantime, get used to the fact."

"And what's that fact you've been trying to convey to me so romantically?"

"In this great scheme of creation, we're not even ants, honey."

"If that makes you feel better, I hear it, my darling. Now let's go, I want you to see the factory where the spaceship of the future is going be built." ***

The whole team was with Cindy and Trevor. The interior space of the plant pleased Cindy. Before her tour Cindy activated the artificial gravity. Hence, she didn't have to wear the fan driven pack, or FDP in short, with thrust vector. The ceiling was one hundred feet high with cranes and guide rails hanging from it. The roof was made up of three-inch-thick metal plates made from precious alphiron alloy. The plates had the strength to withstand tiny meteors, and all around the plant were layers of sand and radiation absorbing materials. In other words, the view from the plant was blocked from all sides. Cameras connected to the huge display screens and the exterior sensors reproduced what was outside. The plant could also be used as shelter, in case of threats from asteroids or solar flares.

"Why is the floor magnetic?" inquired Anna, who was behind Cindy.

"It's mildly magnetic. It has been kept so for the convenient of movement under zero gravity. Those who'll be working in the plant won't be given the FDPs for economic reason," responded Sage, the humanoid standing next to Trevor.

"Space Race never misses an opportunity to cut the cost. Is it a good sign, Sage?" Trevor asked.

Being equipped with the latest software generated intelligence, Sage was familiar with the company's vision and fiscal policies. Hence, he understood what Trevor had tried to convey to him.

Very calmly he replied, "Cost management is an ongoing process of all business enterprises. If it cannot be executed efficiently, the margin of profit slims down."

"Sage, are you one of the financial advisors the CEO has hired to represent him up here in the orbit?" Trevor asked only to make fun of him.

With a cold calculated voice, the humanoid replied, "No, but I appreciate your compliment, Mr. McLaughlin."

Everyone around them laughed at Trevor. At one point, the captain of the station remarked, "It's quite large, Trevor. I don't get it, why did you want it to be larger."

"In his orientation speech, Professor Stan talked about a city size spaceship, didn't he?"

"Yes, he did. You shouldn't take everything literally, especially if it's coming from the higher ups of the company or politicians. They say many things for motivational purpose. If they promise a mile, you should take it as a yard. I'm afraid that's how the real world is, so please, don't raise a storm over it. Apart from that, I don't think the company can afford to build a plant the size of a city, at least, not at this stage."

"Have you been going through the company's annual reports?" Trevor inquired.

"We've all been doing it, haven't we? Let's talk about something more pressing. How will a spaceship be built if the height of it exceeds one hundred feet?"

"Thanks for coming to my point. As it stands now, either they'll have to raise the ceiling, or focus on assembling sections of the vessel. Later, they can be put together outside the assembly plant," Trevor explained.

"Everything is fine, now please show us the warehouse," Cindy insisted.

"Access to the warehouse," Trevor told Mother, and before their eyes, the floor of the plant parted, revealing the warehouse underneath. The warehouse had five levels. Whenever building materials were going to be needed, the ceiling over the particular item was going to be parted for hoisting the object with the help of the crane or FDP. Sage farther briefed that at any given time, five thousand workers could work inside the plant.

"So, we're looking at thousands of androids working in this plant, right?" Cindy asked.

Sage stared at Cindy with his lifeless artificial eyes, and asked, "Are you uncomfortable with the idea, Mrs. McLaughlin?"

"No Sage, we don't have any problems with it, as long as androids like you don't start telling us what to do, what to eat, or how to act?" with a smile Cindy snapped.

For a few seconds, Sage looked confused, and then responded, "Humans have created us to serve them. I cannot think of a situation when we will be telling them what to do."

"You cannot, but we can, and that's why we're humans, and you're robots," Cindy explained.

While Cindy and her crew concluded their tour of the assembly plant and the warehouse, Mother announced the arrival of the latest shipment of building materials. Cindy and Trevor returned to the bridge, while the rest of the crew went to the gate of the ramp to receive the shipment. At the bridge, Cindy found Bob trying to reach them from the ground control. She didn't feel like turning on the hologram. However, she knew it was against the company directive to have it turned off during a call. She glanced at Trevor and Sage, and then reluctantly, told Mother to connect them to the ground control.

They had expected to see Jeff. It only heightened their curiosity when Bob greeted them with an anxious look.

"We know you have your hands full folks. Honestly, we wouldn't hesitate to lessen your burden if we could," said Bob in a rather slow pace, and the way he said it, prepared his audience for what was to follow. After the brief pause, Bob cleared his throat, and added, "We have been experiencing some sort of technical malfunction with one of the elevators."

Bob refrained from farther disclosing what he had to say. He wanted to gauge the response from his audience. Since it had to do with the elevator, Cindy stared at Trevor for his input.

"Which elevator are we talking about?" Trevor asked with a somber expression.

"The extension of the first one, in between the third and fourth platform. It's stuck. It had been on its way down when it stopped. We tried everything. It wouldn't respond."

"What does the diagnostic tool say in its report?" Trevor asked.

"It didn't find any problem with the operating system. The power is on, the cables, rails and brackets are all intact. We would like you to have a look at it."

"Do you mean, going down and physically checking what's wrong?" asked Trevor with his brows raised.

"I'm afraid that's the only way," said Bob apologetically before adding, "We thought you could fix the problem, after all, you're the expert in this field, aren't you?"

Trevor sighed when Cindy intervened. She said, "You know Bob, this is way more than what we bargained for.

First, we get into trouble with your hacked military robot. Then we face the cluster of asteroids. No sooner had we turned our heads, we get blown away by the Manchurians. And now you come up with this."

The signs of anger and frustration were clearly visible as Cindy vented out what she had to say. Bob instantly knew what she had been trying to convey to them. He thoroughly studied the clauses of the contract between Space Race and the elenauts. Hence, he drew from it, and said, "The contract explicitly states your compliance to what is expected of you. It doesn't matter what the circumstances are. We know it's hard, but that's how it stands."

"Oh yeah, it's all in there. If we could only foresee what we were getting into," Cindy remarked with a sigh.

"Alright, how do I get to it?" Trevor focused on the crisis.

"Get into your space suit with the thruster on it. You won't be doing any heavy lifting, so you don't need the exoskeleton. Just use the first elevator to go down to the fourth platform and see for yourself what the problem is. Don't forget to take your toolbox and a humanoid with you."

"It means, we have to reposition the station in order to have the ramp in place," Cindy pointed out.

"Naa, I think we should do it the hard way. That should save you the trouble," Trevor insisted.

"Hard way!" Cindy exclaimed.

"We'll just float to the gate and manually open the door of the elevator." ***

Cindy, Sage and Anna watched Trevor and SPOT-1 getting into the entrance of the decompression chamber with the exit to the exterior of the station. SPOT-1 carried Trevor's heavy toolbox. He had a thruster on him but wore no space suit.

The fourth platform was in the exosphere. Hence, they were out of the zero gravity environments. The elevator had not been at the platform. This prevented the door from opening. SPOT-1 assisted Trevor to bypass the safety measure in place, and then manually opened the door.

Trevor had turned on the thruster pack and carefully looked down the shaft to check if he could see the elevator. He could see nothing as the shaft disappeared beyond his visual range.

"Alright SPOT-1, we have to use our thruster packs," Trevor yelled at the humanoid.

The braces rushed up as they descended the shaft. The elevator was stuck at hundred kilometers from the planet surface. Before stepping on it, Trevor checked if the capsule would hold. As he stood on it with his thruster pack still on, the capsule held steady. One by one, Trevor checked the various parts of the capsule. He found everything in sound working condition. However, when he had opened the outer covering of the motor connected to the pulley, he discovered the problem. The coil of the motor was burnt out, rendering the capsule immobile. It took roughly one hour to replace the coil and get the capsule moving.

Inside the capsule, Trevor checked if the control panel had been functioning properly. The system responded as it had been expected to. Then Trevor stared at SPOT-1 from the captain's seat, and asked, "How do I look?"

"Just fantastic," the humanoid responded.

"Take a snapshot with your robotic eye, will you?"

Trevor was happy with the snapshot of him, sitting like the captain of the capsule. Subsequently, he told the onboard computer to connect him to the ground control.
***

The buzz was like a blow from a hammer. In the darkness, the hologram display had the time suspended in the air. It glowed like radium in the dark. Eileen could not help exploding. Who could it be calling at three in the morning? Her annoyed expression disappeared when she had noticed Mr. Bates' image at the corner of the display. Anxiety flooded her heart as she received the call.

Without any kind of greetings, the old farmer said, "You folks better come down over here ASAP."

Eileen sprang up from her bed, and while putting on a jeans pant told the communication device to contact the rest of her team.

Jones was the first one to call back. He asked, "What's going on, Eileen?

"Get Noah and Rakesh, and meet me at the farm, on the double," Eileen snapped before hanging up and collecting all her tools in a toolbox. She chose to drive through the desert highway, instead of flying. As she sped through Highway 20, she noticed a number of animals crossing the highway, fleeing northward. The headlights could not distract the animals in a rush to get away. They simply ignored the vehicle moving at more than sixty miles an hour. The darkness all around mingled with the blazing light of the vehicle before her. Eileen struggled to suppress the eerie feeling gripping her heart. She told the vehicle's computer to connect her to her team.

"Where are you guys at the moment?" Eileen yelled as the hologram image of her team appeared on the right side, over the dashboard.

"We're about two kilometers behind you. I think we can see your rear lights," Jones replied.

"I have observed quite a few animals fleeing to the north. Have you guys noticed anything?"

"Yeah, we've seen some animals crossing the highway as well ________,"

Jones could hardly finish when Eileen exclaimed, "Guys, look to your right, do you see anything?"

A few moments passed without any kind of response, and then Jones said, "Yes, we can see the red glow in the night sky. The built-up energy has finally reached the threshold. The charges are already in the night sky. I have told Rakesh to point his device at the sky. Let's find out what the readings say. I'm going to call the radar station too. I'm sure they'll have something to add as well."

A chaotic scene awaited the team at the barn. Mr. Bates and his hired hands had already been there when the team reached the entrance of the barn. The mooing of the cattle, the squealing of the pigs, the neighing of the horses, the howling of the dogs, and the cluck of the chickens had turned the barn into a natural opera house when the team inspected each and every shelter. The animals displayed erratic behavior as well.

"So, what do you make of it?" Jones asked Eileen.

"It's coming, no point denying at this point. It might strike at this very moment, or it might take several days, but it's coming Jones," Eileen said with a straight face.

"Do you want me to send out the alert?"

"You return to the lab and do that. In the meantime, let me drive to the pool and collect the samples of the pool water," Eileen suggested to Jones.

"Is it safe Eileen?" asked Noah.

"The risk is part and parcel of our job, Noah. Can't always afford to work from the safety of our office." Then Eileen turned to Mr. Bates and said, "Mr. Bates, how many drones do you have?"

"Four," replied the old farmer.

"Are they operational, right now?"

"Their batteries are being charged. In the morning they'll be fully ready."

"How long can they operate, once they're charged?"

"It depends. If they remain stationary, the charge can easily last more than a week, but usually that's not the case. So, normally they last for a few days."

"We'll need to connect our GOES and Terra Satellites to your drones for a better view of what's been happening down here. For the time being, those satellites will take over the control of your drones, is that okay with you?"

"For how long do you plan to use them?"

"As soon as the threat recedes, we'll handover the control to you."

"No problem, be my guest."

"In that case we need to have your formal approval and the access codes. I'm going to send you the form, please fill it up, along with your fingerprint and access codes, and we'll take it up from there."

It took ten seconds for Eileen to send the form and the request to Mr. bates from her S-Pad. By then the clamor inside the barn had become a cacophony. Subsequently Mr. Bates told his men to release the animals. The barn door slid open automatically as the sensor attached to it detected the pen and stall doors opening. The animals rushed out as if they were being chased by the angel of death. Yuba Farm had several barns like that, and the animals in them were also released. The animals kept roaming in the dark restlessly, looking for a way to escape from the farm.

However, one development farther puzzled Eileen and her team. They could not find a single ant on the surface of the ceiling which had been completely enveloped by the insect army the previous day.

"Where did they vanish?" Noah exclaimed.

"Perhaps, they've returned underground," Mr. Bates shrugged his shoulders.

"Why would they return? The threat has not receded. They must be somewhere around," Jones insisted.

"Everyone, check every inch of the barn," Eileen howled.

The team spent the next half an hour scouring the whole barn. Not a single ant could be found. For a few moments, they placed their arms on their hips and stared at each other, when Eileen said, "Let's check outside."

The landscape around the barn was shrouded in a thick blanket of fog and mist.

"Don't you have flood lights, Mr. Bates?" Eileen inquired.

Mr. Bates howled, "Turn on the flood lights."

A mystical view transpired before them as if a magician had brought into being a strange unrecognizable world of shadows and light. In this struggle between the artificial light and the darkness beyond the perimeter of the barn, the visitors crouched in all directions, looking for the signs of the subterranean dwellers. They rubbed the soft grass with their feet, to see if the tiny insects had been hiding underneath the green canopy.

"Isn't that strange?" asked Noah.

"What's so strange?" Jones responded.

"The cottonwoods, look at the trunk, it looks different," Noah replied.

Upon close inspection, they discovered the new shelter of the tiny insects. All of them stepped closer for a better view. The ants had invaded the entire tree. The other trees faced the same fate.

"Why are they up on tress? What's wrong with the roof of the barn?" Noah wanted to find out.

Eileen said, "Perhaps they think the structure is not strong enough."

"Not strong enough for what?" Jones shot back.

"Not strong enough to withstand the quake," replied Noah.

"Since when did the ants become architects?" said Mr. Bates with signs of amusement in his tone.

"We could learn a lot from the bees and the ants, Mr. Bates," Eileen responded.

"I hope so. Now what do you suggest we do?" asked the old farmer.

Eileen turned to her team and said, "You guys get back to the lab, and send out the alert. Make sure that you contact the officials of Space Race. I think they're in deep trouble."

"Take Noah with you Eileen, just in case ______," Jones stammered.

"Just in case what. Jones? Alright Noah, come with me," Eileen surrendered to the suggestion. When she was done talking to her team, Eileen turned to Mr. Bates and his men, and added, "Mr. Bates, I would like you to keep your men and equipment ready for any kind of emergency. Let the animals roam free until the disaster passes."

"Is it imminent Ms. Malone?" asked the old farmer.

"Mr. Bates, I don't know exactly when it will strike, but take my word for it, it's coming, and it's going to be big."

As she was about get into her vehicle, out of nowhere, a goose hopped into it. It kept honking at her, making everyone laugh.

"It sure found in you the safest refuge," Mr. Bates remarked with a smile.

"Come, come, sweetheart, will you go on a ride with me?" very tenderly Eileen addressed the bird as she fondly stroked its long neck.

"They make very reliable guards, honking at strangers" Jones added.

"Yes, they do. These animals are our best friends. Many of us don't realize it," Eileen admitted frankly.

"Alright fella, I think you'll have your ride some other day," remarked Mr. Bates as he gently removed the goose from the vehicle. ***

On her way to the Emerald Pools, it occurred to Eileen that she should warn her parents, living in Seattle. She remembered her parents, taking her on tours of the downtown Seattle from their home on the Bain Bay Island when she was a kid. She hated living in the quiet atmosphere of the suburb. She thought the bustling city life had much to offer. It was only when she had graduated from her university that she learned to appreciate what nature had to offer. In comparison, man's urban dream was nothing but an illusion and waste of resources.

Mr. Sweeny Malone and Mrs. Rose Malone lived in their suburban cottage almost their entire life. Eileen often boasted to her colleagues and friends about her parents' undying love even at their old age. They were one of those few who managed to stick together through thick and thin. Both received a fair share as inheritance, allowing them to purchase the cottage of their dream. When she was eighteen, Eileen had completed her high school from the nearby school and then went to Washington State University for her undergraduate and post graduate degrees on geology. Both Mr. and Mrs. Malone were happy with the career their daughter chose.

Mr. and Mrs. Malone had been watching the evening news on their holovision when they received the call from their only child. The hologram image of her daughter driving with her colleague aroused curiosity in the old couple.

"Where are you heading at this time of the day, Eileen?" asked Mrs. Malone the moment the image appeared in their parlor.

"Mom, I'm on my way to the nearby pool. Is Dad with you? I don't see him." Eileen inquired anxiously.

"He was here, where did he go?" Eileen could hear her mother yelling at her husband.

As Mr. Malone appeared in the image, the two exchanged greetings, and then Eileen said, "Dad, I have called you to warn you two about a quake."

"We haven't had a quake over here for quite some time now," Mr. Malone remarked.

"It's going to be a big one, dad. The signs are all over here. It's only a matter of time before it strikes."

"You noticed the signs where you are. How will it affect us over here?" asked Mr. Malone.

"I get this feeling that this time around the shock might exceed eight Richter scale. Even if it's under eight, Seattle will experience a pretty good jolt from it. So, I want you two remain alert, and try to stock up with food and fuel."

"Oh dear, when do you expect it to strike?" Mrs. Malone threw the question at her daughter.

"Mom, we don't know the exact time. It can happen at any moment now, or it can take a few more days. It depends on so many factors."

"Alright dear, we'll remain alert. One more thing sweetheart, aren't you planning on coming home for Thanksgiving?"

"No promises Mom, but I'll try my best to spend the Thanksgiving with you two," Eileen promised. ***

# Chapter Seventeen

As the wide doors of the Cincinnati Federal Courtroom burst open, Michael and his attorney encountered an army of humanoid reporters working for various news channels. Through their eyes and ears, the world saw what they saw, heard what they heard. Human reporters were no longer viewed reliable and objective. Hence the entire communication industry had stopped employing human journalists and began deploying these humanoid reporters. They simply reported without adding any kind of feelings. This served the owners of the media outlets well, gradually turning it into a trend.

"How do you feel, Mr. Stewart?" one of them asked the billionaire CEO of the Space Race.

"You wouldn't understand,'' Michael snapped.

Another humanoid reporter responded, "We wouldn't, but our viewers would."

"We can't see your viewers so please leave us alone," the old lawyer said.

"Mr. Stewart, we have report that the plaintiff of this case died in an accident only a few days back. Do you have anything to say about that" another reporter inquired.

Michael was about to respond when Me. Kruger placed his hand before his client's face, stopping him from responding to the question. Glaring at the reporter the veteran lawyer warned, "Now you've crossed the line, humanoid. One more question, I'll file a lawsuit against your media."

After the encounter, the old lawyer escorted his client to their vehicle through the crowd with the help of a police officer. Once inside their vehicle, Michael frowned at Mr. Kruger, "Oh James, you didn't need to be so rude. You know how these reporters can make or break one's image."

"You gotta control your impulse to talk Mike. You're off the hook because the jury gave you the benefit of the doubt. But this is just one case. The big one is yet to pass. Anything you say can be used against you to prove your guilt in Lillian's murder."

"Has it now been confirmed that it was not an accident"?

"Of course, haven't you seen the video of her vehicle being tampered?"

"The Manchurians are clearly involved in it, aren't they?"

"That's one narrative, but has it been proven yet? No"

Aren't we going to have something from the Pentagon?"

"No. The other day they sent me a note.  They're saying they have no plan to reveal the incident which clearly indicates the Manchurian government's motive behind framing you.  Indirectly they're saying that they are not going to testify on the ground of national security, and you know when the military decides to evoke the clause related to the national security, there's not much anyone can do. The court will simply refuse to summon them, and without their testimony, I'm afraid the charge against you will look very very convincing. You're in deep shit, Mike."

The vehicle had been flying at one thousand feet from the ground. Every now and then Michael observed the low clouds rushing past the flying vehicle. For a while Michael watched the exciting world outside and then turned his head. He asked" You're not very fond of euphemism, are you?"

"What does it mean?" asked the old lawyer.

"Expressing something unpleasant in a more acceptable manner,

"I mean referring to something like shit as human excretion, right."

Mike had to smile when he responded, "Yes, something like that."

"Well Mike, I've been trying to prepare you for the shit that's heading your way. I think you should tell your son to be ready to take over your business on a very short notice."

"Is the situation really that bad, James?"

"Yes, Mike. I hoped for some sort of lift from the Pentagon or the State Department. Unfortunately, it never materialized. Could you think of any reasons for the military to wish for your removal from the Space Race?'

"Why would they want that?"

"Yes, I have the same question, ever since I got the letter from them. It doesn't make sense. The Manchurian government has been clearly trying to sabotage your project, yet the response from the military is like, I see nothing, hear nothing."

"We live in a strange world, James. Sometimes, the line between patriotism and betrayal is so thin that one can easily confuse betrayal for patriotism."

The drink from Mike's goblet spilled over as the craft dropped almost hundred feet due to the air pockets, and for the next couple of minutes, it was a roller costar ride.

Michael sensed the old lawyer's discomfort as he watched him wriggle like a worm in his seat. Mr. Kruger relaxed after the ordeal was over. The vehicle landed smoothly on the concrete tarmac where Michael's rocker jet had been waiting for them. Michael was going to drop Mr. Kruger at Los Angle and then head for Hanford.

The flight crew of Michael's rocker jet made every effort to make the flight from Cincinnati to Los Angeles as pleasant as possible. The refreshments were the very best any airliner could offer. Prior to the flight from Cincinnati to Los Angeles, the pilot informed the flight attendants about the special guest. They understood that perhaps the future of their CEO and the owner depended on the performance of the old lawyer. Hence, the crew did their best to turn the entire journey into a luxury cruise.

At one point, the old lawyer muttered to his client, "Look Mike, even the best attorney has certain limitations. Sometimes luck plays a dominant role in this kind of cases. I don't know why I have this feeling that luck has been conspiring against you." A pause followed, and the veteran lawyer used the pause to gauge his clients thought, staring straight into his soul. In the end, he didn't want to dishearten his client. So, he continued, "Nonetheless, I will not leave any stone unturned to ensure a fair trial."

On the tarmac, a limo stood not too far from the rocker jet. The old lawyer stooped at the door of the limo with his client right behind him, getting ready to bid farewell. Instead of stepping into the limo, Mr. Kruger turned around and asked, "By the way, did you talk to your son about Lillian's death?"

"Yes, I did. It was Bob who informed me about the accident."

"How does he feel about this?"

"He was very upset. He wanted to find out if I had anything to do with it."

"What did you say?"

"What I told you?'

"Did he believe you?"

"I don't know if I was very convincing at first. After this assault on the space station and the video footage you showed me, I don't see any reason for him not to believe me."

"Did he witness the strike on your space station?"

"He was at the ground control when it happened. He saw the whole incident. Not only that, but I also showed him the video clip of the parking lot and the identity of those assailants."

"Then he just connected the dots, right?"

"Yeah."

Mr. Kruger lowered his head and smiled and then stared back at his client, and remarked, "It's a good thing that at least your son knows the truth. Albeit I'm not sure how the jury is going to take it."

Michael looked awfully exhausted. He presented a dry smile and said, "Don't kill yourself over it. At the end of the day, I believe in destiny. While fate guides us to our destiny, we find out who our friends are, and who claim to be our friends. I have complete faith in you, James." ***

One by one, the managers presented their recommendations to the committee set up to prepare a draft proposal. Jeff didn't waste time informing the committee after getting the red alert from the CISN. Jeff's robotic secretary converted the verbal recommendations into text before producing the graphic images. Unanimously the committee, decided to bring back the elenauts as soon as possible. Bob suggested that Mr. and Mrs. McLaughlin should be given the option to extend their stay at the station. They were to be joined by the couples who were going to be selected as the next batch of elenauts as part of the plan to permanently raise children who were going to be born in space. If the elenauts succeeded, it would provide valuable data about permanent human presence in space. The other two members of the committee agreed to Bob's proposal and finalized the steps to be taken in case of a quake. Then Jeff told his secretary to invite the head of the CISN at Carson City to the meeting. Eileen was in the lab behind the covered van, when she received the request.

As her somber face appeared before the whole crowed, Jeff introduced himself after the greetings, and said, "Ms. Malone, we're very worried about the quake alert you sent us. As you can see, I have called an emergency meeting for coming up with a plan to handle the crisis. Now tell us more about your work, and particularly let us know how CISN has come to this conclusion that a quake is imminent."

Eileen had a test tube in her hand as she responded. She held it up before the meeting, and said, "You see, this is the sample of pool water over here. Last time when I tested the sample, the level of chemicals was slightly higher." At this point she paused and showed the printout of the readings she had collected only an hour ago.

"The level of chemicals likes calcium, sodium, potassium, and magnesium have all shot up. This happens because these chemicals are released into the geologically active pools by earth's crust prior to any major quake. Apart from that we have recorded positive charges in the atmospheres, another major indictor of an imminent quake.

We have also received data from the radar station, reporting a drop in height of the earth's ionosphere. Before these signs, we have been getting reports from a nearby farm of unusual animal behaviors. Mr. Baldman, my instincts tell me, it's going to hit us in the next few days."

"Any idea, how strong it's going to be," Jeff inquired.

"Anywhere between six to seven Richter scale.

"Our project has been designed to withstand a quake of that scale. Still we're going to mobilize our resources to cope with the situation. We appreciate your early warning. It's my pleasure talking to you, Ms. Malone."

The screen was behind Jeff. He turned his revolving chair to face his managers, once the line was disconnected. None uttered any words. The shadow of the impending disaster engulfed their thoughts. Bob had been sitting next to Jeff when Jeff turned around.

"Can't afford to spend time contemplating what might happen, Jeff. Let's move and get ready to face it. Let the evacuation of the elenauts from the station commence. Before that I suggest that you discuss with Mr. and Mrs. McLaughlin the prospect of extending their stay," Bob remarked.

"Yeah Bob, I was about to do what you suggested just now," Jeff responded firmly.

Officially, Jeff concluded the meeting, giving necessary instructions to his managers before focusing on communication with the space station. It had been a hectic day for the elenauts, receiving the latest batch of construction material and storing them in newly constructed warehouse. Cindy was at the bridge when communication was established. Her sunny appearance saddened Jeff. He struggled to find a way to disclose what he wanted to convey.

"Jeff, we're about to conclude our efforts to stock up with the latest batch of building materials. From tomorrow, we can commence working on farther extension of the station," Cindy said confidently.

"Congratulations to you and your team. You have done a wonderful job of making the station adequately prepared and equipped for our next mission." Then Jeff cleared his throat before coming to what he really wanted to convey. In an unusually calm voice he added, "Right now we have an issue in our hands. It's kinda difficult for me to explain while watching your enthusiasm for the project. Not too long ago, we have received a warning from CISN. It's an organization which monitors events prior to a quake, and issues alerts. They're saying a big one is about to strike within the next few days."

After the disclosure, Jeff paused deliberately, expecting some sort of response from his audience. Trevor moved forward and asked, "How strong is it going to be?"

"Somewhere between six to seven in Richter scale," Jeff muttered.

"We're safe up here, aren't we?" Suzy interrupted.

"Oh yeah, you guys are safe up there. Our concerns are regarding the shaft," Jeff chuckled.

"As far as I know, the structure incorporates anti-quake technology, right Jeff?" asked Cindy.

"Yes, it does, but we don't know how effective it is. It has never been tested during a real crisis," Jeff explained.

"Well, I guess we're about to find out," remarked Trevor with a touch of humor in his voice.

"Yes, we will. I hope things turn out the way we expect them to. In the meantime, we're going to bring you guys down. The period mentioned in the contract has been fulfilled, so it's due anyway."

"Is it because the contract period has been fulfilled or is it some sort of precautionary measure?" asked Anna who had been standing right behind Cindy.

"Both reasons are valid. If something happens to the shaft, we don't want you guys to get stuck up there in the orbit. As it stands, it'll take considerable time to prepare the conventional vehicles for a rescue mission. Therefore, it's a better option to bring our resources down. Yes, you could see it as a precautionary measure. When things will return to normal, we can resume sending men and materials for our missions in space. There's something else, but I prefer discussing it privately with Mr. and Mrs. McLaughlin."

Inside their private quarter when the line of communication was re-established, Jeff said to Cindy and Trevor, "We have an option for you two. You can either return or stay up there for indefinite period."

Jeff knew, his audience was about to respond, so he paused.

"What do you mean, we can stay up here for indefinite period?" Cindy shot back with signs of disbelief in her eyes.

"Mrs. McLaughlin, one of the objectives of this project is to raise a space generation, born and brought up in space __________,"

Jeff couldn't finish when Trevor interrupted, "What's the purpose of this objective Mr. Baldman?"

"Before I can explain it to you, I have to ask a question, Mr. McLaughlin."

"Go ahead, we're listening," Trevor snapped.

"What do you think is the obstacle against the kind of space travel we've been thinking of?"

"The distance between the constellations and the galaxies. It'll take thousands if not millions of years to reach them, even if we manage to travel at the speed of light," replied Cindy.

"Well, you're partly correct, but this is not what I expected. The human body is the greatest obstacle before us. It has not been designed to travel at the speed we've been trying to achieve, and that's just one part of the problem. We still don't know the effect of permanent exposure to zero gravity environments on human body. We have seen how long-term exposure to it weakens the bones, how it creates problems for our cerebellum to function properly. We believe it's because we're used to living under natural gravity. Therefore, we must have astronauts totally habituated to living under artificial or zero gravity, and there's a silent consensus among the scientific communities that only those born and raised in space can effectively cope with that kind of environment. If we can achieve this milestone, there's no limit to what we can achieve as far as space travel is concerned. Hence, this project aims to bring couples to space, couples who'll give birth and raise children in space. We would like you two to be the pioneers in this endeavor."

"Are you sure permanent exposure to zero gravity or artificial gravity won't cause undesirable mutations in human cells?" Trevor asked.

"We intend to find out, Mr. McLaughlin," with a smile on his lips the head of the project elenaut replied.

"In other words, you want us to be the guinea pigs of your noble experiment, right? No Jeff, we have no interest in giving birth in space. By the way, how do you know we've been thinking of conception?" Cindy sounded agitated.

"You have been married for a while, and you have no children. We assumed you might be interested in our proposal."

"No Jeff, we have no plan to be the parents of a bunch of mutant children. I think it's time for us to return home and lead a normal life."

Now the head of the project appeared a bit desperate, as he said, "For the sake of science, for the sake of progress, this much sacrifice we expected from you two."

"This much sacrifice!" exclaimed Cindy, "You are asking us and our unborn children to be your guinea pigs. You are one sick bastard, Jeff! You're one sick asshole!"

Jeff realized he was heading nowhere with his preposterous proposition. Clouds of disappointment were palpable as he said, "Science progresses through experiments, no matter how unacceptable we find them at times. That's the bitter truth Mrs. McLaughlin, that's the hard fact."

Both Cindy and Trevor felt relieved when the holographic image of Jeff vanished from the quarter. Trevor could sense Cindy's indignation. It made him conceal his interest in Jeff's proposition. He held her in his arms and said softly, "Don't let anyone ruin our day. Let the company do what it wants. In the end, we'll do what serves our interest." Trevor allowed a brief pause to give Cindy the time to divert her thoughts. He wanted her to calm down and think it over. He stared at her deep, dark eyes before kissing her passionately.

"Ah what a relief!" whispered Cindy.

"Let's turn on the artificial gravity, I want to feel the weight of your body pressing on mine," Trevor said softly.

"Cindy laughed quietly, and said, "Not here honey, we might fly in the wrong direction."

"Why not? So, what if we chose not to give birth in space, we might be remembered as the first couple to make love in space."

Now Cindy couldn't hold herself. She burst out in laughter, and said, "I don't want to take any chances dear. One awkward push, and I might end up flying through the ceiling."

"It'll be quite a scene, don't you think so?" Then Trevor paused for a moment before stating what he wanted to say. He said, "I thought you were always interested in doing something for the sake of science."

Cindy stared quietly at Trevor. She understood the implication of her husband's remark. Something had rung the alarm bell in her. Very gently, she let go his arm from around her, and said, "You are interested in Jeff's proposal, aren't you?"

"Not really," Trevor sounded confused, and continued, "but it's true that science progresses through experiments. If everyone follows our cue, how will they uncover the mysteries that block the progress of science?"

Cindy raised her brows. Now she was visibly upset. In a tense voice she said, "Oh come on Trevor, you know there will be no shortage of volunteers. Why don't you just say what you want us to do?"

"I wouldn't want us to do anything against your will honey, but I think we should have given it a thought, no harm in it, is there?"

Cindy closed her eyes, and for a few moments she contemplated the prospect of an ugly quarrel up there in space. It's not that they never had quarrels. However, getting into a quarrel up there in the orbit would add another dimension to it. She couldn't let that happen, especially when she wasn't even certain of their impeccable privacy. Somehow if it leaked out, it would turn them into a laughingstock before the whole planet. Therefore, she organized her thoughts, and very calmly said to her husband, "Honey, listen to me carefully. I'm not going to get into an argument with you up here. Who knows they might have hidden listening devices. The chances of a healthy fetus developing in the womb under zero gravity are almost zero. It just can't happen. You need natural gravity for the development of organs, and especially the brain. Just imagine our deformed baby struggling to breath before our very eyes. I can't take it Trevor. I just can't take it. I don't know about you, but the mental trauma would be too much for me to handle. So please, please, don't push it."

Trevor realized one more push, and things would get out of hand. He gave up, raising his two arms, indicating he was in no mood to continue. Cindy knew she had done it. She took a deep breath and embraced her husband fondly. She loved when he surrendered to her will. It never failed to embolden her confidence. ***

# Chapter Eighteen

The blipping red dot in the air indicated to Jeff that Professor Stan's phone was ringing. Jeff wasn't sure if the professor was going to receive his call. Hence, when he did, it was more like a sweet surprise to Jeff.

"Jeff, I haven't heard from you since I left the place. I hear that under your competent leadership, the project has been hopping from success to success. Congratulations! Now tell me, how you've been doing."

The old professor's hair was untidy. Jeff could see the professor very busy in his lab with the electronic note pad in his hand. Jeff already knew that the old professor had returned to his previous job. Jeff thought perhaps he should start the conversation by talking about the professor's research work. He said, "Stan, I'm as busy as you are with your research work. I hear that you have joined your Ivy League colleagues."

"I always maintained communication with them. When they heard about my dismissal, they suggested that I join the research work on the revolutionary ion propulsion. You know I always enjoy working on propulsion. Now tell me what you have on your mind, Jeff. I know you don't have time for courtesy calls."

Jeff began by expressing his gratitude for being so receptive. He made no effort to conceal his disappointment at the CEO of Space Race for his failure to appreciate what Professor Stan had tried to do. Jeff didn't worry about secrecy for he was quite aware of the old professor's security clearance. All of them were under an oath not to disclose anything even after their dismissal or retirement. Gradually, Jeff's focus turned to the pressing issues. One by one, narrating to the Professor the events which took place after the professor's departure. Albeit he had described the hacking of the humanoid, the strike on the space station by the Manchurian military, and the onslaught of the asteroid cluster, in details, his emphasis was on the present crisis. Jeff wanted to consult with his predecessor the structural integrity of the shaft, and particularly the tolerance level of the shaft to vibrations or quakes.

"The design of the shaft is sound. Apart from that, the metals and the alloys which have been used can easily withstand a quake of magnitude six to seven. California has a pretty good record of quakes exceeding seven Richter scale. If one like that strikes, no one knows what the outcome will be," the old professor remarked.

Jeff wasn't sure if he should raise the issue of ongoing investigation regarding Lillian's death. It was a sensitive topic. The outcome of the trial had the potential to destroy the image of the company. He decided to avoid it, and said, "I'm worried about the plan to have couples giving birth in the orbit. The proposal was turned down by the McLaughlin couple. I think Mrs. McLaughlin has a pretty good idea about the possible outcome of this experiment."

At this point, the dismissed professor's suppressed contempt revealed itself in his comedian like gesture. His thin gray hair over his ears, the bald top, big round eyes, sharp nose, and thin lips gave him the appearance of a stage performer. Pointing his fore finger at Jeff, he said, "You know what, I thought you were the smartest black man I'd ever met. I expected a lot from you, considering the struggle you went through to reach where only a few could dream of. It's an irony that I have a bald head, while you carry the last name Baldman with a head full of thick curly hair. You should have been the last man to behave like a man owned by another. Listen Jeff, the Project Elenaut has a lot of loopholes in it. Loopholes which might cause it to collapse like a house of cards, and the plan to have the elenauts conceive up there is one of them. I won't be surprised if secret dungeons are found somewhere below the training facility or the shaft to hide the mutants produced by this experiment. This was one of the main reasons why I found myself in Mike's black book. I opposed the idea on humanitarian ground. We have no right to experiment with fetus like this. Every fetus has the right to develop naturally, under natural environment. Zero gravity is no natural environment for a fetus. I objected to the idea unequivocally and it's on record. Of course, I understand you don't see it that way for the sake of science. But at the end of the day, when things will fall apart, remember, your CEO won't take the fall for you. You'll be made the fall guy. You have proven your loyalty to an individual. Hence, you have been chosen."

"What could I do, Stan?"

"No Jeff, I didn't expect you to resign, but you could have pointed out the loopholes to the man, and the dangers of ignoring them, in a more acceptable way. I hear that you are clever with words, aren't you?"

"The man wouldn't listen, and you know it. He's bent on making this work within his budget. Keeping a lid on the cost is one of his priorities, and I understand why. Are we being fair to the man while criticizing? This is no government project. He has to convince his investors about the possible return."

"But slashing the cost in the wrong place, at the wrong time and wrong manner, is a recipe for disaster." The old professor paused for a second, raising his arms as if he wanted to surrender, and then continued, "Alright, alright, it's my fault. I should have given you some examples before getting into an argument. Do you know that the diagonal bracings of the shaft are made of plain steel?"

Jeff smiled as he replied, "Oh Stan you know the cost would have shot through the roof had we used the scarce alphiron for the entire structure."

"But your quake resistance equation assumes the whole structure is made of alphiron. Don't tell me you can't figure out the implication of this."

"The structure doesn't stand on the diagonal braces________,"

Come on Jeff, I didn't expect it from you. No, the structure doesn't stand on the diagonal braces, it stands on the horizontal braces, but those horizontal braces derive their strength from the diagonal braces. Now you tell me what that means."

"I didn't call you for a debate, Mike_______."

"Wait, that's just one part of the story, now tell me about the weather over there."

"It's cloudy. Most probably a storm is brewing. Why do you ask?"

"Have you noticed that the weather has been like this ever since we erected the shaft? I recommended an anti-ionization coating. Unfortunately, for keeping the cost down, it was ignored. The change you see in the weather is due to ionization induced by the shaft. Soon you'll have ice and sleet accumulating on the rails and the brackets, and of course, you're aware of the consequence, aren't you?"

"We have de-icing tools ready."

"For how long can you de-ice part of the structure which is twenty thousand feet tall? The sleet will form within minutes if not seconds after de-icing. If the recommended coating was used, both ionization and sleet would have been prevented."

"Stan, your concerns are well founded. The problem is, your position and mine are not same. You didn't have to wait after your dismissal, your previous employer was too happy to cover your back. On the other hand, I might have to wait for ages to get a suitable job. For this reason, I must be very careful how I raise these issues before Mike. Nonetheless, I promise I'll bring it up at the right moment. I owe it to Space Race. Now I expect some suggestions from you about the latest crisis we've been facing."

Having said so, Jeff paused, allowing the old professor to calm down. From his gesture it became clear that he was ready to listen. Subsequently, Jeff narrated to him the events after getting the quake alert. He said, already another shipment of building materials was on the way to the station. At the time they received the quake alert, both elevators had been on the third platform. According to CISN, quite a big quake could strike the region in the next few days. Now, I could recall the elevators, unload them, and send them back up for evacuating the elenauts, or let the elevators reach the orbit with the load. In that case, the elenauts and their robots have to unload the shipment before returning. It's a dilemma for both approaches have their pros and cons."

"The station has only one ramp, so even if they want to, they cannot unload the cargo simultaneously. They have to be done with one elevator, reposition the station, and then unload the other elevator. It'll take much longer. As I understand, time is what you don't have in plenty right now. How many handlers do you have in each of the elevators?" asked Professor Stan.

"Two in each."

"Alright, bring back one of those elevators. Let the other one reach the orbit. It'll take half the time unloading and securing the shipment of only one elevator. I assume, the elevator has only one forklift in it. So, with only one forklift it'll take at least two hours to unload all the pallets. Moving the pallets to their respective spots inside the warehouse would then take another two to three hours. Therefore, from the third platform to the warehouse in the orbit, the entire operation would require forty-eight to seventy-two hours to complete. And then of course, you'll be bringing down your elenauts. If your luck runs out before that, I have no idea how it's going to turn out."

In his revolving chair, Jeff had been sitting with hand to his chin. He looked troubled by what lay ahead of him. The old professor felt pity for his former associate. He no longer displayed the contempt for what had happened. With reassuring words, he tried to encourage Jeff.

He said, "Jeff, it's pointless worrying about what might happen. Space Race has the brightest engineers and scientists, and therefore, even if events don't unfold smoothly, they know how to handle every possible scenario."

Jeff had to nod at the last part of Professor Stan's speech, and then came to the point what had been troubling him. He was obviously very nervous when he asked, "Stan, is the structure going to hold?"

"I don't know, Jeff. Let's just hope for the best." ***

At the gate of the Space Station, the blinking red lights, and the blaring siren heralded the arrival of the elevator.

Cindy and Trevor watched from the bridge as Greg led the team supervising the unloading. The forklift and the exoskeletons were being used by the androids. The pallets piled up in the space before the decompression chamber. Cindy sent Andrew and Mark to the warehouse for receiving the pallets and placing them at the designated spots. Greg suggested to Cindy that artificial gravity be turned off for the convenience of transportation, or else the heavy pallets had to be dragged to the assembly plant. The risk associated with loading or unloading under zero gravity made Trevor object to the idea. However, taking into consideration the time factor, Cindy went with Greg's suggestion, telling Mother to shut down artificial gravity. All the doors from the gate of the decompression chamber to the assembly plant were kept wide open so that the pallets could simply float to the intended location.

One by one, like a freight train, the pallets began floating in the direction of the assembly plant with just a slight push. At the other end, Andrew grabbed the pallets and pushed them down through the opening in the floor of the assembly plant, and into the warehouse where mark placed them onto slots with bolt locks. As the operation neared completion, the lights began flickering, signaling some sort of breakdown in power supply. Mother's cold, lifeless voice warned them of a breakdown in the fusion reactor. The intervals between light and darkness began growing. For a second or so, Andrew was distracted by the flickering lights and Mother's repeated warnings. His reflexes failed him the moment darkness disappeared. Andrew noticed the pallet only a few feet from him, pushing him and eventually slamming him onto the metal wall of the assembly plant.

A cold chill went through Cindy's spine as they watched the accident occurring right before their eyes. They heard Andrew cry out in pain as the heavy pallet crushed him against the wall. From down below, Mark heard Andrew's cry. He sprung up to see what was going on. From the other end, Ted, Mehmet and Suzy rushed to the scene. Mark pushed the pallet to release trapped Andrew. Blood oozed out of Andrew's mouth when the pallet was pushed away. He stood there in upright position, as if he had been glued to the wall. Absence of gravity would not let him drop, but everyone could see that he was unconscious. Mark scanned him with his bio scanner. Two of his ribs were broken. The scanner did not register farther injuries.

Questions arose if the injured elenaut should be sent to the clinic inside the station or the one in the elevator. They also felt the need to run the diagnostic tools to find out the problem with the fusion reactor. Mother's initial report showed that the reactor was operational. Perhaps it was the result of a software malfunction, speculated Cindy. In the meantime, the power source was switched to solar panels, stopping the fluctuation in power supply.

For consultation, Trevor re-established communication with the ground control. Jeff looked disoriented by the news of the accident and power disruption. He felt like the world was closing in on him from all directions for he had already been troubled by the quake alert. Thin line of sweat appeared on his forehead. He loosened the knot of his tie as all eyes had been on him for directives.

Cindy could not comprehend why they had a fusion reactor for power supply instead of solar panels. When she finished briefing Jeff about the situation, she couldn't help asking, "Why do we have a fusion reactor for power? I thought solar panels were a safer option."

"The solar panels we have cannot provide the kind of power we need Mrs. McLaughlin. Apart from that, we have a plan for a space station the size of New York. Hence, the fusion reactor was a more viable option."

Upon saying this, Jeff struggled to breathe. His countenance rapidly took the appearance of a collapsing man. Everyone rushed to assist him, but the two android medics requested everyone to move away so that they could check his condition and administer medical aid. One of the robots scanned Jeff's system while the other one checked the pulse. Absence of pulse led to mouth-to-mouth resuscitation from the android's air sack while the other robot pressed down his chest for compression. The oral CPR continued for several minutes as the staff at the ground control and the elenauts in the orbit observed anxiously. When the method failed to revive Jeff, one of them swiftly removed the clothes from his chest, while the other one raised his two palms. The skin of the palms had slid under the wrists, exposing the metal underneath. The robot rubbed its palms for a few seconds before placing them on Jeff's chest. The patient's chest shook violently as the robot administered the shock. The voltage of the three consecutive shocks was gradually raised from two hundred to seventeen hundred. The spectators cheered as Jeff coughed after the third shock.

The robot scanning Jeff's system detected altogether twenty-three blockages, including three in the left anterior descending artery. It was a miracle that Jeff lived with so many blockages. The sheer number of blockages precluded any possibility of surgery or plaque removal by laser. The robot preparing the report recommended heart transplantation. Bypass surgery was yet another option, but the surgery would require much longer time, and even if successful, complications could arise in future. Bob had the printout of the report and the recommendations in his hand. He needed Jeff's approval before he could let the robots go for any of the options. Jeff was then moved to the clinic, and as soon as his vital signs stabilized a bit, Bob sat next to his bed, softly telling him about his condition. Once the recommendations had been read out, Jeff knew Bob needed his approval to proceed. He gestured to Bob to get the bio-metric device. Bio-metrically he gave his consent for the transplant surgery. TB2 was the most successful artificial heart genetically developed from the stem cells. However, it had to be transported from the US Heart Foundation in Dallas, more than two thousand kilometers from the ground control. His father's rockerjet was the first thing to cross his mind when Bob was told about the TB2 because he knew that was the only place where it was available in the US.

Luckily, the craft was available after the monthly servicing it went through. Mike didn't hesitate to lend it when he heard about Jeff's condition. He also instructed his pilots not to use the usual flight route. Instead, they were to fly the trajectory used by re-usable aero-space vehicles. This would considerably reduce the flight time, hence, expediting transportation of the valuable cargo.

As the craft was about to land on the tarmac with its precious cargo, the dark clouds, the swirling dust and fog, and the darkness of the approaching storm formed an eerie picture. The chopping noise of the rotors added an extra dimension to it. Two androids stood at the tarmac, waiting for the craft to settle down. They climbed up the stairs, and in the next few minutes, received a refrigerated box containing the cargo.

While the androids carried the box, Jeff had been shifted to the operating theatre of the clinic. Six medical androids were assigned for the urgent surgery. A conspicuous glass wall surrounded the operating theatre, allowing the physicians and the experts to have a view of the entire procedure. One of the robots, referred to as sterilized incubator pump, had a cylindrical shaped body, limbs and a head with scanners and sensors. The hands of every humanoid had been transformed into laser scalpel, scissors, speculum, ready for versatile functions like incisions, drilling, zapping the targeted organs with laser, and stitching or gluing together the organs. For the androids, it was an operation of the robotic assembly plant seen inside the flying car or aircraft plant.

As soon as the robots had sedated the patient, LHS-1 (Licensed Humanoid Surgeon) made incision with its laser tipped forefinger, while LHS-2 ripped apart the outer layer of the chest and held it tightly. Then the actual work of replacing the ailing heart commenced. One by one, LHS-1 and 3 severed the arteries coming in and out of the heart, connecting and fusing them with the artificial arteries popping out of the SIP, in a matter of seconds. During the surgery, from one end of the heart, LHS-4 kept injecting killer micro robots into the blood vessels, while LHS-5 kept retrieving them from the other end with a magnetic device. LHS-6 was busy spraying the air over the operating table with disinfectant and getting rid of the unwarranted bleeding with a suction tube.

In little over an hour, the surgery was over. The brand-new heart had been transplanted, and Jeff was moved to the chamber for the convalescent. A sense of relief had returned among the colleagues, while Bob focused his attention on the crisis brewing in the orbit. Earlier, Mike officially declared his son the acting CEO until farther notice. Now Bob was free to handle everything the way he wanted to. Albeit only thirty-two, ten years of service with the Space Race prepared him for the post he held after his father's temporary departure.

Bob was aware of the danger from the fusion reactor. However, he didn't want to demoralize the spirit of the elenauts. He kept quiet. He needed to be certain of the problem with the power source. He turned his attention to

Cindy and said, "Mrs. McLaughlin, please brief us about the situation up there."

"The solar panels have restored the power, though I'm not sure for how long," replied Cindy, and then added, "right now, mentally and physically, we're all ready to return."

"Don't worry, the power will last as long as the solar panels are turned in the right direction, and the sun is not blocked from the station for long. Now I want you to run the diagnostic tools for the main power source. It'll take approximately fifteen to twenty minutes."

"When do you want us to begin our descent?" Cindy asked anxiously.

"Oh yeah, that's another pressing issue. You sound homesick. Don't you feel safe up there?"

"We just don't want to get stuck, in case something happens to the shaft. Besides, now we have a member with broken ribs. He needs surgery, and Mark alone cannot perform the surgery. We have the facility up here, but not the necessary manpower."

"For your information, I think half of your humanoid associates are licensed surgeons. Where is your patient right now?"

"In the clinic."

"Shift him to the elevator's clinic. You are going to start the descent right after you get the diagnostic report on the condition of the main power source."

Cindy decided to stay in the bridge for the diagnostic report, while asking Trevor to shift Andrew and the belongings of the elenauts to the elevator.

After the accident in the assembly plant Cindy asked Mother to activate the artificial gravity. On a wheeled hospital bed, Andrew was taken to the elevator by Anna and one of the androids. The rest of the elenauts began packing their luggage for the return journey.

As soon as the report was in, Cindy passed it down to the ground control. The reactor was still running, and the diagnostic tool found no problem with the reactor's operating system. The steam turbine malfunctioned due to a crack in one of the turbine blades. To fix it, Mother recommended replacing the entire turbine wheel. To Cindy, the recommendation didn't make any sense.

She said, "Bob, why do we have to replace the whole turbine wheel? Why don't we just replace the broken blade?"

"It's simpler than replacing just one single blade, the new wheel comes with a new set of blades attached to it. Placing the blades on the wheel is a complicated task for it's the most delicate part of the turbine. The angle of the blade must be consistent with the other blades, there's no room for discrepancy. Apart from that, the blades are fused with the wheel to prevent unwarranted vibrations. In other words, the blades come with the wheel." At this point Bob paused for a moment, and continued with a sigh, "I'm not really troubled by the broken turbine for I know none of you, including the robots you have, are qualified to do it. Even if you could, we simply don't have the time. It would take hours even if the robots were to do it."

"Then why do you look so petrified? Let's just get the hell out of here," Cindy exclaimed.

"The ramp has to be detached from the decompression chamber, or else the quake could bring down the station along with the shaft."

"And what's so complicated here? Before boarding the elevator, we'll retract the ramp remotely from the decompression chamber."

"And for that you need power to the ramp Cindy."

"Are you trying to say the ramp isn't connected to the solar panels?"

"Yes, the ramp gets its power from the main power source."

"I don't understand why you people designed it this way."

"The ramp requires plenty of power, it would use up half of the stored power in just a few minutes, and the ramp is just one of the features of the station requiring substantial amount of power. When you re-align the thrusters or the shield, they require plenty of power too. Solar panels we have right now cannot produce that kind of power in a sustainable manner. Hence, it's designed to support only the basic requirements such as life support, lightings etc."

"So, how do we retract the ramp from the decompression chamber?"

"You can't retract it from there without any power source connected to it. You must retract it manually from the gate of the station. There are two wheels on either side of the gate. They must be turned simultaneously."

"It means someone has to stay behind. I'm sorry, not one but two people have to stay behind since the wheels have to be turned simultaneously," Cindy fumed in a clearly upset tone.

"Yes, and there's more to it ______,"

Cindy would not let Bob finish when she exclaimed, "More to it! What did you guys get us into, Bob?"

In order to appease Cindy, Bob raised his arms, and in a conciliatory tone said, "Calm down, please calm down Mrs. McLaughlin. No one plans for accidents. Accidents are just part of life. How you handle them, tells what you're made of."

"Enough of your motivating lectures Bob. Now tell us what else we have to do."

"That's much better," a paused followed, while Bob took a deep breath. Then very softly he said, "The reactor is still running, but the power produced has no way out. As a result, pressure has been building up."

Now Cindy realized the gravity of what Bob had been trying to convey. For a moment she closed her eyes, trying to visualize the horror that awaits them. Almost like a whisper she said, "Are we looking at a possible melt down?"

Bob couldn't say anything, he just nodded.

"Why don't we shut down the reactor?" Cindy knew there was definitely a very good reason. Still, she wanted to hear it from Bob."

"It's a long and complicated procedure. We have the people down here who can do it, but in this kind of situation, we can't send them up there, Mrs. McLaughlin."

All this time Cindy had no idea Trevor was right behind her. He had finished packing their belongings and assigned a humanoid to carry the luggage to the elevator. The other elenauts were also on their way to the elevator. Cindy did not expect Trevor to return so quickly. Quietly, he had heard everything, so he didn't hesitate to intervene. He said to Bob, "Let's not waste precious time in irrelevant talk about what could have been. Tell us what our options are."

"Mr. McLaughlin, some of you have to stay behind. We're looking at a possible melt down."

"How much time do we have?" Trevor asked.

"Maximum forty-eight hours. It can happen earlier. It depends on the rate at which the pressure has been building up."

"What do you want us to do?"

"We're going to discard the reactor ___________,"

"Discard the reactor! How the hell are we going to discard the reactor?" exclaimed Trevor.

"There's no need to be so excited Mr. McLaughlin. Please calm down and pay attention to what I have to say." Bob wanted to make sure that his audience was paying attention, so he paused for a moment, and then continued, "The entire complex housing the reactor, the turbine and the generator, is connected to the station by ten metal beams. Those beams, along with the air-bridge, are attached to the outer wall of the station by means of locking devices. Each locking device has a lever the size of a small boy. When the lever is pulled, the device unlocks and detaches the complex from the station. Once the complex is detached, it must be physically pushed away as far as possible."

"Pushing away the entire complex the size of a football field!" exclaimed Trevor, and the next moment it occurred to him that in space, size and weight didn't matter. Subsequently, he changed his tone, and said, "Oh yeah, it's space, I forgot."

Bob smiled at him and said, "You'll need two people to do it. Now you decide which one of you will stay behind."
***

# Chapter Nineteen

The packed courtroom had been awaiting a verdict when the door of the courtroom opened and general Normandy, escorted by his adjutant and a military police man, entered. All of them were dressed immaculately in line with the military tradition. The medals and the ribbons on the coat spoke loudly of the general's military career, quantifying all his achievements.

The adjutant held a rather short note in his hand. He asked for the permission of the court to pass it to the judge. Upon being given the permission, with due respect, the adjutant approached the judge, and handed him the note. The following minute, the judge read the note very carefully, passing it to the jury for their opinion when he was done. On behalf of the Pentagon, general Normandy asked for the opportunity to submit evidence to expedite the case. One by one, the five members of the jury browsed through the note. They were fully aware of the significance of the note. By nodding their heads, they gave their consent to the judge. Finally, the military establishment had changed their previous stance, and decided to reveal the evidence connecting Lillian's murder to the real culprits. The evidence exposed the real motive of the murder. Hence, saved the day for the beleaguered defendant.

The final deliberation exonerated the defendant of all charges. The news channels somehow noticed the defendant's gloomy countenance. When they asked about the possible reason, as usually the case, his attorney intervened, rescuing his client from farther scrutiny. ***

"What!" exclaimed Trevor when Cindy said she wanted to be with him in the mission to save the station from a nuclear melt down. He was dismayed by her frantic response. He stared right back at her, and said, "You are the team leader, you need to be with the rest of team."

Don't worry, the team will survive without me. By now, every member knows what to do in any kind of emergency."

"No honey I can't let you do that. I'm full of praise for your leadership. You have already shown your metal. Now let me handle the rest. This is not the time or the place for an argument, so please desist. I won't listen to your demand, not now. I have seen those levers out there. They are quite heavy. This is simply not the job for you. I'll take Sage with me. Now go, join the rest of the team in the elevator. They have been waiting for you. I'm confident, you are going to get them home safely. When you see them, send Sage to me. Tell him we have a mission for him."

Cindy knew her husband all too well. His gestures, his voice, his look told her he was not going to budge. This was one of those rare moments when she felt powerless against him. She had to listen to him. She lowered her gaze, indicating her compliance. The next moment she put her arms around his neck and drew him closer. Almost like a whisper, she uttered, "Listen you heartbreaker, I don't want to return to an empty home. Don't you dare break my heart."

"How many times did I disappoint you, sweetheart?"

"Let this be the first and the last time."

"I'm sorry honey, I had to do it. Pray for us, will you?"
***

Cindy found the rest of the team, anxiously waiting for her in front of the decompression chamber. The elenauts had already shifted their belongings to the elevator. They were a bit surprised to find Cindy alone. The question in their eyes demanded an explanation about Trevor's absence. Very gently Cindy explained, "Trevor has decided to stay behind. The reactor complex needs to be detached and safely disposed. At any moment there could be a nuclear melt down." Then she turned to Sage, and said, "Sage, you have been a wonderful associate. We are proud to have you in our team. Now you have one last mission before we go home. Trevor needs your assistance in discarding the reactor complex." A brief pause allowed Cindy to organize what she was going to say next. She said, "I don't know if you can feel how we humans feel when we say goodbye to friends in this kind of situation. Let me say it again, you have been a good friend to us all. A friend we could trust, a friend we could count on. We know you don't need any protective suit, but still, I want you to wear the especial suit. You might need it. On behalf of my team, I wish you the best, and make sure that you bring back my man in one piece. Farewell my friend, farewell."

After a warm handshake, the humanoid walked away with steady steps towards the bridge where Trevor had been expecting him. From the locker, they took out the specially made suits equipped with miniature rocket thrusters. They also carried with them several explosive devices, laser cutter, communication box, and a toolbox before heading for the other decompression chamber with an exit to the exterior of the station.

Inside the decompression chamber, Trevor stared at Sage with pity, not quite sure who should be the object of pity. With a faint smile on his lips, he said, "Sage, do you feel sorry for yourself?"

"I don't understand, why you ask me this question. Why should I feel sorry? I have my eyes on the very purpose behind my creation, and I'm glad, of all the androids, I have been chosen to assist you in this dangerous mission."

"By the way, what do you think is the purpose behind your creation?"

"Serving mankind."

Trevor laughed quietly, and then asked, "Are you sure, serving the CEO of your company isn't the real purpose?"

"Yes, I'm sure. I do not have any directive like that in my operating system."

"Glad to have you with me buddy," Trevor remarked while gently slapping the humanoid's upper arm.

As the count down in the display above the door hit zero, the door slid open.

"Don't use the thrusters now, we're going to need the fuel. Let us just use our limbs for movements as long as possible. As they stepped out, Sage connected the safety line to the hook beside the exit. Instead of moving freely in space, both Trevor and Sage had their grip on the exterior of the station while moving towards the beams connecting the reactor complex to the station. ***

The other elenauts, except Greg and Anna, sat right behind Cindy. At the rear of the three columns, were the androids. Greg and Anna were next to Cindy while Mark was with his patient in the clinic, strapped to their respective seat and bed. The androids wore lab suits, but others had to be in their space suits, making the descent somewhat uncomfortable. The sheer thrill of the ascent only a few weeks back was replaced by constant consternation. All of them knew, at any moment a quake could strike them. What would happen if the magnitude of the quake exceeded the threshold? This unpleasant question hung heavy in the hearts of the elenauts.

When they commenced the descent, it was six in the morning. By the time they reached the second platform from the top, it was quarter past six. The androids used the forklift to transport the pallet having the luggage and boxes to the next elevator. They were no longer under the zero gravity environments. Hence, the march towards the next elevator was rather slow and tiresome. The two android medics carried Andrew on a stretcher while Mark stayed next to them to see if his patient needed anything. Cindy was the last one to leave the first descending elevator. Before stepping out, she glanced at the interior again. The elevator had different paint work. Everything else was identical. As she sighed, the headset in his helmet crackled. It was Bob. He said, "Is everything okay with you guys?"

"So far, we haven't faced any troubles. I'm about to step out of the top elevator. The other members of my team are already on their way to the next elevator."

"Mrs. McLaughlin, Dr. Straus would like to talk to you about Andrew. He's our chief medical officer down here. Please brief him about Andrew's condition."

"Go ahead, give him the micro-phone."

"Hello Mrs.  McLaughlin."

"Hello Dr. Straus, I can hardly hear you. The signal is quite poor over here. You have to be a bit louder."

"Mrs. McLaughlin, I would like to hear from you about Mr. Fergusen's condition. I have seen his x-ray and ultra-sono report. How does he feel right now?"

"He has been sleeping; I hope he's well," Cindy replied.

"Tell you what, connect me to your camera, let me have a look at him."

"He's not with me right now. He has been carried to the clinic inside the next elevator. I'm on my way to it now. I'll hook you up with Mark's camera. He's with him right now."

"Alright, you might as well do that."

At sixty thousand feet, the dark space above the earth's exosphere was clearly visible. Cindy pulled down the night vision goggle over her visor, to see what had been happening to the station up there. She did not notice separation of the reactor complex from the main module of the station. She glanced at his watch, perhaps it was too early. Then she turned around. At other times the spectacular panoramic view would have fired up her imagination. This time around, she just sighed, and resumed moving towards the next elevator.

Inside the elevator, another unexpected crisis greeted Cindy. Though he was put to sleep, no one noticed that Andrew had been bleeding through his nose and mouth. When the dark visor was lifted, to give Dr. Straus a glimpse of Andrew's condition, the bleeding was exposed.

"Oh God, look at that!" exclaimed Suzy who had not yet occupied her seat in the elevator.

Mark was about to remove Andrew's helmet when Dr Straus yelled, "Don't! Check the cabin pressure."

Cindy had not yet entered the elevator.

"Mrs. McLaughlin, you have to hurry, we have a situation in here," through his microphone, Mark yelled.

By the time Cindy arrived, the vital signs of Andrew had dropped below the danger level.

"Close the door and pressurize the cabin," yelled Dr. Straus.

In the next ten seconds when the cabin pressure had been normalized, the veteran doctor continued, "Take off his suit and tell one of your androids to get ready for a CPR. He must have lost plenty of blood due to internal injury."

"But I sealed the vessels with laser," said Mark.

"The injury is somewhere else, most probably his lungs have been damaged," responded Dr. Straus in a tense tone.

"The x-ray and ultra-Sono report showed nothing," remarked Mark.

"They won't, you need CT scan detecting bleeding from the lung's walls. If you can't stop the drop in his vital signs, he's going to have an angina due to low diastolic blood pressure. Right away, administer a shot of EpiPen. If it doesn't prevent the drop in his vital signs get ready for a CPR and infusion of blood. You're going to need a surgery to stop the bleeding in the next half an hour.

"Surgery in this flimsy clinic!" Cindy objected.

At this point Bob intervened from the ground control. He said, "Mrs. McLaughlin, from laser scalpel to endotracheal tube, this flimsy clinic has every little tool you need for a successful surgery, and as surgeons, you have four LHS (licensed humanoid surgeons) robots among the androids. Of course, Dr. Paski is there for supervision, and from down here, Dr. Straus will be monitoring the surgery. The clinic has a small blood bank as well. We knew something like this might happen. Subsequently, we equipped all our elevator clinics with the state-of-the-art medical tools. I guess you never had a good look at the infirmaries, did you?"

"No, I didn't. I never thought it would come to this," Cindy admitted with a sigh.

"Trust us, we have invested generously so that our elenauts have the best chance in any given situation."

Soon after EpiPen had been administered, Andrew's diastolic blood pressure stabilized. In ten to fifteen minutes, the humanoid surgeons got ready, EpiPen had lent them the time to prepare for the operation.

In the meantime, the descent to the third platform began. Cindy was to facilitate the surgery when the elevator had reached the platform. Through the portholes, the team could see the sunrise over the eastern horizon. Ever since the mission started, one after one, it was plagued by sad incidents. During a conversation it came out of Anna. She said that the project could be jinxed. The team members laughed at her and scorned her for being so reckless about her remark. If it had leaked out, she could have been ousted from the project. This kind of remark from a team member had the potential to damage the image of the company. However, privately they admitted, they felt pretty much the same way.

Cindy could feel the sinking feeling of her crew as the elevator descended. Her eyes had been closed when she felt Anna's hand over hers.

"Don't worry, things will work out fine in the end," Anna whispered to her team leader.

Cindy sensed something in Anna's voice which consolidated her confidence. "Thank you so much Anna, I needed it," Cindy responded very softly.

"You have been a great team leader. We have no complaints. I guess luck has been conspiring against us," Anna added.

Greg heard what Anna said. He said, "Don't blame everything on luck. We had our fault too. We were being reckless when we shifted the cargo under zero gravity. Faster is not always better."

Cindy felt betrayed by Greg's remark. She said, "Sometimes faster is the key to survival. The tragedy has been imposed on us, first by the quake alert, and then by the power failure. Of course, you could argue that Andrew should have been more careful, but it would not have occurred had there been no failure in the power source. In this kind of situation, even a second matters. The darkness that preceded the incident affected Andrew's judgment. The bottom line is, we cannot turn the clock back."

"I'm sorry for being so insensitive," Greg apologized.

"You're not being brutally factual Greg, you're being partly factual, and it's worse than being totally wrong. When someone is totally wrong, people just laugh, but when someone is partly factual, people are misguided for it creates an illusion of being the whole truth."

"Whoo, heavy staff!" Greg tried to brighten up the atmosphere, and then added, "Anyway, I apologize, I didn't mean to offend anyone."

"Apology accepted, let's move on guys," having her confidence restored, Cindy said calmly. ***

The noise of the blaring alarm tossed Eileen from her bed. Habitually she stared at the clock on the end table. It was seven in the morning. She was asleep when the first shock rattled her bed. The seismic recorder was connected to the clock, recording the magnitude and exact time of the shock. As she stood up, she felt the second shock. It was a lot milder than what she had expected. She rushed to the toilet. She was going to have a very long day. She wanted to be totally prepared before heading for her office. In five minutes, she was out in the lawn of the home where she had been lodging for the last few months. Her landlords were a retired couple in their sixties. They were also out in the open. She advised them to stay out for the next few hours.

Like a frisbee, Eileen's vehicle flew only a few feet from the ground. When she rode like this, she always made sure the wheels had been deployed, instead of tucked inside the vehicle's chassis. It was a precautionary measure, in case the vehicle touched the road.

Eileen wanted to call her associates. She hesitated for she had been flying too close to the ground. A slight distraction could end up in disaster. To activate the autopilot or auto drive, she had to climb to three hundred meters or drive on the road. A quake could throw the vehicle off the road, so she increased the speed and climbed to three hundred meters before giving the control to the onboard computer.

The first thing she heard from Jones was, "Did you feel the jolt Eileen, did you feel the jolt?"

Jones was in Noah's vehicle. His voice sounded more like a trumpet. He was clearly very excited as he received Eileen's hologram call. The loud rap music inside Noah's vehicle annoyed Eileen. Noah's pearl like teeth glistened against his black face as he hailed Eileen.

"Noah, would you please turn down the volume? I can hardly have a conversation," Eileen pleaded with Noah.

As Noah brought the volume to a tolerable level, Eileen continued, "Are you guys coming to the lab?"

"Yes, we would like to track the epicenter of the quake," Jones replied.

"I thought so. I'm heading for the lab too. I think we need to visit the farm as well."

"I don't think it's a good idea, all of us visiting the farm at this time," Jones remarked.

"No, no, I don't want the whole team to be there. Let Noah and Rakesh visit the farm. We two can monitor the events from the lab," Eileen suggested.

Noah, who had been silent all this time, asked, "Eileen, what will happen if the towering behemoth crashes down on us?"

"What are you talking about?" Eileen sounded confused.

Jones explained, "He's talking about the Space Race elevator shaft."

No signs of anxiety or alert were visible in Eileen as she replied, "I don't know Noah, I find the prospect quite worrisome though. Perhaps this is why they've built it in the middle of the desert."

Noah wasn't convinced. He continued, "It's eighty miles tall, do you think it might come crashing down over our heads?"

Eileen took it as a joke. She laughed as she replied, "Don't worry Noah, we're out of its range."

"Are you sure? From now on, I'm thinking of wearing those hard hats," with a grin Noah remarked.

Jones could not help but laugh when he remarked, "Do you think your hard hat is going to save you from the two-thousand-ton behemoth? You better dig a rabbit hole, Noah." ***

At the lab, Eileen and Jones worked frantically, collecting and deciphering data received from their seismogram. Eileen told Jones to get print out of the readings while she prepared a report for the head office at Pasadena. As soon as the report was prepared, she sent it to the head office for evaluation, along with the seismogram readings. At Pasadena, data from across the US were going to be collected. It would take an hour to assess and then figure out the epicenter of the latest quakes.

The third wave of tremors struck a few minutes after Eileen had sent the data to Pasadena. The shock waves continued for more than a minute this time around. Something was wrong with the seismogram. On the display, they could see no fluctuation in the pulses. Jones ran to the lawn outside to check if the seismograph and seismometer dug into the ground had been functioning properly. He reset them to ensure they captured the vibrations accurately. The seismograph responded to the new setting and produced the desired result. The magnitude of the latest jolt was 3.2 Richter scale. Apparently, the tremors had been getting weaker. This trend puzzled Eileen and her associate because they had expected a devastating blow.

No sooner had the third wave of shocks dissipated, the cold artificial voice of the communication device announced an incoming call from CBN, a local news channel.

"Hello there, I'm Daniel Hunt from CBN news," the news anchor greeted Eileen.

"Hello, I'm Eileen Molone from CISN," Eileen responded with a tense voice.

Like a professional, the anchor went straight to the point. He said, "Ms. Malone, we have been getting reports of quakes from across the west coast. Is this what you warned us of a few days back?"

"Yes, it is. We thought it was due a week earlier though. That's how these events are, you never know exactly when or where they are going to strike."

The anchor would not let Eileen continue. He said, "Earlier we were warned of a very devastating quake, but what we have experienced so far, doesn't really fall into that category. What do you have to say about it?"

Eileen looked a bit annoyed by this inconvenient question. She remarked, "I don't understand how you guys have come to this conclusion that it's over. Often smaller foreshocks precede a massive quake. This might well be the case this time around. So, I ask everyone not to lower their guards yet, and thank you for your cooperation."

Eileen disconnected the line the moment she had finished her statement. She didn't want any more awkward questions from the anchor. ***

Meanwhile, the picture at the Yuba Farm took both Noah and Rakesh by surprise. The chaotic scene they had encountered the previous day no longer persisted. The animals had been in the open fields, hardly making any noise or movements, while workers attended to their daily routine.

"Your drones have been quite useful to us, Mr. Bates," Noah remarked as they completed their tour.

 Mr. bates had been standing before his residence with a pale face when he replied, "We've been trying our best. You gotta give us some feedback."

"So far there have been no damages or casualties in any of the cities or counties. The tremors were unexpectedly milder. We hope the entire saga will be over within a week or so. We've been lucky, lucky, lucky!" reassured Noah with a smile while nodding wildly.

Obviously, this was what Mr. Bates wanted to hear. He nodded his head to express his pleasure, smiled back and said, "I like the sound of it. I like the sound of it." ***

# Chapter Twenty

Ever since Michael returned from Mr. Kruger's office, he had been drinking. He dismissed the entire staff managing his mansion and estate until farther notice, the very moment he had returned to his billion-dollar estate. The day at the court was nerve wrecking. He needed to be alone. He felt like the world had crashed down on him like a heavy hammer. His acquittal offered little reason for celebration, albeit his attorney saw it differently. He roamed around the place, emptying bottle after bottle of the hard liquor. Sometimes he would cry, and at other times he would laugh uncontrollably. He would swear at Lillian, "You did it bitch! You did it! I hope you burn in hell now!" And then he would whimper at his late wife, "I'm sorry honey, I shouldn't have taken you there. I had no idea this would happen!"

By the time the first tremors struck his estate at seven in the morning, Michael was totally intoxicated, drowning in his miseries. He was unrecognizable with his untidy hair hanging over his ears, his eyes drooping, his cuffs unbuttoned, and his shirt dangling out of his belt. He still had his shoes on as he stumbled across the great hall-room and the adjacent lawn which was separated by a huge glass door. For a while he tried to kick the empty gasoline cans. He swayed as he tried to stand still before aiming at the cans with his right foot. The pungent odor of gasoline dampened the air of the ground floor. Apparently, Michael did not miss anything, spraying gasoline over every item with the help of a nozzle fitted to the neck of the gasoline cans.

When he sensed the ground had been shaking, he slurred out, "Even the world cheers at my miseries!" Raising his two arms like an opera conductor, he spun on his feet like a ballet dancer with a bottle of whisky in his hand. He would stop, swallow the liquor, and then resume spinning, while trying the tune of the American anthem as best as he could. When the ground had stopped shaking, he stomped on it, shouting, "What's the matter, don't like it anymore? Whad ya know, the generals came to me, waving the flag, waving the godamn flag!"

A brief pause followed as he threw the bottle away and yawned.

"Jesus, I need a good sleep!" he stammered, and then added, "when I'm done with this sacred business of mine!"

A cigar was next in line. Carefully placing the lighter in his pant pocket, he began making circles with the exhaled smoke. Abruptly, it occurred to him that the occasion demanded befitting music. The audio system was on voice command mode, all he had to do was utter the track and the heavy bass of the music filled the great hall-room. The music had transported Michael to the world of fantasy when his hand took out the lighter, lit it, and threw the flicker onto the thick Persian carpet. The carpet simply exploded, turning the great hall-room into a raging inferno within seconds. ***

Captain Rayan Smith had just begun his paper-works when the blaring siren threw him into a frenzy. The satellite in service with the Hanford Fire Department reported fire at 54 Grangeville Boulevard. Everyone in the town knew who lived there.

"Holy shit!" cried out the fire chief as he sprung up from his seat. He, his deputy Jim Rodney, and Nancy Barn were the only human staff members of the Hanford Fire

Department. The rest were all humanoid robots made from anti-flammable substances. There outer shell could withstand extremes of heat and cold. Captain Smith called out to his deputy, while putting on his traditional fire suit and hat.

Hanford Fire Department had five androids working for the department. These self-sustainable robots didn't require food, rest, or re-creation. Above all, they were expandable under the most atrocious of circumstances one could imagine. Hence, they were the ideal candidates for the highly risky missions. These androids were of E-2161 series with embedded intelligence at its best. They carried their individual names given by their owners. Chuck, Morris and Doug had been servicing the brand-new fire truck while Hawk, Condor, and Eagle worked on the older ones.

The brand-new fire truck was the pride of the Hanford Fire Department, incorporating features, only a handful of fire trucks in the country could boast of. Though it could not fly, its sheer size ensured that it could carry the entire fire department with it. It boasted a command-and-control center, a drone, and a specially built water tank with sprinklers attached to its belly. The tank was designed like a hovercraft, able to lift itself to a height of a few hundred meters from the ground. This flying tank also carried $CO_2$ canisters which acted like bombs. These bombs extinguished a flame in two stages. At first, the explosion used up the oxygen in the area of deployment, hence, depriving the flame of its fuel. The remaining pockets of fire were then enveloped by a layer of $CO_2$ released from the canisters. The optical devices and the infra-red sensors installed in the drone conveyed to the operator of the flying tank the location and intensity of the flame, and from the command center, the operator guided the tank to its optimum position. Thus, the operator of the flying water tank used the craft like an attack drone.

The fire chief didn't expect to find his deputy in front of the dressing room, ready to accompany him to the Stewart Mansion. With his brows raised, he frowned, "Where the hell are you going?"

"Are you sure Smith, you don't wanna take me with you?" asked Jim who was disappointed by the fire chief's tone.

Smith lowered his voice, and said, "I want you to stay here with Nancy. We have been receiving plenty of distress calls. We might get emergency calls from other places. If you receive such a call, take Hawk and Eagle with you, and get to the spot. I'm taking Doug and Morris with me. Nancy will stay here with Condor and coordinate our activities. I have a feeling, these small tremors we've been having, are just foreshocks. The big one's coming."

"Whatever you say, you're the chief," with a smile Jim responded. He watched the fire chief slide down the fire pole while Doug and Morris waited for him in the truck. With the siren blaring from the roof of the truck, Doug drove it like a professional. The fire chief sat next to him, getting briefed by the police chief who had been at the scene. Morris stood at the rear of the truck with his hand telling other motorists to maintain safe distance from the truck.

On Saturday morning there was hardly any traffic on the road. Most of the vehicles were seen using the holoways. When the truck reached the Grangeville Boulevard, pedestrians watched curiously as the truck rushed towards the other end of the boulevard.

The two chiefs were well acquainted. Hence, Smith skipped the usual greetings, and asked, "Did you people see anyone coming out of the mansion?"

The police chief was a tall, thin man with a clean shaved appearance. His crew cut grey hair was hidden under his police cap which looked bigger for his relatively small head. With his thumbs tucked in, his hands hung from the belt as he approached the fire chief. "We have been here for an hour, we saw nothing," the police chief reported.

"Doug, take the hose and get inside. Morris you take the axe and break open the gate and then see if you can find anyone alive," the fire chief told his humanoid subordinates. Upon setting them up for the task in hand, the fire chief climbed up into the command-and-control center, turning on the communication devices, the remote control for the drone and the flying tank. As soon as the drone became active, Smith fed into it the necessary commands and the co-ordinates of the designated target. In the next couple of minutes, the drone commenced relaying the images and other necessary data. The eastern part of the mansion had already been raged to the ground, while the rest of the mansion was partially damaged. The drone guided the flying water tank to a position over the central part of the mansion where the flame had been burning most intensely. It dropped three of its CO2 munitions, and the following explosions extinguished the flame in seconds. The sprinklers let lose a steady stream of water, killing in a few minutes, the remaining flickers.

Morris carried with him an unconscious man to the barricade of vehicles before the front gate of the mansion. By this time, an air ambulance had arrived at the scene. The unconscious man had third degree burn all over his body. The medics administered a kind of life saving gel which could reverse tissue damage. Soon after the air ambulance had left, it was revealed that the sprinklers inside the mansion had been turned off.

The fire chief stared at the police chief, and in a somber tone said, "It's an irony, isn't it? This is the man who donated the brand-new fire truck to the Hanford Fire department." ***

"Mark, stop the procedure, the shaft is shaking!" Cindy shouted.

"We can't, not now, the bleeding must be stopped, or else we're going to lose him," Mark howled back.

The operation table rattled, but the jolts could not stop the androids. One by one, they zapped the injured spots in the lungs. Before the third shock, the surgery was completed. During the third wave of shocks, the ground control discovered that the ramp connecting the space station to the shaft had not been retracted.

"Sage, the ramp has not been retracted. Stop whatever you're doing! Go back into the station. Take Mr. McLaughlin with you and retract the ramp. On the double, on the double!" Bob exclaimed.

"We still have four levers that need to be unlocked," Trevor reported.

"Don't worry, Mr. McLaughlin, you still have twenty minutes left. The first wave of foreshocks has already struck us. The big one could bring the station down with the shaft, if you guys fail to retract the ramp," frantically, Bob conveyed to Trevor.

Sage and Trevor could no longer ignore the danger. As fast as they could, they rushed to the gate. When they had retracted twenty-meter ramp, Bob told Mother to use the

thrusters to move the station farther away from the shaft.
***

"Jones, we have the epicenter, it's hundred kilometers to the east from the San Andreas Fault Line," Eileen yelled.

Jones scrambled from his seat to get the printout of the report. He was halfway to the printer when the floor began shaking violently.

"It's the big one Jones, it's the big one!" Eileen cried out.

"Let's get out of here, the roof might collapse!" Jones shouted back at Eileen.

Like two drunk people, Jones and Eileen rushed out of their office building. The shock continued for more than a minute. From the open lawn, they could see, the sections of the city, just collapsing like card boxes. ***

"Hold on everyone!" Bob cried out, as the entire complex shook violently. Paints and plasters came off several spots of the roof and the walls.

On the ninety-six-inch LED screens, with sheer horror, everyone in the ground control watched the shaft sway like the treetop during a vicious storm. If the tremors continued, at any moment, the shaft would come crashing down.

"Mrs. McLaughlin, climb to three hundred meters from where you are," Bob suggested to Cindy.

Instead of asking, Cindy pushed the joystick forward. The abrupt upward movement made everyone dizzy. It took only thirty seconds to climb to the prescribed altitude. Then Bob explained that there were rails passing through diagonal braces, allowing for the elevator to be ejected safely like a capsule. The red ejection button was on the right arm rest of Cindy's seat. Once pressed, the thrusters attached to the side wall of the elevator would hurl it along the rails, eventually ejecting it out of the shaft. From the roof of the elevator four chutes would then be deployed to slow down the descent. ***

After the ramp had been retracted, through the transparent walls of the station, Trevor and Sage watched the shaft sway wildly. It wasn't a scenario Trevor wanted to see. He figured the magnitude of the tremor down there had to be more than eight Richter scale to make the shaft sway like that. In the past he studied the images of structures damaged by tremors of not more than five Richter scale. He did not dare imagine what was happening down there. The less than two minutes of the devastating quake seemed like an endless nightmare. At any moment, the shaft was going to crash. Trevor thought of Cindy and her companions when he felt the vibration in his pocket. *"The line is not down yet. It's a good sign,"* Trevor muttered to himself. Trevor's voice activated the hologram image of Cindy frantically trying to communicate with him.

"Honey, this may be our final moment. Pray for us. We're about to eject. The structure can't take it much longer. I have never felt tremors of this magnitude."

No sooner had Cindy finished, the transmission ended. Sage said something to Trevor, but he didn't respond. Sage raised his voice, and repeated, "Mr. McLaughlin, we should be moving."

Trevor came out of his worst nightmare. He said, "Yes, yes, I'm sorry, I should have paid attention to you. How much time do we have?"

"Fifteen minutes."

"I thought we had twenty!"

"In this kind of situation, people tend to lose track of time," the humanoid said in a cold tone.

"Alright, let's get back to work."

By then, the count-down to disaster up there had begun. *"Time flies like a cannon ball,"* whispered Trevor. When Trevor unlocked last piece of the lever, they had five minutes before the cataclysmic explosion. Earlier Trevor saved the fuel of their powerful thrusters for this moment. The thrusters were on full throttle, rapidly pushing the complex away from the station. Sage could see Trevor panting and sweating in his suit, more out of anxiety than exhaustion. Due to poor transmission and the loud noise of the thrusters, he could not clearly hear what Trevor was saying. Trevor realized and switched to hand gestures, conveying to Sage that they were going to push the complex for two and a half minutes before turning back, and taking shelter behind the protective shield and the station. Trevor wanted to wait behind the station when Sage said, "The station is going to be blown away or severely damaged, there's no point waiting here."

"Alright, let's dive into the atmosphere," Trevor yelled.

They had been at least eight kilometers from the station when the blast simply vaporized the shield and part of the station exposed to the blast. In the exosphere, Trevor managed to maintain the angle of dive required for a safe entry into the atmosphere. Sage was a few meters behind him. ***

Five seconds after being ejected from the shaft, the onboard system deployed the chutes. As the chutes had slowed down the rapid descent, communication with the ground control was restored. The scopes of the ground control had their focus on the space station and two tiny dots dropping through the upper atmosphere. From the elevator capsule, Cindy and her companions could also see the images, as they were connected to the communication device of the ground control.

With signs of utter horror in her eyes, Cindy watched Trevor lose his balance due to increased air pressure. Out of reflex, she screamed at him, "Trevor, don't give up! Sage, help him!"

"If he cannot stop the uncontrolled descent, it will break every piece of bone in his body," Bob remarked quietly.

Finally, Sage closed in, and grabbed his backpack containing the chute from the rear, thus stopping the uncontrolled descent. A loud applause and cheer filled the ground control and the elevator capsule which had just landed safely on the Mojave Desert. The jolt of the landing shook everyone inside the capsule. Cindy was the first one to unbuckle her seat belt. One by one the others followed. Cindy stepped forward and removed the curtain separating the clinic from the rest of the capsule. The androids were seated in their seats. The vital signs of Andrew were stable. Quite miraculously, he survived the ordeal. Cindy thanked the androids for what they had done for Andrew.

Before stepping out of the capsule, Cindy took off her suit and helmet, and advised others to do the same. During its descent, the wind drifted the capsule away from the structure. It landed miles from the compound perimeter. Cindy took a few steps away from the capsule. Far away, over the horizon, she could see the structure. There were no signs of the recovery team. Being exhausted, she returned to the capsule and sat on the exit of the capsule. A few minutes later, from behind the sand dunes, appeared the air ambulances. Five of them landed a few hundred meters from the capsule. From one of them, Bob stepped out, and walked straight to the capsule.

"Where is Trevor?" Cindy yelled at Bob.

"Look behind you," Bob responded.

Cindy turned and saw nothing at first. As her eyes got used to the bright light of the desert sun, she noticed the two specs dropping from the sky, couple of miles to the north.

"Take me there," she said to Bob.

"Just give me a few minutes. Let me have a look at Mr. Ferguson's condition."

When Bob entered, the rest of the team had been getting ready to come out with their belongings. Andrew was still on the wheeled bed of the clinic. Bob glanced at his vital signs and smiled. No sooner had Andrew been transferred to the stretcher, he regained his senses. Bob shook hands with him and congratulated him for making it back to the planet alive. Bob walked along the androids who had been carrying him to the air ambulance, waiting only a few hundred meters from the capsule. Bob boarded the air ambulance carrying Cindy. The rest of the elenauts and their humanoid companions shared the remaining four air ambulances.

On their way to pick up Trevor and Sage, Cindy hardly said anything to Bob. Bob understood her mental state, so he refrained from any type of conversation. The air ambulance skimmed over the desert surface at two hundred miles an hour. Trevor had regained his senses even before his chute was deployed at sixty thousand feet. He had a mildly strained neck. Otherwise, he was okay. Trevor and Sage landed on their feet almost simultaneously.

When the air ambulance reached the spot, Trevor and Sage had been busy managing their chutes. Cindy got off from the air ambulance and took a few steps towards her

husband approaching her with steady strides with the chute underneath his right arm. Trevor was limping slightly. Cindy didn't mind. She didn't care about his status. She just put her arms around his neck and passionately kissed Trevor. A few meters away, Bob and Sage smiled at the couple. To them, this was the best part of the whole saga.
***

Uninterruptedly, the news channels aired the images of utter destruction and miseries along the coast of the State of California. Parts of Arizona and Nevada was also affected by the devastating quake. The quake demolished wholly or partially more than sixty percent of the structures in the city of Los Angeles. Robots were in short supply. Hence, the city officials deployed dogs to sniff out the dead and the survivors from the piles of rubble across the stricken city. A somber atmosphere prevailed inside the air ambulance, as Cindy, Trevor and Bob watched the hologram images of the rescue efforts being transmitted by one of the news channels from Washington state. The channel also interviewed Ms. Eileen Malone, the CISN quake expert from Carson City, who saved millions by conveying the alert well ahead of time. She explained to the viewers what really happened, and how it happened. She said, their devices recorded the magnitude of the quake as 8.8 Richter scale.

"At one point I thought the structure would not hold. The way it swayed, I just couldn't believe it," Bob remarked.

"Where's your dad?" Cindy asked.

"At the hospital."

"A quake victim!" Cindy exclaimed.

"No, he tried to kill himself," Bob snapped.

"What!" Trevor couldn't believe his ears.

"But why?" Cindy was puzzled.

"I don't have the answers yet, but we're about to find out" Bob replied. ***

When Michael regained his sense, he could not remember what happened to him. Most of his body was wrapped in bandage. Under the bandage, the new transplanted skin would take several weeks to settle down permanently.

Bob and Professor Stan stood next to his bed, and behind them were the elenauts. Michael stared at Bob and struggled to say something to his son.

Bob brought his ear close to his mouth, and heard him whisper, "I'm sorry about your mother. It was an accident."

"I know dad, I believe you. Look who's here to see you." As Bob turned, everyone came forward. And then, very gently Bob uttered, "You are our real hero. The shaft stands tall even after the devastating quake."

When Bob was done talking, Michael was put to sleep, and at the door of the cabin, three military brasses led by General Normandy congratulated Bob. Mr. Kruger was also with them. The veteran lawyer informed Bob about the agreement Michael had agreed to. According to the agreement the military accepted the debts of the company, and in return, from then on, the military was in charge of the Project Elenaut. The agreement also stipulated that Bob could continue as the CEO of the company, as long as he wanted, and his father would retain twenty percent share of the company. ***

It took nearly three months for Michael to get back to normal condition. Induced by the ointment used over his wounds, his new skin grew at an astounding rate, expediting his release from the hospital. His grand mansion at Henderson had been rebuilt, though he never returned to it. Ever since his release from the hospital, he was on a vacation on Goldstein Island with the Coyote Bob adopted. His aim was to rebuild his empire. This time he was going to have Goldstein as his partner. Goldstein was full of praises for the humongous structure in the Mojave Desert. Michael would often show the images of it to his friends and would be partners.

Every morning, he set out for the morning walk with his coyote in warm balmy climate of the Caribbean. While enjoying the sunrise, he would think of the ways to buy his company back from the military. He knew, it was a farfetched dream. Nonetheless, he was not a man to accept defeat. In the meantime, the military prepared their plans to send thousands of their experts to the orbit. The aim was to build a military industrial complex in deep space, geared towards exploring and colonizing every single planet and the moons of the solar system. The military had no shortage of funds. It expected to complete the project in the next two to three years. Through his channels, Michael kept an eye on the progress of the project. Often the military asked for his opinion on how to move ahead with the project. As for the plan to have a generation, born and raised in space, the military would not disclose anything. Finally, it was decided that Michael would run for the Senate from the state of California. Goldstein decided not to directly contribute to his campaign. He had wealthy and powerful friends who promised to do everything in their power to get the bold entrepreneur elected as their representative at the Senate. ***

# The Epilogue

At the gate of the shaft stood a contingent of androids armed with weapons, guarding the space station. The work on building the space vessel was on full swing. Jeff was the only human being at the assembly plant. Under him, worked ten thousand humanoid workers and experts. In the next two years, they were expected to complete the hull of the super-sized space vessel. The vessel was like a ball. It would spin at one thousand mile an hour, producing the necessary gravity required to have a sustainable echo system inside the vessel. From time to time, Jeff sent images of the vessel to his former boss. At his desk, Michael stared at the images, and dreamed. He dreamed of the day when was going to lead the drive to conquer the solar system. He shared the images with Bob, who was also involved as the acting CEO of the Space Race. Once Michael was going to be elected, he had a plan to introduce bills to curb military involvement in private ventures.

www.ingramcontent.com/pod-product-compliance
Lightning Source LLC
Chambersburg PA
CBHW020315160726
47992CB00004B/1554